Marc struggled to keep himself from reaching out to McKenzie. "You don't have to do anything you're not ready for. We agreed to take things slow."

McKenzie looked at him. "Thanks for understanding, Marc." She stood and headed toward the door. Just as she neared the front door he reached her, then pulled her back into the den.

"Do I scare you, McKenzie?"

She squared her shoulders and stood facing him. "No, I think I scare myself."

"Are you sure you want to go home?"

McKenzie nodded, afraid that if she spoke her words would indicate otherwise. "I can call a taxi."

"You don't have to do that. I'll take you."

"That's not necessary, Marc."

He held up his hand. "Just give me a minute to grab my jacket."

McKenzie said nothing during the short trip to her home. Just as he parked the car, she jumped out. Marc got out, too, much to her surprise.

"You don't have to walk me to the door, Marc. I'll be all right."

"I'm walking you."

Marc stood on the step below her. They stood head to head, staring at each other. He reached for her then, and planted a kiss on her lips. Pulling her closer in his arms, he whispered in her ear, "Merry Christmas, Dr. Ashford." Without looking back, he left.

BOOK YOUR PLACE ON OUR WEBSITE AND MAKE THE ARABESQUE ROMANCE CONNECTION!

We've created a customized website just for our very special Arabesque readers, where you can get the inside scoop on everything that's going on with Arabesque romance novels.

When you come online, you'll have the exciting opportunity to:

- View covers of upcoming books

- Learn about our future publishing schedule (listed by publication month and author)

- Find out when your favorite authors will be visiting a city near you

- Search for and order backlist books

- Check out author bios and background information

- Send e-mail to your favorite authors

- Join us in weekly chats with authors, readers and other guests

- Get writing guidelines

- AND MUCH MORE!

Visit our website at
http://www.arabesquebooks.com

FAMILY TIES

Jacquelin Thomas

ARABESQUE
BET BOOKS

BET Publications, LLC
www.msbet.com
www.arabesquebooks.com

ARABESQUE BOOKS are published by

BET Publications, LLC
c/o BET BOOKS
One BET Plaza
1900 W Place NE
Washington, D.C. 20018-1211

First Printing: July, 2000
10 9 8 7 6 5 4 3 2 1

Printed in the United States of America

Prologue

Los Angeles, California

"My mother's dead," Marc said quietly. He rested his mother's hand on her breast, then stood. She was dead, and so was the chance for them to make their peace. He looked at her a moment longer, her confession lingering ghostlike in the room. Without a word, Marc walked over to the hospital window and stared out at the dark solemn night, his fists convulsed with suppressed rage.

Jim Rawlins followed him. "I'm sorry, Marc. I wish there was something I could say. . . ."

Marc Chandler shook his head. "I just can't believe it." He turned to look at the stocky man standing next to him. His mother had just died, but instead of grief it was anger he felt. "How could she do that to me, Jim? How could she keep something like that a secret? Why would she keep such a secret?"

Jim, his longtime friend and confidante, clapped a strong hand on Marc's shoulder. "Don't hold it against her, Marc. She did what she thought was best."

"I don't believe that!" Marc spat out the words with contempt. "There had to be another solution. She didn't have to—"

"Marc, you don't know all the particulars. As for me, I believe Lillian did what she felt she had to do at the time. Before she died, she asked for your forgiveness. Don't hold this against her."

"I can't forgive her. I can't. Not right now." He shook his head in disbelief. Turning his gaze back to Jim, Marc fixed him with a level stare. "Why didn't she tell me about it before now? She had plenty of opportunities." Slamming his fist against the wall, he muttered a curse. Nonetheless, the pain shooting through his hand did not compare to the ache Marc felt in his heart.

"Marc." Jim rushed over and examined Marc's hand. "Old man, you've got to be careful. You could've hurt yourself some- thin' fierce!"

Snatching his throbbing hand away, Marc uttered, "I don't give a damn."

"You're just angry right now, Marc, and you're hurting."

Marc raised pain-filled eyes. "You're damn right. I'm very angry. Hell yes, I hurt!"

"I'm sorry. I truly am."

Marc felt as if his guts had been ripped out. Every time he closed his eyes he could see his mother, sad and asking for forgiveness. *No. You won't get forgiveness from me,* he swore inwardly. *How could you have looked me straight in the face all these years and lied to me? You were the only woman I believed in. The one woman I could depend on to be honest with me. I hate you for this.*

Jim steered him toward the door. "Why don't you go on home now, Marc? There's nothing more that can be done here at the hospital. Taylor Funeral Home will be here tomorrow to pick up the body. I've made all of the arrangements."

"She's gone." Marc looked up at Jim. "She's resting in peace while—" He stopped short, disgusted, not able to continue, and threw up his hands in resignation.

"Yeah, I know. Lillian's gone and left you with a lot of un- answered questions. But remember one thing, Marc, she's made her peace. Now you'll have to find a way to make yours."

Marc chose to remain silent. Glancing back at his mother one last time, he felt his insides turn over. He had to get out of there—he was beginning to feel sick. Without a word he stormed out of the room, leaving Jim behind. Marc walked briskly through the long sterile corridor and out the automatic doors to the parking lot.

Once outside in the fresh night air, he took deep breaths to calm the overpowering feelings of loss and fury that swept over him.

Marc drove to his mother's house in Marina Del Rey. His *mother's* house. It was no longer Lillian's house. She was dead! His lying deceitful mother was dead.

He tried to discern her reasons for what she did, but couldn't. Marc didn't think he could ever forgive her for deceiving him. She had left him with one legacy: Lillian, like all women, could not be trusted.

One

Three years later
Orlando, Florida

"I still don't understand why you had to go and accept that position in California," said Calvin. "And what about us? You know how I feel about you."

Seated in Austin's Restaurant, McKenzie sighed inwardly. She waited until the waitress served their dinner before saying, "Calvin, please don't make this any more difficult than it has to be. Designing an effective vaccine for HIV is a high priority for this company. Working for Chandler Pharmaceuticals will provide me with the opportunity to do what I've always dreamed of doing." Noting the stubborn jut of Calvin's jaw, McKenzie attempted to change the subject. Motioning toward his plate with her fork, she asked, "Aren't you going to eat?"

Calvin slanted a defiant glance at her. "But there are pharmaceutical companies located right here in Florida. You don't have to move so far away."

She realized he wasn't going to let the subject of her moving to California drop. A soft sigh trembled on McKenzie's lips. "Calvin, I've really given this a lot of thought. Yes, there are other pharmaceutical companies, but Chandler is a huge drug discovery and development company. They've had some financial problems over the last few years, and their strategy to get them back in the black is to focus all of their efforts on life-threatening and chronic diseases." Giving him a placating smile and pointing to herself, McKenzie added, "I want to be a part of that."

Calvin played with his entrée, moving it from side to side with his fork. "Mack, I understand that this job is very important to you. But I was really hoping you'd decide to stay here. We could get married. . . ."

Moved by the flash of pain on his face, McKenzie placed a slender hand over his large chubby one, to still his fidgeting. "We're just friends, Calvin. That's all. You know I don't have room in my life for a serious relationship, much less marriage. You wouldn't be happy, and you deserve to be."

"You know how I feel about you. How I've always felt about you."

The hurt and longing lay naked in his eyes. Her heart squeezed in anguish at his pitiful look of appeal. Calvin was in love with her, but McKenzie knew she would never be able to return that love. All she felt for him was a sisterly affection. "I know you care about me. I care about you, too. You do know that, don't you? I'm just not interested in anything more. Not right now."

It was Calvin's turn to sigh. Shaking his head sadly, he said, "Mack, you never gave us a chance."

McKenzie glanced around the busy restaurant. She didn't want to have this discussion right now, but he had given her no choice. Almost desperately, she said, "Please, Calvin. This is my last night . . ."

Calvin apparently didn't want to ruin their last evening together, because he quickly changed the subject. His dark chocolate face melted into a bright smile. "So what are you going to do at Chandler?"

"Well, Chandler's program is currently focused on the HIV protease, a—"

"A what?"

McKenzie smiled at the perplexed expression on Calvin's

face. "A protease. It's a key enzyme that plays an essential role in viral replication."

Calvin shook his head in confusion. "Well, that certainly explains it."

McKenzie giggled. "Chandler plans to improve its current protease inhibitor."

"What's that?"

"It's an orally active compound that will inhibit the enzyme based on its three-dimensional atomic structure."

"And that translates to what in English?"

"Protease inhibitors block infected cells, and prevent them from producing new viruses. When the cells are blocked, the HIV virus can only make defective copies of itself."

Scratching the back of his ear, Calvin said, "I don't understand why you get off on this stuff. It's boring. *Geez*. A protease something or other. That's not exactly exciting stuff."

McKenzie's laughter bubbled over. "Stop being sarcastic, Calvin. *It is* exciting to me. Just watch, one day I'm going to develop a vaccine for AIDS."

Calvin joined her in laughter. "I'm sure you will, Dr. Ashford. Lord knows you've given up your life to do so."

She sobered. "No I haven't."

His left eyebrow rose a fraction. "Come on now, admit it. This stuff is all you think about."

McKenzie was quiet for a moment. "No, I don't just think about my research. I think about . . . other things."

"Yeah? Like what? You most certainly don't think about me."

Although she detected a tinge of bitterness in his voice, McKenzie said nothing.

"Are you ignoring me now?" Calvin's gentle nudge brought her back from her daydreams.

"Of course not, Calvin. I'm not ignoring you. I'm just tired. I've had a lot to do in order to prepare for my move to California."

He placed his hand over hers this time. His hand was rough,

and gave her a sense of protection. "I care about you, McKenzie. I hope all this works out for you. I really do."

McKenzie nodded. "I know that, and I appreciate your concern. I want you to understand that this is something I have to do."

Calvin sat back in his chair. "I do understand. I know how important your career is to you."

Gazing into his deep-set eyes, she said, "Calvin, I've given this a lot of thought. I really have." Putting a piece of meat into her mouth, McKenzie chewed slowly, savoring the juicy taste of grilled steak, all the while trying hard to ignore Calvin's hurt expression.

They finished the rest of their dinner in silence. As soon as McKenzie took her last bite, Calvin signaled the waitress for their check.

Neither spoke as they drove along International Drive. Calvin soon pulled into a vacant parking space in front of her condo. Turning the car off, he sat quietly, staring at her.

Her anguished gaze sought and found Calvin's. McKenzie leaned over, kissing him on the cheek. "Goodnight, Calvin. I know it seems as if I'm abandoning you—"

Calvin shook his head. "That won't happen. We've been through too much together. If you need anything—"

McKenzie cut him off while brushing a lone tear from her cheek. "I know. Well, I guess I'd better go finish packing. I have a plane to catch in the morning."

Calvin's eyebrows shot up in surprise. "Girl, you haven't finished yet?"

McKenzie shook her head and shrugged. "You know how I am. I always wait until the last minute. I hate packing." Twisting her mouth into a frown, she added, "I hate moving, period."

Calvin laughed as he reached over to hug her. "I'm gonna miss you, girl. I'm gonna miss whipping your butt out there on the basketball court."

"I don't think so. The way I remember it, you can't keep up

with me . . ." McKenzie tried to keep her tears at bay. "I'll miss you, too. Thank you so much, Calvin . . ."

"Aw, girl. Go on upstairs and finish packing. I'll see you in the morning."

Gently, he thrust McKenzie from him. His eyes were bright with unshed tears. She smiled as large drops of her own tears slid down her face. "Calvin—"

"Go on, now. You know how I hate emotional women."

She nodded. "I'll see you in the morning."

Upstairs, McKenzie stood in the doorway until she could no longer see Calvin's car. She really was going to miss him. He was her best friend. Closing the door to lock up for the night, McKenzie wiped away her tears with the back of her hand. Leaving was going to be harder than she'd thought. On the verge of fresh tears, she took the stairs two at a time to her bedroom.

Fifteen minutes later, McKenzie put the last shirt in her suitcase and closed it. Smiling, she dropped down on her bed, feeling pretty pleased with herself. She was finally packed. Tomorrow morning she would board a plane to California. McKenzie scanned the room once more. Suitcases and cardboard boxes were everywhere.

Leaving her bedroom, McKenzie headed downstairs and slowly wandered through the condo, stopping here and there. Saddened by the thought of leaving the place, she swallowed hard and squared her shoulders. It had been her first real home since her grandmother's death, something she'd cherished greatly after losing her mother.

On Saturday, Calvin would come over to let the movers in. McKenzie hoped to be in an apartment by the time her furniture arrived in California. When McKenzie mentioned putting her place on the market, a coworker had immediately made an offer to buy the luxury condo.

She watered her plants and silently said her good-byes. They, too, would be left with the new owner. "I'm going to miss this place," McKenzie whispered in the empty condo. A hot tear slid slowly down her cheek as she turned to climb the stairs.

Back in her bedroom, McKenzie picked up a small leather-bound book that she had placed on top of her suitcase earlier. She sat down on the edge of her bed and began writing in her journal. She recorded her thoughts on this day—her last in Orlando—and her hopes for the future.

As she continued to write, she thought about her visit to Barbara's grave earlier that day. She'd told her mother about her plans to move to California, and her new job at Chandler. Memories of her mother and the way she died flooded her mind, and McKenzie could feel the bile rising in her throat.

McKenzie had been fifteen at the time of Barbara's death. She was on her way home from school, and very excited. She had just found out she would be able to graduate and attend college at sixteen. She flinched, remembering how she'd come home and found her mother dead of a drug overdose. Terrified, McKenzie had called an ambulance, but it had been too late. There was nothing that could be done to save her.

After Barbara died, all McKenzie had left were her memories and her hunger for justice. Her anger and thoughts of revenge aided her in times of grief, and allowed her to keep going. One day, the person responsible for her mother's death would be forced to pay!

Culver City, California

"Good morning, Marc."

Marc looked up from the prospectus he was reading and grinned at the woman standing before his desk. Medium height with a slender frame, Carla was pushing back errant strands of her hair. The dark-brown curly mane fell to just below her shoulders. Tiny freckles peeked from beneath her thin veil of face powder.

"Good morning, Carla." Marc had recently promoted her to Vice President of Research and Development. "When is the new scientist coming on board?"

She handed Marc a cup of steaming hot coffee. "She arrives today at one o'clock. David's picking her up from the airport. After our orientation, I thought I'd take her to lunch." Sipping from her own cup, Carla walked over to a navy and burgundy plaid couch and sat down. "You know, Dr. Ashford is coming from Mason Research Laboratories in Orlando, where she served as research head for infectious diseases."

His brows flickered a little. "Really? How long has she worked at Mason?"

"She came to Mason as a research associate following her postdoctoral work at Harvard Medical School, and has been there until now. I believe you're going to be pleased with her. Dr. Ashford will bring a wealth of expertise to the Chandler Management team. Our R & D division will benefit from her experience and fresh perspective."

Stroking his chin, Marc regarded Carla carefully. "She has certainly impressed you."

She laughed. "Once you meet her, you'll be impressed, too."

Marc stopped her with a raised hand. "Carla, you should know by now that I don't impress easily."

Biting her lip to stifle a grin, Carla warned, "I'll remind you of that later, after you've met her."

"Since you've piqued my curiosity, I'll tell you what. After your orientation and company tour, I'll take you both to lunch. It will give me a chance to garner my own impressions of your Dr. Ashford."

Unable to control her facial expression, Carla broke into a wide open smile. "Great. I really think you're going to like her."

Marc exchanged a smile with her, shaking his head. "I doubt that. Scientists and doctors tend to bore me."

Seeing the amusement in his eyes, Carla laughed. "You're terrible, Marc."

He threw back his head and laughed. "Haven't you ever noticed that you're the only one I spend time with? Besides, I only keep you around to decipher the lingo."

Carla ran her hand through her bouncing curls as she continued laughing.

He enjoyed the gentle sparring as much as she did. Carla and Marc were very close, having met years ago in college. They'd never had a romantic interest in one another, but had remained close friends. When Carla graduated from college, Marc introduced her to his father, who was President and CEO of Chandler at the time. She had been with the company since then.

While they continued their light banter, Marc stood and escorted Carla out of his office.

Twenty minutes later, he returned to his office. After settling into his leather chair, he reviewed his appointments for the day. He quickly had his secretary, Clara, call and cancel his lunch meeting with a sales representative from Med-Tech.

Marc flashed back to his conversation with Carla. Did she really think some dowdy scientist would impress him? Dr. Ashford was probably just another plain-faced know-it-all. Knowing Carla was up to her old habits of trying to find him a wife, Marc shook his head and laughed. Would she ever give up?

McKenzie walked over to a slender young man holding a large sign that read, Chandler Pharmaceuticals. She smiled at how embarrassed he looked. He turned with a start when she lightly touched his arm.

"Oops. I didn't mean to scare you." She pointed to the poster. "You can put away the sign. I'm Dr. McKenzie Ashford." She shifted her briefcase to her left hand and held out her right.

He shook her hand. "Hello, Dr. Ashford. I'm David. I guess you could tell I was uncomfortable, huh? I sure felt stupid holding up this sign."

McKenzie took note of the handsome young man. He was tall and slim, his smooth cinnamon complexion flawless. His medium brown hair lay in tight curls. A thoughtful smile curved her mouth. "It was a nice gesture. And you didn't look stupid to me."

She could tell from David's expression that he was studying her. McKenzie knew he was trying to calculate her age. Used to getting that kind of response, she was no longer bothered by it. Although she was only thirty years old, most people assumed she had to be much older. Few people knew that she'd attended college at sixteen.

"I hope your plane ride was enjoyable. Me, I hate to fly. You can't get me up in a plane. Every time I travel, I go Greyhound or Amtrak."

McKenzie shook her head. "Not me. I couldn't bear sitting on a train or bus for three days."

David rattled on. "Huh! Wouldn't bother me none. Not at all. I figure this way—if the good Lord above had wanted me to fly, he'd have given me some wings."

McKenzie laughed. "Come on, let's get my luggage." They headed to the baggage area.

While they waited for her suitcases to appear, she asked, "So, David, are you from California?"

He bobbed his head up and down. "Yeah, born and raised. It's a nice place to live. It could be a great place if we could just get rid of the smog. For April, this weather is perfect. In the past, it's been like the middle of summer."

"Smog or not, I think I'm going to like it here. It gets pretty hot in Florida, too, so the heat won't bother me. At least it's not humid."

They grabbed her luggage and headed to the parking area.

As they drove along the freeway, David pointed out various points of interest. They were soon pulling into the parking structure next to Chandler Pharmaceuticals in Culver City.

Carla greeted McKenzie as soon as she set foot in the building. She had met Carla three months before, when Carla had given a lecture at the University of Miami. McKenzie had traveled to Miami just to engineer an introduction. She had immediately expressed an interest in working for Chandler.

Carla called her three weeks later, telling her about the HIV program and the company's plan to improve Chandler's orally active protease inhibitor. She'd also mentioned wanting to design and develop a vaccine. When Carla asked McKenzie if she would be interested in heading the program, she flew into Los Angeles a few days later for an interview. During her three-day visit, McKenzie had hoped to manipulate a meeting between Marc Chandler and herself, but he had already left for a symposium in Paris.

"It's good to see you again, Dr. Menton."

"Just call me Carla. We don't stand on formalities around here. I've made arrangements for you to stay at the Marriott until you find a place to live. I've also made an appointment for you to meet with Allie Marshall. She's a real estate agent, and a good friend of mine. She'll help you find a nice place to live."

"Thanks. I'm hoping to find a place by the time my furniture gets here."

"I don't think that'll be a problem. Allie already has a few places lined up for you to look at. Why don't we head up to my office?"

McKenzie followed her to the elevators. "When is the appointment?"

"I made it for tomorrow afternoon. I didn't think you would feel up to it your first day in town."

"Do you think I can arrange to see her today? I really hate living out of my suitcase. I want to find an apartment as soon as possible."

Carla nodded. "I know what you mean. Having your own home gives you a sense of security."

"Yes, it certainly does." McKenzie walked beside Carla down a brightly lit corridor.

Carla checked her watch as she unlocked a door and entered the tastefully decorated corner office. "She should be in her office. I'll give her a call right now."

McKenzie surveyed her surroundings as Carla phoned Allie. She had a brief impression of cherrywood furnishings, floor-to-ceiling bookshelves, landscape paintings, and unique African statues. Her eyes focused on a photograph placed on the credenza. It featured Carla and an older man. McKenzie recognized Dr. Charles Chandler, the founder of Chandler Pharmaceuticals, from photographs in medical journals and textbooks.

Propped against her desk, Carla covered the mouthpiece of the phone and asked, "Is four-thirty today okay with you?"

McKenzie nodded.

Carla confirmed the appointment, thanked her friend, and ended the call. She stood up and walked over to the file cabinet, where she pulled out several documents. She handed them to McKenzie as she spoke. "We think that the easiest way to design an effective vaccine is to know what immune responses protect against the specific infection and construct a vaccine that stimulates those responses."

McKenzie settled back in her chair. "It's not going to be easy, since we don't have a human model of protection to guide us. Unfortunately, no one knows whether a natural protective state against HIV can exist."

Carla nodded. "This is true. However, there is evidence that some people appear better able than others to resist progression of the HIV infection."

McKenzie sat forward in her chair. "Hmm . . . if exposed but uninfected individuals can be proven to have resisted HIV by an active immune mechanism, they could possibly represent the natural protective state upon which we can model a vaccine."

Carla appeared to be thinking this over. "I think you may be onto something. If we . . ." She glanced down at her watch. "Oh dear, it's almost two o'clock. We're supposed to be meeting Marc Chandler for lunch. Are you hungry?"

McKenzie's stomach chose that exact moment to rumble. Embarrassed, she said, "Yes, I guess I am."

"Good. We'd better be on our way. Marc is probably already there. He's a very nice man. You're going to like him."

"I can't wait to meet him," McKenzie said with a smile. "I've followed his father's work for years, but I must admit I don't know much about Marc Chandler, beyond where he attended college and a list of several organizations where he holds board positions."

Two

Marc was already seated when McKenzie and Carla arrived at the restaurant. He stood up when he spied them coming his way. Slowly he shifted his gaze from Carla to Dr. Ashford. From a distance, she seemed to be just another scientist—a plain, skinny one at that. Yet even as the thought crossed his mind, Marc could see that his first impression had been wrong.

There was beauty in her unblemished mocha-tinted face, which was completely devoid of makeup. Her extremely short hair, the black of a starless night, lay in tiny waves. Marc observed her slender form, her narrow waist and boyish hips, finding nothing to his liking until his eyes found her full breasts. These were swollen to womanhood, natural and taunting. Dr. Ashford looked to be no more than twenty, but according to her credentials she had to be much older. She carried herself confidently.

As McKenzie neared the table, they made eye contact. He noticed there was strength in her dark brown eyes, and they never wavered. To his astonishment, she leveled him with a stare as subtle as a bullhorn. Looking at her with a slightly lifted brow, Marc could not believe her audacity. It never occurred to him that he had just been doing the same thing to her.

Marc pulled out a chair for her and held out his hand. With unveiled amusement, he asked, "Are you through staring, Dr. Ashford?" His deep rich voice held a trace of laughter that seemed to have the desired affect on her.

McKenzie's smoldering gaze registered something he could not identify. She seemed to be struggling for something to say. Marc wondered why she suddenly seemed rattled.

She spoke softly. "I—I apologize. You look familiar, that's all."

Marc's gaze sharpened, and he observed her more closely. There was a definite undercurrent of tension in her voice. He supposed it was due to weariness, or new surroundings. "No harm done. I admit to being curious about you, as well. I've heard a lot about you, Dr. Ashford." He made a conscious effort to sound nonchalant without appearing rude. Marc didn't want to risk having her make the wrong assumptions about him. It served to protect him from entanglements that could potentially turn nasty. It was his intent to make sure she viewed him as her employer, nothing more.

McKenzie felt her heartbeat escalate rapidly, and her breath hung in her throat. She could not believe it. He looked like . . . *Could it be?* It had to be. *He* was Marc Chandler. McKenzie made a conscious effort not to display any emotion. She took a deep breath, and with a firm grasp she shook his hand, her eyes never leaving his face. "I've heard a lot about you, as well, Mr. Chandler." She reacted to his searing touch as if she'd been burned, and McKenzie resisted the impulse to rub her hand.

Her back straight, her chin at a tilt, she stared Marc directly in the eye. At so close a range, she still couldn't believe he was standing there. She eased into the chair he'd pulled out for her.

Acutely aware of him still watching her, McKenzie flashed him a forced smile, displaying none of her true emotions. She might have looked happy, but deep down she felt anything but— here was the man responsible for her mother's death!

Marc's eyes narrowed fractionally, and she found it hard to put into words what those eyes revealed. It wasn't exactly interest in her—it was a look of wariness. He looked as if he were waiting for her to say something more. When she remained silent, he motioned for the waiter. "While we're waiting for our waiter, Dr. Ashford, why don't you tell us about yourself?"

The waiter quickly appeared, granting McKenzie a temporary reprieve. She chose this time to gather her thoughts. Marc Chandler was suspicious of her. Her throat tightened. And was he deliberately baiting her? Was it possible he recognized her, as well? If not, then why had he been sitting there staring at her? *Calm down,* she told herself. She couldn't let him see that she was tense.

While the waiter took Marc's order, McKenzie's eyes froze on his long lean form. Marc's amber-colored eyes were startling against his warm tawny skin. He wore his midnight black hair cut close to his head. Over the years he had certainly acquired polish, McKenzie observed. Shifting in her chair, she straightened her back and prepared to be cordial in spite of her true feelings.

Lunch wasn't going to be easy, McKenzie acknowledged while scanning the menu. Marc was the last person she wanted to eat with, and she cautioned herself to keep her cool. She didn't want to make an enemy of him, especially this early on, but that didn't mean she would embrace him as a friend, either.

When the waiter left with their orders, Marc turned to face her. "You were about to tell us about yourself."

McKenzie sent Carla a quick glance before saying, "There's really nothing to tell. I'm just a simple person with dreams of saving the world. I've devoted much of my life to trying to make those dreams a reality." Her hands twisted nervously in her lap.

While they waited for their food to arrive, McKenzie felt the heat of his gaze on her. "Mr. Chandler, you're doing it now." When he seemed puzzled by her comment, she explained, "It's you who's staring now."

Marc lifted his brow. The amused look had suddenly left his eyes, in its place, a flash of grudging respect. "I apologize."

Carla cleared her throat loudly and reached for her water glass. McKenzie didn't miss the look she gave Marc, but she didn't dwell on it. Her thoughts at the moment were so jumbled she almost didn't hear the question Carla had asked. Catching herself, she asked, "I'm sorry, did you ask me something?"

"I was asking what your impressions of Chandler were thus far."

"Dr. Ashford, are you okay?" Marc inquired.

Looking up into liquid pools of brown, McKenzie nodded. "I'm fine. I guess the flight took more out of me than I thought. With the time change and everything—I think after I eat . . . I'll feel better."

Carla nodded her understanding, while Marc weighed her with a critical squint. McKenzie pretended not to notice.

A momentary look of discomfort crossed her face. "I'm very impressed with the company," McKenzie admitted honestly. "Using the application of structure-based drug design technology for the treatment of HIV infection and AIDS is a brilliant idea. You have a wonderful company, Mr. Chandler."

"Call me Marc. Mr. Chandler was my father. And I thank you for the compliment, although I can't take credit for it. Credit goes to Carla and her talented team of scientists and research assistants." He pointed to himself. "I'm just a plain and simple businessman."

Putting up a hand, Carla shook her head. "Now wait a minute. We can't take the credit, either. Your father was a distinguished scientist born years before his time. He deserves all of the credit. This was his vision."

McKenzie nodded in agreement. "I'm very familiar with your father's work. Dr. Chandler was a genius."

"He certainly was," interjected Carla. "It's just a shame he died before he could really see his work come to fruition."

From the expression on his face, Marc seemed caught up in memories. Looking past McKenzie, he said quietly, "Some people called him crazy, but he had the last laugh. When he started this company he only had one product, five thousand dollars, and a very big dream. No one ever expected his all-in-one hcG pregnancy tests to become so successful. That's still our biggest moneymaker."

Their food arrived.

While Carla chewed daintily on a morsel of turkey, McKenzie ate as if there were no tomorrow. All the while, Marc watched her, as if trying to decipher her mood. She didn't ignore him, but neither did she shower him with overt attention. McKenzie merely accepted his presence without being influenced by it one way or another. In fact she gave him the same consideration she gave her knife and fork.

"So tell me, Dr. Ashford, are you from Florida originally?" Marc asked.

McKenzie looked into his eyes, searching for a spark of recognition. "Please call me McKenzie. And yes, I'm . . . from Orlando," she lied. She wasn't ready for him to make the connection to Miami. McKenzie paused to watch his reaction. Seeing none, she relaxed and continued, "I left after my mother died. After I graduated from Harvard, I moved back." She took a deep breath. It was time to see how truthful Marc would be. "Have you ever lived in Florida? You seem familiar, somehow. In fact, I'm sure I've seen you before." She waited anxiously for his answer.

Marc dropped his fork on his plate. A muscle leaped in his lean jaw, but his voice was soft and even. "Yes. As a matter-of-fact, I'm originally from Miami. We moved away when I was a little boy. As for being familiar, you may have seen a picture of me somewhere."

"You're probably right." McKenzie struggled to remain calm. "Do you ever go back . . . to Miami, I mean?"

Marc suddenly seemed tense. She wanted to question him further about his time in Miami, but Carla quickly changed the subject.

"McKenzie graduated from high school at the tender age of fifteen, Marc. Can you believe that? It was right after her mother died."

"Really?" He eyed her for a moment. "I'm impressed. That had to be a terrible time for you. So many changes."

His tight expression seemed to relax once more.

"My mother was my best friend, and then one day my mom . . . my mom was suddenly taken from me." McKenzie fought to keep her anger out of her voice. "Some days it was harder than others, but I kept going."

Marc's face registered his surprise. "You were alone after your mother died? What about your father? Didn't you have any family?"

"I went to live with Granny Mae—that's my grandmother— but then she died shortly after I started college. So there I was again, no family, no home." McKenzie refused to tell him that she never knew her father—he'd left her mother as soon as he found out she was pregnant.

"I'm sorry you had to go through something like that, especially at so young an age," Carla murmured softly.

Marc nodded his head in agreement.

Her hunger for revenge was renewed, and it took all of McKenzie's strength not to throw her soup at him. *He* was the very reason she'd had to grow up without her mother. He didn't know the meaning of the word sorry, but he would, she vowed silently. Before it was all over, she intended to make sure he felt the same pain she'd endured all these years.

Carla placed her hand over McKenzie's. "I'm sure your mother's watching over you, and is very proud of all your accomplishments, McKenzie. Some people would have crumbled in the face of such sadness."

McKenzie merely shrugged. "As I said, I did what I had to do. Life doesn't always leave us with very many options. I guess that's one of the reasons I went into medical research. There are so many people in this world with terrible diseases. Feeling they no longer have choices, they just give up and die. I wanted to give people options."

Carla broke into a wide open smile. Looking over at Marc, she said, "I told you she was really something." To McKenzie Carla added, "I'm really glad to have you on our team."

Marc nodded his agreement. "Welcome to Chandler Pharmaceuticals, Dr. Ashford."

McKenzie smiled as she gazed boldly into Marc's eyes. "You'll never know how grateful I am to Carla for giving me this chance."

Picking up her chicken breast sandwich, McKenzie pretended not to see the inquiring look Marc gave Carla. Stealing a glance, she found Marc still watching her. Although uncomfortable under the heat of his gaze, McKenzie was relieved to find no signs of identification in those eyes. She was grateful when Carla sought his attention.

While Marc and Carla discussed the order of tasks that needed to be undertaken, McKenzie polished off the last of her coleslaw.

Marc signaled for the waiter and requested the check. They were soon on their way back to Chandler Pharmaceuticals.

When they reached Chandler, they found Allie Marshall waiting in the lobby. Carla rushed over to her. "Oh, Allie, I'm sorry we're late, Have you been waiting long?"

Having just ended a conversation, Allie stuck her cellular phone into her Coach handbag. "Actually, I just got here myself. My last appointment ran over, and then traffic was hell . . ." Her bubbly voice drifted, and her long micro braids swung in motion as she gave McKenzie her full attention. "Hello. You must be Dr. Ashford. Welcome to California."

Smiling, McKenzie reached out to shake Allie's outstretched hand. "Thank you."

She turned around, crashing into Marc. "I'm sorry. I should look where I'm going," McKenzie croaked.

He smiled. "I shouldn't have been following so closely."

Too close. The elevators were in the opposite direction. McKenzie wanted to know why he was following her. "Did you need to see me?"

"I was just going to reiterate how happy we are to have you on our staff. I look forward to working with you."

"Same here, Marc."

He nodded. "Happy house hunting. Good seeing you, Allie."

"You, too, Marc."

McKenzie rolled her eyes as Allie watched him stroll confidently toward the elevators. She was practically drooling after him.

"That's one good-looking man, don't you think?" she asked.

"Good-looking men are nothing but trouble," McKenzie muttered. "I try to stay away from them as much as possible."

Bursting into laughter, Allie shook her head in disbelief. "Well, we should get going. My car is right outside."

She drove McKenzie around Culver City and Marina Del Rey. They looked at several places before McKenzie found one she really liked. It was a three-bedroom town house, and available for lease with an option to buy. After filling out the necessary paperwork, Allie dropped her off at the Marriott on Century Boulevard.

By the time she reached her room, McKenzie could barely keep her eyes open. She was exhausted, but knew she wouldn't be able to fully relax until after a nice hot shower. Right now, she was too tired to think about Marc Chandler, or anything. Now that fate had placed him directly in her path—he wouldn't be going anywhere.

Lying in bed, McKenzie shivered and pulled the covers to her chin. It was freezing in her room. Clad only in silk thong panties, matching bra, and a pair of white socks, she jumped up from the bed, braving the cold temperature to turn up the thermostat. Picking up her overnight bag, she quickly returned to the warmth of her bed, muttering, "Now, that's much better."

Settling back, McKenzie retrieved her journal and started to write. As she described her thoughts on meeting Marc Chandler, she admitted he was a very handsome man, but she wouldn't let that distract her from what she had to do. He had to pay somehow for what he'd done. She'd promised her mother. She would make him pay for her mother's death. McKenzie vowed to hurt him as much as he'd hurt her. She recalled the obvious pride she'd heard in his voice earlier that day. Chandler Pharmaceuticals was his baby—his pride and joy. McKenzie intended to expose him for what he truly was. She wondered what the stockholders would do when they found out the truth about Marc—a drug dealer who just happened to own a pharmaceutical company. All she needed was evidence.

She dragged her thoughts to the way Marc had watched her all through lunch. Knowing he'd only seen her twice before today, McKenzie felt reasonably sure that he didn't remember her. Her mother had always tried to keep her boyfriends away from McKenzie. There could be no name recognition because she'd dropped her first name and her last, using only her middle name and her grandmother's maiden name, after Barbara died.

She wrote hastily and, upon finishing, put her journal away. Stretching out on the bed, McKenzie savored her plan.

Reluctantly, she scrambled off the bed to start the dreaded process of unpacking. She chose a comfortable pair of Guess jeans and a teal-blue polo shirt to wear for her first day at Chandler. She had a lot of unpacking to do at the lab, too. The thought made McKenzie frown. *I hate all this packing and unpacking. That's all I've done my whole life.* Her mother had often used rent money to buy drugs, causing them to steal away in the night to Granny Mae's house. They would then stay with her grandmother until they could find another place.

When she was finished, McKenzie lifted the empty suitcase off the bed. An old faded photograph fell out. Before she even bent to pick it up, McKenzie knew what she would see. It was a picture of her mother and her boyfriend at the time—her mother and Marc. His face was blurred, but McKenzie could tell who it was. Marc was only one of several younger men Barbara had dated over the years. He had to be about forty-three now, McKenzie calculated.

Filled with sadness, she sank down on the bed, tears spilling from behind closed lids. "M-mama, why? Why couldn't you leave the drugs alone? Why didn't you love me enough to quit?"

McKenzie felt alone and frightened. "I needed you, Mama." Wiping tears from her eyes, she took one last look at the photograph before putting it in the bottom of her purse. "I'm not going to let you down like you did me, Mama."

All the unpacking done, she put on a pair of black leggings and an oversize T-shirt. After locating a copy of the room service menu, she decided to order in. McKenzie didn't feel like being around people right then.

She was about to pick up the phone when it began to ring. The unexpected loud noise of the telephone startled her. Her first thought was not to answer, but curiosity won out and she changed her mind. "Hello."

"Hello, McKenzie. This is—"

"I know who you are, Calvin," she exclaimed with intense pleasure. "I haven't been gone long enough to forget you. How are you?"

"I'm doing okay. I know you've only been gone since this morning, but I miss you."

Tears formed in her eyes. "I miss you, too." She and Calvin had been friends since she was fifteen. After her mother died and McKenzie went to live with her grandmother, she met Calvin. After graduating from high school, she enrolled at Howard University, where he was attending college. Her grandmother died shortly after she started her freshman year.

When they returned to Miami for summer break, McKenzie stayed with several friends before finally moving into a cheap and dirty motel. One day, Calvin showed up at her door after following her to the motel. He demanded to know what was going on. She broke down and confided that she didn't have anywhere else to go, and would not be able to return to Howard. Not having any answers himself, Calvin took her to see his mother, who immediately came to McKenzie's aid. Mrs. Dixon helped McKenzie secure funding for school, and she opened her home to her.

McKenzie lived with Calvin and his mother whenever she had a break from school, until she reached the age of twenty.

With a bachelor's degree to her credit, she landed a job at a hospital in Miami, then moved into her first apartment. After working for a year, she decided to attend medical school. With Calvin's encouragement, McKenzie applied to Harvard and was accepted. Calvin had been a good friend to her. When she landed a permanent position with Mason Labs, he, too, transferred to Orlando, and started his own company. She only wished she could return his feelings.

". . . so the furniture won't be there for another week."

"Huh? Oh that's fine, Calvin. I should be in my town house by the weekend."

"You already found a place to live? Girl, you don't waste any time, do you?"

"You know how I feel about hotels."

"Yeah, I know. Hey, I had a guy come by and make an offer for your car."

"Really? Well, what do you think?" She would be glad to get rid of that old piece of junk.

"I think it's a fair one. You should probably take it. I'll wait for a couple of days and see what happens before I call him back."

"That sounds good to me. Go with whatever you think is best. I'll have most of my money transferred to a bank here by the end of the week, but I don't want to close my account there. Not just yet. Anyway, you'll be able to deposit the money directly into the account. Calvin, you're—"

"I know, I know, I'm a good friend. Now go. You need to get rested up. You have a big day ahead of you tomorrow."

Feeling somewhat better after talking to Calvin, she dialed room service.

McKenzie was deeply engrossed in her notes when her food arrived. Putting them aside, she tore into her sandwich with enthusiasm.

McKenzie didn't sleep much that night, with everything that had transpired during the day—the most significant of which had been seeing Marc Chandler. Tomorrow she would find a detective and have him perform a thorough background search on Marc. *I'm going to uncover all your secrets*, Mr. Chandler.

Three

Birmingham, Alabama

"*Sherrie*. What the hell's taking you so long?" Pierce Phillips yelled as he settled back on the sofa. A shadow of annoyance crossed his tawny-colored face.

"I'll be out in a minute, honey," a singsong voice complete with a Southern drawl called from the bedroom. "You don't have to yell." She pronounced it as yale.

Pierce grumbled under his breath as he riffled through the pile of magazines under the glass coffee table. He finally selected a copy of *Ebony*. Noting the date and the year, he frowned. "If you're going to keep me waiting, you could at least have some current magazines around here for me to read," he grumbled. "Look at this. This magazine is older than your niece. *It's two years old.*"

"I'm collecting them, Pierce."

"I bet you don't even know what's in it. All you do is order magazines. You never read 'em."

"I buy them so I can win the sweepstakes. You know they just throw away the entries from people who don't order anything," Sherrie yelled from her bedroom.

Pierce skimmed page after page, then a certain photograph caught his eye. His luminous brown eyes widened in astonishment. For a minute his heart stopped, and he tried to call Sherrie, but could not find his voice. He tried again. "Oh my God! Hey, Sherrie!"

"What, honey? I told you I'd be out there in a minute. I'm fixing my hair right now."

"Come here. *Quick.*"

An ample-bodied, ivory-skinned woman rushed out of the bedroom. "Pierce, honey, what is it? Are you okay?"

"Will you take a look at this?" He thrust the magazine at her.

"Oh my!" Sherrie shook her head in disbelief. "Is this—"

Pierce shook his head. "This man's name is Marc Chandler. It says here that he's the CEO of Chandler Pharmaceuticals. You never saw this article before?"

"Naw, I sure didn't. I would've said something if I had. I have heard of Chandler, though. They have an extensive HIV and AIDS research program." She looked at Pierce. "Do you know what any of this means?"

Pierce shook his head. "I have no idea. I do know one thing though—I'm gonna find out." He thoughtfully touched the mole just above his lip. "I have to find out." He glanced down at the picture again. "This is too weird." Letting the magazine drop to the sofa, Pierce stood up and walked to stand in front of the huge picture window, gazing out, but seeing nothing.

Sherrie ran a hand through her waist-length blond hair. She watched him for a minute before joining him, encircling him with her arms. "You know, honey, this could actually work in our favor."

Pierce turned toward her. His eyebrows raised inquiringly. "How do you mean?"

"Think, Pierce. A pharmaceutical company . . ."

He smiled. "I guess you're right. This could prove to be *very* helpful. But how do you think he'll react? Look what it's doing to me." His whole body was trembling. *How could this be?* he wondered. So much was going through his mind. Over the years he had often felt as if a big part of him was missing. Pierce had often felt a strong connection to something or someone. He was never sure until now what it was.

"So, honey, what do you think we should do?"

Pierce led Sherrie over to the couch before answering. "I don't know, baby. I don't know if I should do anything. I mean, what if he doesn't want to see me? I'm sure he probably doesn't know a thing about me. At least, I think he doesn't."

"We can always write him a letter or give him a call—"

Pierce shook his head. "No, I think something like this should be done in person. Remember what happened last time?"

"But honey, it wasn't your fault. It wasn't a good lead."

"No, it wasn't. I just hate the fact that because of the letter we sent, it opened a can of worms."

Sherrie shrugged in resignation. "Well, honey, it's your decision. Whatever you decide, I'm behind you one hundred percent."

"Even if I want to go to California?"

Grinning, she said, "Even then."

His light brown eyes glittered with amusement. "Are you serious? Just like that? No questions asked?"

"You should know by now that I'd go anywhere with you. I just want to be with you."

Pierce settled back on the couch. "Sweetheart, do you really have your heart set on going out tonight?"

"Naw, honey." Sherrie was suddenly worried. "What's the matter? Don't you feel like it?"

"I feel okay. I just don't want to go out. You know, be round a lot of people." He pulled her down next to him. "I would rather stay here and be alone with you."

Sherrie snuggled next to him as she whispered, "Honey, staying home with you is just fine with me. I love times like these the most."

"You mean to tell me that I could have saved all that money I've spent taking you out to dinner all these years?"

Sherrie giggled. "Naw, don't get me wrong. I love those

times, too. Speaking of food . . . I'll call and order." She picked up the phone and ordered a vegetarian pizza to be delivered.

While they waited for the pizza, they watched television. Pierce feigned interest in the movie, but in reality, his mind was clouded with thoughts. What kind of man was Marc Chandler? Would he welcome Pierce with open arms, or would he simply slam the door in his face?

Culver City, California

"Hi, honey."

Marc looked up to see Glenda Reynolds, a petite woman handsomely attired in a hot pink suit. Her shiny, auburn, shoulder-length hair was held back in a matching pink-and-gold barrette. She was a delicate beauty, but as determined as they came. Getting involved with her had been a mistake. And Marc intended not to make the same mistake twice.

"How did you get past Clara?" His greeting contained a strong suggestion of reproach.

"The witch wasn't at her desk. She's probably lurking in the halls somewhere in this massive building." She walked over to the couch and arranged herself so Marc could view her shapely legs. "Is that all you have to say to me?" she asked huskily.

"What more should I say?" he asked, spacing the words evenly.

Glenda pouted prettily. "Oh, Marc. You can't still be mad at me, can you? Why, it's been ages now since we had our little misunderstanding."

"Our what?"

"Darling, I've missed you terribly. Why don't we have dinner tonight? We can kiss and make up."

"I'm busy," Marc said in a nasty tone. "I have a dinner meeting."

"Marc," she whispered in a broken voice. "Would it hurt you so much to attempt to be pleasant?"

"I'm not feeling very pleasant at the moment, and I don't think it's a feeling that will pass anytime soon. Maybe you should leave."

Glenda stood up. "Marc, I'm not here to cause trouble. I was in the neighborhood, and I just stopped by to say hello. I'll talk to you later." She made no attempt to move.

Marc closed his eyes and pretended she was gone. Women were always the cause of some form of trouble, he thought with some irritation.

"I hate you, Marc Chandler, and I wish you were dead."

He soon heard her exasperated sigh, as well as the slamming of his office door. He smiled to himself.

Marc still had his eyes closed and was deep in thought when Jim Rawlins walked in.

"Sleeping on the job, old man?"

Opening his eyes, Marc leaned forward in his chair. "Oh, Jim. I didn't hear you come in."

The heavyset man chuckled. "Nothing, man. What's got you so preoccupied?"

"I've been thinking about my mother. Then, on top of that, Glenda decided to just drop by unannounced. She was her usual seductive self, which didn't work."

He chuckled. "I know. I saw her just as I was getting off the elevator. She looked madder than a rattlesnake."

Marc shrugged nonchalantly. "She'll get over it." He was quiet for a moment. "Man, I still find it hard to believe. You know, after all this time I can't let go. Mom really did a number on me. It still hurts."

Jim nodded. "I understand, Marc. From what I know of your mother, I can't believe it, either. But I do know this—she never meant to hurt you. She loved you more than she loved her own life."

His blood soared with unbidden memories. "I'm still angry with her, Jim. I can't find it in me to forgive her deceit."

"You're going to have to let it go. It's not right for you to go on like this. Being an unforgiving person can only lead to more pain."

He frowned, his eyes level under drawn brows. "I don't agree, Jim. Getting involved with women can only lead to more pain. Take Glenda, for instance. I caught her making love to another man. We had a date, and I guess I arrived a little too early. She didn't even have the decency to lock the door. I walked in, and there they were. Now she wants to call it a misunderstanding. I'm amazed at the lengths women will go to when it comes to lying."

"You're not being fair, Marc."

Marc leaned forward in his chair. "How so? Every woman I've ever met has been a liar." His tone was bitter.

"That's because you haven't met the right ones," Jim explained. "There are some good women out there."

Shaking his head, Marc stated flatly. "I'm not interested."

"You shouldn't condemn yourself to a life without love."

"Jim, I'm fine with the way things are. Woman are not to be trusted. My own mother proved that. Besides, I don't see you rushing down the aisle. I've seen the looks you give Carla. Why don't you do something besides gawk at her with that dumb expression on your face?"

"Like what? That woman won't give me the time of day."

"Have you ever asked her out?"

"No."

"Why not?"

"She's too classy for me. I'm just a country boy. Now, enough about my nonexistent love life. Okay—"

"Just drop it, Jim. I'm not interested in love. I have everything I need. I have a company to run, a new product in the works, and we've just recently hired a scientist with an impressive background in AIDS research."

"That's wonderful. Who's the scientist?"

"Dr. McKenzie Ashford. She studied at Howard University, and then received her doctorate from Harvard. But get this, she graduated from high school at the age of fifteen. By the time she was twenty, she had already completed four years of college."

"She sounds like a woman who is not only intelligent, but very focused."

"I met her earlier today, and she does appear focused. She's barely been in town one day, and she's ready to get to work. But I've learned that things aren't always what they seem."

"I wouldn't be so skeptical. Sounds to me like you've got yourself a winner."

"Time will tell. She might be trying to impress the boss. Dr. Ashford may be a damn good actress."

"Man, don't be so hard on women," Jim admonished. "I told you, there are some good ones out there."

"I don't know any other way to be." Again Marc's distrust for all women rekindled in his heart, and he swore he would be wary of his attraction to McKenzie. "All women are trouble-some creatures I would rather live without. Besides, love seems grossly overrated. Marriage, I imagine, is, too."

"You don't really mean that. You have needs, man."

Marc would not make the mistake of ever trusting another female, but that did not mean he didn't intend to enjoy what they had to offer. "Oh, I intend to satisfy those needs, but without all the entanglements."

Jim laughed. "I don't think you have control over your feelings, as much as you'd like to think. It's just not that easy. Mark my words, one day you're going to meet your match. Just watch. Some woman is going to steal your heart before you even realize it."

"I doubt that seriously." Marc had not been in love for a long time. And he certainly didn't intend to pander to that crippling emotion now.

Four

"Morning, Carla," McKenzie said as she entered the lab. Carla, breezing by, was shuffling through a black and white composition notebook. She glanced up from her notes. "Good morning." Motioning toward a steaming coffeepot stationed on a nearby Formica counter, she asked, "Would you care for a cup of coffee?"

McKenzie wrinkled her nose and shook her head. "No thanks. I'm not a coffee drinker."

"I'm a bear until I've had my first cup."

"I'm that way about hot chocolate." McKenzie pulled out a packet of cocoa mix from her briefcase. She heated a cup of water in the microwave before mixing in the powdery contents of the packet.

Carla helped herself to a cup of coffee. She took a sip before asking, "Did you sleep well?"

"I had a good night, but I think it's going to take a couple of days before my body fully adjusts to California time." McKenzie opened the door of a nearby closet and selected a bright white lab coat, putting it on over her blue jeans and polo shirt. Reaching into her briefcase, she pulled out a shiny black and gold eyeglass case. After putting on her glasses, she strolled around the sterile blue and white laboratory, each stride fluid.

Carla propped her body against an empty desk area, sipping her coffee. "By the way, how did it go yesterday?"

McKenzie paused before taking a sip of hot chocolate. "With Allie, you mean?"

"Yes. I hope she treated you well."

"She was great. And so patient. Would you believe I actually found a place?"

The heavy lashes that shadowed Carla's cheeks flew up. "Already?"

McKenzie's head bobbed up and down. "Yes. It's a three-bedroom, tri-level town house on Canterbury Drive, here in Culver City. It's only three years old."

"I've seen those before. They're beautiful. You really don't waste any time do you, McKenzie?"

McKenzie laughed. "Not if I can help it. I really hate living in hotels. I had to do it once. After my grandmother died."

Astonishment showed clearly on Carla's face. "You lived in a hotel all that time?"

"No, for the first few weeks I lived with friends, going from place to place." She gave a small laugh. "I soon ran out of friends. I lived in a hotel for almost two weeks until my friend Calvin and his mother took me into their home. Good thing, too. I was running out of money."

"Oooh, McKenzie."

McKenzie couldn't stomach the pity she heard in Carla's voice. She forced a smile through unshed tears. "Hey! I turned out okay, don't you think? The events of my life were great motivators. It all kept me focused."

Carla nodded, unable to speak for a moment.

"Enough of my past. I'm ready to get started trying to prolong someone's future." McKenzie slid gracefully into a comfortable-looking leather chair and flicked on her computer monitor.

Carla emptied the last of her coffee in the stainless steel sink. She quickly rinsed her cup and left it on a nearby rack to drain. "Do you need any help setting up your things?" Checking her watch, she added, "I have a few minutes to spare before I have to leave."

McKenzie glanced up. "Are you going to be out of the office all day?"

"For most of it, anyway. If you need anything, David can help you."

"I'm sure I'll be fine."

"Do you want to meet me somewhere for lunch?"

McKenzie shook her head. "Can I have a rain check? I have an appointment this afternoon. But thanks for the offer."

Carla turned and headed toward the door. "No problem. If I don't see you later, I'll see you in the morning."

"Have a good day."

"You, too." Carla disappeared in a flash.

McKenzie marveled at Carla's stamina. She seemed to have an unending source of energy. With white legal pad in hand, McKenzie stood and walked around the lab, making notes here and there.

Later, completely unpacked and with her office organized to her satisfaction, McKenzie settled back into the chair at her desk, scouring over the latest issue of *Nature* magazine. A copy of the June *Journal of Infectious Diseases* lay on a file cabinet next to her desk.

With her perfectly arched eyebrows furrowed together, McKenzie was so deeply engrossed in reading the article that she didn't hear Marc enter.

He stood for a few minutes silently watching her.

"Dr. Ashford?"

McKenzie jumped. "Oh! You scared me." The sound of his deep baritone voice affected her deeply, and she had to quickly pull her thoughts together. *What was Marc doing there?* She tried to assess his unreadable features.

"I'm sorry. I didn't mean to scare you. I wasn't sneaking up on you." He scanned her from head to toe.

Pushing her feet as far under her chair as possible, McKenzie instantly regretted wearing her worn plaid sneakers. Ignoring the questions in her head, she chose not to speculate about why she cared what Marc thought of her shoes. McKenzie raised her head, finding him watching her. He seemed to know what she had been thinking, and it amused him.

Peering over the magazine in her hand, Marc asked, "What are you reading?"

"N-nothing you'd find interesting, I'm sure."

Marc gently took the magazine from her and appeared to be reading the article. "You know, I read somewhere that HIV-positive women are three times more likely to have this type of cancer than HIV-negative women."

"I've read that, too." McKenzie pushed her glasses up. "There are thousands of new cases occurring annually. Cases of HIV-positive women with cervical cancer."

Marc shook his head sadly. "I hope we'll soon find a way to fight this disease. I know you scientists feel that based on T-cell counts—"

McKenzie interrupted, "Not all scientists believe that treatment strategies should be based solely on T-cell counts. During the MACS studies—"

Marc stopped her this time. "The what?"

"MACS studies," she repeated. "The Multicenter AIDS Cohort Study. The MACS researchers found that the level of HIV RNA—"

"The genetic material of HIV?"

McKenzie raised her eyebrows. "Yes, the level of genetic material of HIV in a person's plasma is a better predictor of the risk of disease progression than the T-cell count. The ability to predict HIV disease progression more accurately may help doctors better manage their patients."

Marc was so near she could see the rise and fall of his chest under his expensive white shirt and paisley patterned tie as he took each deep breath. Looking into his bottomless eyes, she felt herself almost gravitating toward him. *No, no,* her mind kept telling her. McKenzie tried to deny the pulsing knot that had formed in her stomach.

As Marc stared at her, perspiration beaded on her upper lip, and her heart pounded in her ears. McKenzie shrank back in the chair, unable to take a breath. She wrenched herself away from her ridiculous preoccupation with his arresting face.

They discussed her strategy for designing a preventive vaccine. Then, hearing someone enter the laboratory, they both turned. It was David. She and David had become fast friends since he'd picked her up at the airport. He stood shifting from foot to foot, looking uncomfortable. David started to speak, cleared his throat, and tried again.

"Uh, excuse me. Clara just called down here. She's looking for you, Marc. She says your next appointment has arrived and is waiting upstairs."

Marc's brown eyes sparkled with humor as he turned to face her. "I would like to continue our discussion another time. Duty calls."

McKenzie ignored the insinuating look David sent her way, behind Marc's back. As soon as he and David left, she took off her lab coat and grabbed her purse. She was running late.

Seated in nearby Coco's restaurant, McKenzie met with a burly man dressed in durable black pants, polyester shirt, and club tie. The private detective, Dan Edgars, fingered his thick mustache as he took notes.

McKenzie took a sip of water. "I want to know everything about Marc Chandler. Especially during his stay in Florida."

"What part of Florida?"

"Miami."

She passed an envelope containing money to him. "This should more than cover your retainer and travel expenses."

Dan counted the money, then plastered a grin on his solemn face. "This will do it. I'll call you as soon as I have something." He stood up to leave. "Thanks for lunch, Miss Reynolds."

As McKenzie watched Dan amble off, she felt a twinge of guilt. Marc Chandler was her employer. Chandler Pharmaceuticals was one of the top companies in its field. Did she really want to destroy the company Dr. Charles Chandler worked so hard to build? Was her need for revenge so great?

* * *

Marc sat back in his chair, his hands behind his head and his feet propped up on the corner of his desk. Thinking about his earlier conversation with McKenzie brought a faint smile to his lips. He recalled the way her face was illuminated as she discussed the results of different combination drug regimens for HIV infection. Marc could tell she really loved her work. He could certainly understand. It was the same way he felt about his company. He loved Chandler Pharmaceuticals more than his own life.

McKenzie had incredible eyes, wide and almond-shaped. Marc smiled. He liked the fact that she wasn't afraid to disagree. He also remembered her reaction when she caught him staring at her shoes. He thought the plaid sneakers were cute. Seeing her dressed in jeans and tennis shoes made her appear even younger.

Marc turned, hearing a knock on his door. He buzzed his secretary as he beckoned for Jim to come in.

"Clara, please hold my calls," he instructed while waiting for Jim to be seated. "How's it going?"

"It's going, old man. It's going. I just met with the detective. This is what he's found so far." He handed a large manila envelope to Marc.

Frowning upon seeing the contents, Marc slammed his fist down on the desk. "Damn! I really hoped . . ." He couldn't finish. Marc sighed heavily, his voice filled with anguish. "Another roadblock."

"We're not going to give up, Marc."

"We've been searching for three long years. Maybe we should just give up. This is so damn frustrating!"

"Is that what you really want to do?" Jim questioned. "I can call Laine and the detective right now, if you want me to."

Marc shook his head. "No, I really don't want to give up. I need to know. I have to know."

"Then we'll keep searching. We're bound to turn up something."

"We don't even have a name, for sure." Marc stood with his back to Jim, his hands shoved in his pockets, his shoulders hunched forward. "The detectives say it's as if he just disappeared from the face of the earth."

"I think we can safely conclude that the first name never changed. Just the last. At least that's what Lillian said before she died."

"We've got to find him. After all this time . . ."

Jim placed his hand on Marc's shoulder. "We're going to, Marc. It may take us from now until pigs fly, but we will. You just have to have some faith. That's what my ma always used to tell me."

"It's been three years already, and not one positive lead. I'm trying to have faith, Jim—I really am. But it's getting tough. For all we know, he may be dead."

"Even so, you need to know for sure. Be patient, Marc. We're going to find him. I can feel it in these old bones."

McKenzie rolled up the sleeves of her red sweatshirt. She grimaced as she surveyed all the cardboard boxes sitting neatly together in the middle of the floor. Plastic covered furniture was scattered everywhere.

"I hate unpacking!" she fussed as she opened the cardboard box labeled *kitchen*.

No matter how much she hated the task, McKenzie had no choice but to get it over with. She was about to open the box closest to her when she heard the doorbell. "Now who in the world can that be?"

Swinging open the door, she was astonished to see Carla standing there. *"Carla.* What a pleasant surprise. Come on in, and please excuse the mess."

"Hello. I thought you could use some help." She held up a

large pizza box and a six-pack of diet soda. "I even brought lunch."

"That was so sweet of you." McKenzie hugged her. "And I could definitely use some help. Thanks." She relieved Carla of her burden. "Why don't we eat first? I'm starved."

"Fine by me."

McKenzie ran to the kitchen and quickly returned with a stack of paper plates and napkins. "It's a good thing I'd just opened the box of kitchen essentials."

Carla accepted a paper plate from McKenzie. "I almost called Marc, to see if he would come and help."

As casually as she could manage, McKenzie said, "I'm glad you didn't."

"Why not?"

"I'm not sure we really hit it off. I know it's still too early to tell, but I got the distinct impression that he doesn't trust me."

Carla laughed. "I know he can be distant at times, but he's really a nice guy. You just have to get to know him. And he doesn't give his trust easily. You have to earn it."

"It would probably take my whole lifetime for that," McKenzie muttered to herself.

"What?"

"Nothing. I just don't think Marc and I are going to become friends. He's my boss, that's all. Besides, I think he's a little arrogant."

"A lot of people confuse confidence with arrogance. However, in my opinion all men are arrogant at one time or another. Some women, too." She looked pointedly at McKenzie.

McKenzie stopped eating. "Are you implying that I'm arrogant?"

"Are you?"

She was thoughtful. "I guess I can be."

After devouring half of the pizza, McKenzie and Carla worked long and hard, finding homes for most of the furniture. Hours later, an exhausted McKenzie called it a day.

"Thanks so much, Carla. I really appreciate your help."

"No problem. Do you want me to come by tomorrow and help you with the rest?"

"No. It's just a bunch of small stuff. I can handle it. I plan to do a little bit each day until I have everything exactly where I want it. Moving the furniture was the big part." McKenzie rubbed her back for emphasis.

"Well, the offer still stands. If you need any more help, just give me a call." Carla picked up her purse and headed toward the door.

Walking behind her, McKenzie murmured, "I will. Thanks for your help, and for lunch." She was still rubbing her lower back.

The two women embraced. After Carla drove away, McKenzie locked up. Spinning around the room, she let out a whoop of joy. *Home.* She had a home—not some impersonal hotel. She was exhilarated over being in her own place. She would be able to cook her own food, bathe in her own tub, even decorate. Glancing over at the boxes that needed to be unpacked, she groaned.

"I'm not going to unpack another box. Not tonight."

McKenzie was on her way upstairs when her doorbell rang. She was surprised to find a young woman with a huge fruit basket standing outside.

"Are you Dr. McKenzie Ashford?"

"Yes, I am."

"This is for you, then."

McKenzie took the basket and put it on a box near the door. "Hold on. I need to get my purse." She left and returned with a five-dollar bill. Giving it to the woman, she murmured a quick thank you.

As soon as she closed the door, McKenzie tore into the basket. As she opened the card, her mouth dropped open when she discovered the identity of the sender. Marc had sent the basket. She had assumed incorrectly that it had been Calvin.

So, Marc Chandler had been the sender. Grudgingly, McKenzie acknowledged that it was very thoughtful of him. However, she wasn't fooled by his gesture of kindness. Beneath his handsome veneer was a cold heart.

Biting into a juicy red apple, McKenzie savored its sweetness as she scanned the television channels in search of a good movie. She ate the apple quickly, disappointed when it was gone. Reaching over her head to throw the apple core into a nearby wastebasket, McKenzie was painfully reminded that her back ached from moving all the furniture from place to place. After finding nothing on TV, she felt a deep sense of melancholy. She was alone in the huge town house. For the first time in her thirty years, McKenzie was beginning to feel as if her life was passing her by. She knew her feelings of loneliness were somehow tied in with Marc—and nothing to do with her mother's death.

Tonight, feeling vulnerable, McKenzie wished to hear a man acknowledge that she was beautiful and desirable. She was in need of having her ego stroked. McKenzie reached for the telephone, intent on calling Calvin, but was disappointed to find he wasn't home.

The nagging pain in her back persisted, so she decided to take a long hot bath. Maybe a soak in the tub would be just what she needed. First she had to find the box marked *towels*. McKenzie groaned.

Minutes later, McKenzie sat in the Jacuzzi tub letting the hot bubbly water wash away her fatigue while the jets soothed her throbbing muscles. She thought of Marc and recalled his keen probing eyes and inscrutable expression. A wave of apprehension swept through her. The fact that Marc was rich and very powerful scared her. He could destroy everything she'd worked so hard for in a matter of seconds. Even so, McKenzie knew she could not change her mind. She had come too far to turn back now.

* * *

A light rap on the door drew Marc's attention from his computer. "Come in, McKenzie."

She stood near the door, wearing a crisp white shirt and a pair of faded blue jeans underneath a white lab coat. Her short hair lay flat against her scalp. "Clara wasn't at her desk—"

"It's okay. Please, take a seat." He motioned to a chair.

Taking off her glasses, McKenzie stuck them in the pocket of her lab coat before sitting. Her heart did a funny kind of flip, and her throat closed. The way he was watching her made McKenzie feel strange. She found him intensely attractive. McKenzie supposed that was one of the features her mother had fallen in love with. She had a weakness for good-looking men.

She was sexy as hell, Marc thought as he leaned back in his chair. "What can I do for you?"

"I wanted to say thank you for the fruit basket. It was really very thoughtful."

"You're welcome. How is the new house? Did you get all moved in?" Marc's gaze flicked over McKenzie. She looked uncomfortable, a taut expression on her face. He wanted to reach out and reassure her, but felt it improper to do so.

"I'm still a long way from getting it in order, but at least I have a place to come home to."

Silence fell in the room as the two eyed each other warily. Finally in a quiet silky tone, Marc asked, "You have things all worked out, haven't you?"

Stunned, McKenzie wasn't quite sure what he meant by the comment. After a slight pause she asked, "Excuse me?"

Marc felt a beginning spark of distrust. There was more going on here. He could not explain how he knew, but Dr. Ashford had a hidden agenda. "Carla tells me you've already given her your initial findings."

A sweep of relief washed over her, and McKenzie relaxed. "I've been doing research on HIV and AIDS for a few years. I really feel I'm onto something."

Something in her eyes renewed Marc's suspicion that she was

hiding something. Leaning forward, he sat with his hands folded together on his desk. "You know, McKenzie, I pride myself on my ability to read people. There seems to be something bothering you. Have I done something to offend you?"

Her body stiffened. McKenzie shook her head. "W-why would you think that?"

"Well, for one thing, whenever I'm around you seem tense." McKenzie was quiet.

"You can speak freely, Doc."

"Marc . . . it's really nothing. Getting this job and relocating to California was a big dream for me. I guess I really want to prove myself. I know that you're watching my every move—so much so that I feel you're just waiting for me to make a mistake. And I must admit that I don't like it very much. I have a job to do, and I give you my word that I intend to do my best."

Her directness took Marc aback.

McKenzie stood up. "Thanks again for the fruit. I'd better get back to work."

Before he could respond she was gone, leaving behind a faint floral scent.

Marc smiled. She was a feisty one, all right.

Five

Stifling a yawn, McKenzie headed out to her car. She was exhausted, and intended to head straight home. Right then all she wanted was a hot bath and her bed.

"McKenzie, do you have a moment?" Marc, walking fast, caught up with her beside her car.

As she placed her briefcase on the trunk of her car, McKenzie's eyes came up to study his expression. "Sure. What did you want to talk to me about?"

"I've been thinking about what you said, and I want to apologize for making you feel uncomfortable."

"You don't have to do that. It's not a big deal, really."

"It bothered you. I want to be honest with you though. You're the type of person who has the ability to hide her true feelings. Whenever I'm around you, I find myself wondering what's going on in that head of yours."

Maintaining her composure, McKenzie replied, "I think as long as I'm doing my job, you really shouldn't worry about anything else." She unlocked her car.

"You're probably right. However, I do care about the people who work for me."

Putting her briefcase into the backseat, she said, "That's admirable of you, Mr. Chandler."

He studied her for a moment. "Why is it that I get the feeling that we're adversaries?"

He could see that his question threw her, because of the way her mouth dropped open.

Marc gave a small laugh. "Are you surprised that I picked up on it?"

As casually as she could manage, she said, "I don't know what you're talking about."

Marc saw the pensive shimmer in her eyes. Alarm bells ringing in his head, he said, "There's something going on between us. Something I'm not quite sure I know about, but I intend to find out. Have a good evening, Doc."

Having said that, he strolled to his waiting car.

"You just wait, Marc Chandler. You may be perceptive, but what I have planned for you—you won't see that coming," McKenzie muttered as she stepped into her car.

Marc glanced in his rearview mirror before driving out of the parking lot. McKenzie was still sitting in the parking lot. He'd hit a nerve. "What are you up to, Dr. Ashford?" Until he found out, Marc decided, he would have to watch her very carefully.

McKenzie glared at the detective. "Dan, is this all you have?" Shaking her head in denial, she pleaded, "Please don't tell me this is all you have." Flinging the folder down on the table, she added, "This makes him sound like a Boy Scout."

"This Mr. Chandler had some problems in his youth, but he's clean. There's nothing else." The detective coughed into his handkerchief.

"Sounds like you're coming down with something," McKenzie observed. "Have you seen a doctor?"

"I have an appointment this afternoon."

She handed him an envelope. "I need you to check again. This time, I want a thorough check. I *know* he's hiding something."

Obviously surprised and slightly insulted, Dan said stiffly, "It's your money. But I'm telling you, Mr. Chandler is clean."

"I don't believe that. I—" She stopped short. Marc was there, and had spotted her. He was coming her way. McKenzie quickly dropped the folder into her purse.

"McKenzie, hello." His curious gaze traveled over Dan. "It's a surprise seeing you here." He was staring pointedly at Dan, as if waiting for an introduction.

"This is an acquaintance of mine." Her eyes beseeched the detective to keep quiet. "Dan, this is Marc Chandler."

"It's nice to meet you, Dan."

"Likewise." Checking his watch, Dan said, "I think it's time I left." He rose to his feet, saying, "I have an appointment. Good seeing you again." He navigated through the restaurant and disappeared.

She glanced up at Marc. "Would you like to join me?"

He sat down in the chair recently abandoned by Dan. "For a minute. How do you know that guy?"

"Excuse me?"

"How do you know him? He just doesn't look your type."

She leaned back in her chair, her arms folded across her chest. "Mr. Chandler, how would you have any idea what my type would be?"

He had the sense to look sheepish. "I overstepped my bounds. I apologize."

McKenzie broke into laughter. "You don't need to apologize. Dan is an old friend of mine, that's all."

"I didn't realize you had friends in California."

"There's a lot you don't know about me, Mr. Chandler."

"On that I have to agree." He looked around the restaurant and stood up. "My lunch companion has arrived."

Glancing behind him, McKenzie spotted a petite woman with a cute pixie look coming their way.

"Marc, how long have you been here?" She looked over at McKenzie and smiled. "Hello."

"Glenda, have you met Chandler's newest scientist, Dr. McKenzie Ashford?"

"Why, no I haven't." Holding out her hand, she said, I'm Glenda Prescott-Davis. I'm a sales rep for Med-Tech, Inc."

Shaking her hand, McKenzie responded, "It's very nice to meet you, Glenda. Is Reggie Howard still with Med-Tech?"

Glenda's eyes lit up. "Why yes, he is. He's my boss, in fact."

Marc looked surprised. "You know Reggie?"

McKenzie nodded. "Yes, Reggie and I attended Howard together. We kind of lost touch after he got married. Please tell him that I said hello."

"I sure will. It's a small world, isn't it?"

McKenzie was aware of Marc watching her. Wanting to dismiss the way her pulse accelerated so rapidly, she suggested, "You two had better grab your table before they think you've changed your minds." She stood up. "I'll see you later, Mr. Chandler."

"It's Marc."

"All right. I'll see you later, Marc. Nice meeting you, Glenda." McKenzie left as quickly as she could.

"Hmm, so it's Marc, is it?"

Looking down at Glenda, Marc frowned. His voice a low growl, he said, "Let's get our table before I change my mind."

"Brute," Glenda muttered under her breath.

Marc sighed his relief when Glenda left. Lunch was over, and she was on her way to harass someone else. She'd talked nonstop over lunch, grating on his nerves to no end.

It had been interesting seeing McKenzie with that man. He looked to Marc to be a policeman or detective. But why would she need one? He shook his head, trying to clear the confusion. What in hell was going on with McKenzie?

He called to mind a conversation with his father. *Keep your friends close, and your enemies closer.* No matter what she said or didn't say, Marc had a strong suspicion that he and McKenzie were enemies. He just didn't know why.

"Why are you in such deep thought?" Carla asked, entering his office. "What's on your mind?"

"McKenzie." He relayed his suspicions to her. To his surprise, Carla burst into laughter.

"What's so funny?"

"Did it ever occur to you that maybe she's interested in you—as a man?"

"No."

"Well, you might want to consider it. I think she's attracted to you."

Marc smiled. "You really think so?" That certainly had never entered his mind. Although Marc didn't believe in office romance, he found himself intrigued with the idea of getting to know McKenzie better.

She nodded. "Well, I just wanted to drop this off to you. I'm leaving for the rest of the day."

"I'll see you in the morning."

"Bright and early."

"And thanks, Carla."

"That's what friends are for. Besides, why would she hate you? You two never saw each other before she came to work for you."

"You're right about that. That's why it bothered me so much. McKenzie Ashford couldn't possibly have anything against me." He laughed. "At least, not yet. She hasn't worked here that long."

"You're terrible, Marc. I think you have finally met your match. And if you want to know the truth—I think it's a long time coming."

"I'm fine with the way things are. I don't need a mate."

"Marc, life is short, but it's much too long without happiness. I just want you to find some happiness."

He groaned. Carla wasn't going to give up. "Is that why you hired her? Because you thought she'd make me a good wife?"

Carla glared at him, clearly hurt. "I'm not going to even dignify that with a response." She stormed out of his office in a huff.

Marc knew he would have to apologize to Carla. But first he'd let her stew for a while. Maybe it would cure her penchant for matchmaking.

Six

Standing side by side in the lab, Carla and McKenzie went over McKenzie's formula once more. They had been in the lab most of the afternoon, discussing a tentative plan for the development of Chandler's oral vaccine.

Carla suddenly stretched and stifled a yawn. "I can't look at this anymore. I'm tired. How about you?"

Rubbing her eyes with the balls of her hands, McKenzie agreed. "I'm exhausted, too. I've made notes on all of the suggested changes. I'll enter them on Monday."

Carla nodded her approval. "I have an idea. Why don't we go out on the town tonight? You've been here almost three months now, and all you ever seem to do is work. Do you have a life outside of Chandler?"

"Not really." McKenzie shrugged as she moved to sit on a nearby stool. "You're right, Carla. I need to get out, but I don't think I have anything to wear. It's been so long since I've had a social life. I have no clue what the party people are wearing these days."

Carla laughed. "Just throw on something. With your body, no one will even notice what you're wearing."

"You're not going to take me to one of those meat markets I've heard so much about, are you?"

Carla giggled gleefully. "That's exactly where I'm taking you. You need to meet some men. Life is much too short to just let it pass you by."

"I know you're right, Carla, *but* I'm not looking for a man. I'm not the kind of woman who needs a man just to be happy."

"Oh, I'm not, either, but they sure are good to have around some of the time."

"Well, at least it'll give me a chance to sport my new Lexus." Carla laughed. "Look at you."

Smiling, McKenzie folded her arms across her chest. "I was only kidding."

"So, are you going out with me, or are you going to stay home and become a hermit?"

"I guess I'll go. It's not as if I had anything else to do tonight. What time should I meet you?"

"How about nine-thirty?"

"I'll see you there. Write down the address and directions to the club on that." She pointed to the yellow pad of paper lying on her desk.

"I'm so glad we're having this girl's night out. I don't have any female friends who live on the West Coast, so I don't get to socialize much myself. I hate going out alone, and if I don't have a date . . ."

Nodding, McKenzie replied, "I'm that way, too. I have to be honest, though. It's been a really long time since I've been to a club—years. I hope I remember how to dance."

"You're going to be just fine." She glanced at her watch. "Well, I'd better be going. I have some errands to run before tonight."

"Thanks for inviting me."

"No problem. See you later." Carla started out of the lab. "Oh, and jeans are not allowed."

"Wonderful. That's all I wear." McKenzie slumped down in her chair and rolled over to the computer. She was still sitting there two hours later when David strolled by her office. He backtracked and stood in the doorway, watching her for a moment.

Without taking her eyes off the monitor, McKenzie said, "Hello, David. I didn't know you were still here."

"I didn't know you were here, either. Are you planning to move in, girlfriend? You've been here since six this morning. It's now seven-thirty P.M. Why don't you call it a day?"

McKenzie rubbed the tensed muscles in her neck. "I could say the same about you. You should have left hours ago. Why are *you* still here?"

"I had some work I wanted to catch up on. I'm going on vacation at the end of the week. I need to free my mind!"

McKenzie glanced up at her calendar. "That's right. I totally forgot about that."

"Well, I have to leave. I'm meeting my *husband* for dinner. Want to join us?"

"No thanks. I appreciate the invitation, but I'm just going to grab a sandwich before I go clubbing with Carla."

"What? You're going out? I don't believe it!"

"Why not? Believe it or not, I'm not a recluse."

"Go head, girlfriend! Have a good time." David was about to walk away, but McKenzie called him back.

"David, wait! I'm leaving, too. I hate being in this building alone."

"You won't be alone." He grinned. "Marc is still here."

"And?"

David laughed. "You two are so funny. It wouldn't surprise me none if you ended up getting married."

"To each other?"

David nodded.

McKenzie frowned. "I think you're letting the chemicals go to your brain. Me and Marc married? That'll be the day!"

McKenzie stepped out of a red silk dress and spread it on the bed. She glanced at the bed and sighed loudly. Clothes had been thrown all over the room in her quest to find something suitable to wear.

"Ooooh! Why did I agree to this?" McKenzie shook her head. "I don't have anything to wear."

Wearing nothing but a strapless bra and thong panties, she fell across her bed, groaning in frustration. Massaging her temple, McKenzie calmed herself. She meditated a moment longer before climbing off her bed.

"Okay, McKenzie, you can do this," she murmured as she examined the heap of clothing. "You can manage to look like a lady for one night."

Her eyes traveled once more to the red dress that Calvin's mother had given her for Christmas. It really was beautiful, McKenzie admitted. She just hated wearing dresses. A T-shirt and a pair of jeans were always more to her liking.

She tried the red silk on once more. "Not half bad," McKenzie reluctantly acknowledged. "Well, this will just have to do."

Rummaging through her bathroom drawer, McKenzie searched for a floral cosmetics bag containing what little makeup she owned. "Okay, where is the darn bag?" she fumed.

McKenzie found what she'd been looking for. She frowned when she saw that the bottle of foundation was so old that the liquid had separated. Frowning, she threw the bottle away. Bravely, she stuck her hand back into the bag, wondering what other corroded items she would find. She released a sigh of relief when she found a tube of lipstick that didn't crumble upon opening.

"I'd better have a really good time tonight. Going through all this," she mumbled as she applied color to her lips.

Viewing herself in the huge mirror, McKenzie brushed her short hair, running her fingers through the soft waves. "It's time for a trim," she observed. She liked her hair cut close because she had no desire to comb her hair. In fact, she didn't even own a comb. She had been very tender-headed as a child, and getting her hair combed had been an ordeal for her, as well as for her mother and grandmother.

She checked the clock. It was time for her to be leaving, so she grabbed her purse and headed to the door. McKenzie's thoughts centered on Marc. How did he spend his weekends?

she wondered. A handsome single man—McKenzie was sure he had women to spare. It was a most discomforting thought.

Carla was standing outside of Mystique, a popular night spot in Los Angeles, when McKenzie arrived.

Spotting her, Carla met her halfway. "I'm so glad you made it. I was beginning to get worried."

Pulling the snug-fitting dress down, McKenzie said, "I'm so sorry I'm late. Finding something to wear turned out to be a big chore for me. Dresses are not exactly my thing."

"But you look stunning. I love that color on you."

Relaxing, McKenzie smiled. "Thanks, Carla. I would feel a little better if this dress would stop riding up my thighs and I had on a pair of flats." She gave a tiny laugh. "I'm so afraid I'm going to fall on my face."

Carla led her into the club. They made their way toward the bar. "Come on, let's get a drink. I think you just need to loosen up a bit."

"I don't drink. I'll just have a Coke or mineral water."

While they waited for their drinks, Carla said, "You really look nice, McKenzie."

"So do you. But then, you're always so dressed up. You look like you should be on a runway somewhere." McKenzie admired the short, sleeveless, black dress Carla was wearing. "I've always been kind of a tomboy."

Two men eased up beside them.

"You two look like you're in need of some male company this evening. My name is Bo, and this is my friend, Derek. I know you thought I was Wesley Snipes. People always confuse me with him."

McKenzie and Carla exchanged amused glances.

"Hello Bo. Derek," she said, fighting back her laughter. Bo looked nothing like Wesley Snipes.

"It's n-nice to meet you both. I'm Carla, and this is McKenzie," Carla added.

"How 'bout the four of us grabbing a table somewhere? We can all get to know each other," Derek suggested.

McKenzie didn't like the lusty leer Bo was giving her. When she caught him staring at her breasts, he simply grinned, showing a gold tooth.

"Carla and I just got here, and we're just checking out the place for now."

"You can still check out the place with us. We're a couple of nice guys just trying to meet some nice women. How 'bout it?" Bo asked. He placed his hand on McKenzie's arm, pulling her beside him.

She pushed away from him. "I don't know you, Bo. Do not ever put your hands on me," she demanded.

He retreated a step back, holding his hands up. "I'm sorry. Didn't mean to overstep my bounds, pretty lady." He grinned once more, displaying the gold tooth. "Accept my apologies?"

She nodded. "It was nice meeting you both, but I think we should be moving on. Ready, Carla?"

"I'm ready. See you."

"Oh, so now you gonna be like that? Just dis a couple of brothers like that?"

" 'Fraid so," McKenzie replied as she and Carla put as much distance between them and the two men as they could.

"Can you believe the audacity of that Wesley Snipes wannabe?" McKenzie snapped.

Carla laughed. "They were two clowns."

A man wearing a white three-piece suit with a red shirt and red patent leather shoes stood in their path. He eyed McKenzie and grinned.

"Oh, Lord," she murmured under her breath. "Who is he trying to be?"

"I'm not exactly sure," Carla replied. "But here he comes."

"Hey there, honey love," he directed at McKenzie. "You're looking good tonight." Using his fingers, he brushed back his long flowing hair.

"He's got a weave!" Carla stated through lips that barely moved.

Blinking twice and trying to keep from bursting into laughter, McKenzie asked, "What did you call me?"

He gestured toward the dance floor. "You wanna dance?" he asked, ignoring her question.

Clearing her throat, she smiled before saying, "Not right now, but thank you for—"

"Wha— You turning me down? Nobody turns Sweet Daddy down."

McKenzie folded her arms across her chest. "Er . . . Mr. Sweet Daddy, I'm not really in the mood to dance right now."

"Come on. Just one lil' dance with ole' Sweet Daddy," he insisted."

McKenzie was getting angry. "I *said,* no thank you."

"Then what you come to the club for?" he demanded, getting louder and louder.

Aware that they were drawing attention, McKenzie glanced over at Carla, her expression one of frustration.

"What? You and Redbone here got something going on?" He looked at her with disdain. "With all your hair cut off, I guess you the man."

McKenzie's temper snapped. "Look, Mr. Sweet Daddy, or whatever your name is, I don't want to dance right now. It's a free country, and I can do what I want when I feel like doing it. *Understand?"*

"You skinny bi—"

"Is he bothering you, ma'am?" a voice from behind her asked. Turning around, she saw two men who looked like bodybuilders. McKenzie assumed they were bouncers.

"Sweet Daddy don't need to bother nobody. Hell with you, lady. You don't look that good, anyway," he mumbled as he walked away leaning slightly to the side. "Ole' baldheaded heifer . . ."

McKenzie and Carla burst into laughter.

"I'm so sorry, McKenzie."

"It's okay. I never knew men like Sweet Daddy really existed outside of television. The man looks like a caricature of a seventies pimp."

Someone tapped her on the shoulder. Warily, she turned around. She quickly assessed the man standing there. Tall, dark, and handsome came to mind. He seemed to be sane. That was a strong plus as far as she was concerned. Relaxing, McKenzie smiled.

"My name is Joseph. Would you like to dance?"

"Lead the way." She gave Carla the thumbs-up as she headed to the dance floor.

McKenzie found she was able to pick up the latest dance moves fairly quickly.

"Having a good time?" Joseph asked.

She nodded. "I am. It's been a long time since I've been out dancing."

"For me, too."

After dancing to several songs, McKenzie allowed him to escort her to an empty table. When her eyes scanned the club for Carla, he said, "If you're looking for your friend, she's on the dance floor."

They sat down and Joseph ordered a drink for himself and soda for her.

"So, McKenzie, what do you do for a living?"

"I'm a medical scientist. I work for Chandler Pharmaceuticals."

"I see. That's impressive."

"What do you do?"

He seemed to tense up, but it was gone so quickly that McKenzie wasn't sure she hadn't imagined it.

"I'm currently looking for employment. I'm an accountant. I just moved back home."

She nodded. "Where were you living?"

"I was in San Francisco. I did my time there, and now it's time to start over."

"I just moved here myself. I'm from Orlando."

"I've always wanted to visit Florida. Maybe I'll do that some-time next year."

A woman approached the table.

"Joseph! I knew I'd find you here. Who is this thing you're with?"

McKenzie held up her hand. "Wait a minute! I just met him, and all we did was dance. We sat down a few minutes before you came over . . ." Standing up, she said, "But you know what? I'll get up. Matter-of-fact, you can take this chair."

Joseph stood up quickly. "McKenzie, you don't have to leave. I'm not married—"

"You may not be married to me, but we do got three kids together." She looked over at McKenzie. "He just still mad at me 'cause I turned him in. See, I ain't going to jail for nobody."

"Sherika—" Joseph said in a warning tone.

"He tell you he just got out of prison?" she continued.

"Whoa, you've giving me entirely too much information. I don't need to know any of this."

"McKenzie, I can explain."

"No need to." She turned and walked away as quickly as she could. She was met by Carla.

"Looks as if the two of you really hit it off—"

McKenzie shook her head.

"No. What happened?"

"It's not really important. I'll just say that things haven't really changed much in the club scene. How do you feel about grabbing a late-night snack, or an early breakfast? I've had enough for tonight."

"I'm inclined to agree."

Spotting Sweet Daddy standing nearby, McKenzie looped her arm through Carla's. "I think we should make our escape while we can. Ready?"

"I'm ready."

As they passed him, they heard him say, "You need yourself a real man."

McKenzie stopped long enough to reply, "You're right. And

until I find him I'm going to keep looking. I've never been one to accept substitutes."

McKenzie and Carla giggled as they left the club and headed to their cars. In spite of everything, it had been good to get out of the house.

Seven

On Monday McKenzie glanced up from the microscope, sneaking a peek at the wall clock. She needed to get into Marc's office, and now seemed like the perfect opportunity. Glancing over at the lab assistant, she cautiously removed the slide, placing it on the counter before yanking off her plastic gloves.

"Bill, I need to go upstairs to check on something. Think you can handle things until I get back?"

His eyes never leaving the monitor, Bill responded, "Sure can. By the way, if you're going to see Marc, he left about thirty minutes ago. He had to go to some meeting in Los Angeles. He'll probably be gone for a couple of hours."

That's just what I'm counting on, McKenzie thought. Aloud she said, "No, I'm not looking for Marc. I need to run up to the personnel office. I shouldn't be gone long."

"Cool," Bill murmured as his nimble fingers brushed over the keyboard. "Carla wants me to make some changes to the formula. I can work on this while you're upstairs."

McKenzie prepared to leave, but stopped. "Oh, I almost forgot. When you were at lunch, David called. He left all of the reports you'll need on his desk."

Bill muttered something unintelligible under his breath.

Smiling, McKenzie headed to the elevators.

Upstairs, she rapped lightly on the door to Marc's office. When she didn't receive a response, McKenzie opened the door a crack. Good. Marc wasn't there. He had already left for Los

Angeles. And she knew Clara had a dental appointment and would be gone for the rest of the day. McKenzie ignored the warning bells in her head and opened the door wider. She eased into the office, closing the door behind her gently.

McKenzie rushed over to Marc's file cabinet, opening it quickly. Running her fingers across the tops of the folders, she scanned for anything that seemed a bit strange. Disappointed but satisfied that she'd been thorough, she headed to the credenza next.

McKenzie was surprised to find it unlocked. After a meticulous search, she was disappointed to find nothing that would indicate any wrongdoing on his part—nothing incriminating. She knew he probably wouldn't be careless enough to leave anything out in the open, but she'd had to check, anyway. McKenzie then went through his desk, pausing only to make sure everything was back in its proper place.

Just as she was about to leave, McKenzie heard Marc's voice. He was right outside the door. *Oh, no! What do I do now?"* Glancing around, she realized there was no way out.

When Marc opened the door leading into his office, he found McKenzie standing by the large window. She made sure the tension was gone from her face before she turned to him.

Taking a deep breath, she said, "Hello, Marc."

"Hello, McKenzie." Surprise clearly written on his face, Marc asked, "What are you doing in here?"

"I-I wanted to t-talk to you. Do you have a minute?"

"Sure. I was headed into LA for a meeting, but it's been canceled. Luckily, they caught me in the car before I drove all the way there." He strode over to his desk, sinking into the mahogany-tinted leather chair. "Is everything okay?"

McKenzie watched him warily as he sat down. "Yes. W-why do you ask?" Her fingers fluttered to her neck.

"You look somewhat nervous."

McKenzie licked her lips and chose her words carefully. "Marc. I feel that we've gotten off on the wrong foot somehow. I thought maybe I offended—"

Marc held up a hand to silence her. "There's no need, McKenzie. You haven't offended me in any way." When she made no move to leave, he asked, "Is there something else?" Distrust cast a chill of reserve over his eyes. "I don't believe you came all the way up here just to apologize for something that never happened."

What in the world was she going to say that wouldn't arouse Marc's suspicions? She watched as he scanned his office, as if trying to detect if anything was out of place. McKenzie knew she had to come up with something and quick. "Well, I do have a confession to make."

He turned sharp eyes on her. "Oh?"

"I came here to ask you if you would have dinner with me. Your secretary had already left for the day. I was going to leave a note—"

"You want me to have dinner with you?" he interrupted. Marc sat forward and looked at her intently. "Why?"

"I thought . . . we . . . could get to know each other better."

"Let me get this straight. Are you asking me out on a date?" He was grinning from ear to ear.

The nerve of the man, McKenzie fumed. The last thing she wanted to do was date Marc Chandler. However, she did want to kill any suspicions he might be tossing about.

"Well?"

"No, Marc. I'm not asking you out on a date. Not a real date. Just dinner."

"I see. I have one question before I respond. Why? I was under the impression you didn't care much for me."

"I don't dislike you." *Liar,* her inner voice screamed. "That's not it at all."

Marc seemed to give this some thought. "Are you attracted to me? Is that what you're trying to tell me?"

His arrogance was astounding. Marc had her backed against a wall, and he knew exactly what he was doing. She had played right into his hands, and for the moment there was nothing she could do about it—not without exposing her true intentions. "I think I'd better leave. This was a bad idea." The moment the words had come out of Marc's mouth, McKenzie realized he'd spoken the truth. She was attracted to him.

He stood and walked over to the window where she was standing. A slender delicate thread began to form between them, drawing them closer and closer.

"I . . . thank you for asking me out, but I'm afraid I'm going to have to decline. I don't think it would be a good idea for us to get involved."

"Get involved? I was only . . ." her voice drifted off.

Marc turned to face her, then. "What were you going to say?"

His gentle tone added to her mortification. Chin tilted up, she said, "N-nothing. It wasn't anything important."

"McKenzie—"

"I-I'd better leave." Humiliated, McKenzie turned and fled. *How could she have been so stupid?* How could she let him believe she wanted . . . she couldn't finish the thought. She berated herself all the way back to her office. Once there, she realized she couldn't concentrate on her work. She wanted to strike out at the invisible web of attraction that was building between them. *This isn't part of the plan,* an inner voice admonished.

Rather than having to face Marc after making a total fool of herself, convinced he had probably credited her being in his office for all the wrong reasons, McKenzie decided to plead a headache and go home. For some inexplicable reason, his rejection of her hurt deeply.

Later, at home, she stood by the kitchen window, absent-mindedly wiping her hands on her apron. McKenzie couldn't stop thinking about Marc, and how she'd made a fool of herself in his office. And to add to her mortification, she found herself becoming entangled in his web of charm. She had no business feeling the way she did—not when it came to Marc. There was no future for them. It could never be.

* * *

"Hi, Mack."

McKenzie was thrilled to hear Calvin's voice on the other end of the phone line. "Calvin, how are you?"

"I'm good. How are things on your end?"

"Things are fine. I'm staying busy, as always." She forced herself to sound bright and cheerful, lest she alert Calvin to the way she really felt.

"I wouldn't expect any less from you, Mack."

McKenzie rolled up her eyeballs in irritation. "Ha, ha, Calvin."

"Don't get riled up, Mack. I'm just kidding."

"I know. It's just that you make me sound . . . like some kind of strange person."

"You know that's not how I see you."

McKenzie was quiet.

"Mack—"

"I'm all right, Calvin. I was just thinking that maybe I do work too hard."

"Oh, so now you want to slow down? What brought this on?"

"Nothing in particular. I just feel that I've missed out on something. Like living, for instance."

"Trust me, Mack. You haven't missed much. You're dedicated—there's nothing wrong with that. I've never known you to be any other way. Whatever you do, don't try to change. I don't think I could handle it."

McKenzie laughed. "Thanks, Calvin. Now, tell me what you've been up to, and don't leave anything out."

They talked for an hour. McKenzie stifled a yawn.

"Well, it's late here, and I've got an early day tomorrow. You be good, Mack, and don't forget to write."

"Calvin, you know I'm not good at writing letters. I'd much rather call you."

"Take care, girl."

She hung up, her heart swollen with emotion. McKenzie

missed her best friend. Calvin had filled the void that the deaths of her mother and grandmother left.

Heading downstairs to the kitchen, McKenzie went in search of dinner. Pulling out a menu she kept in a drawer in the kitchen, she chose grilled chicken breasts on a bed of fettuccini Alfredo. McKenzie picked up the phone and placed her order.

Hours after everyone else had gone home, Marc was still in his office. He collapsed onto his desk chair and stared thoughtfully at his impressive collection of books. They filled the shelves to capacity. However, his mind was not on his books. It was on a certain wide-eyed scientist. Carla had been right. McKenzie was attracted to him. He still couldn't believe she'd actually come to his office to ask him out to dinner.

A part of him was thrilled. From the first time he laid eyes on her, she'd touched something inside him that defied identification—something dangerously familiar.

Warning bells sounded in his mind. She was getting under his skin, but she was trouble. He knew that like the back of his own hand. No other woman had ever fascinated him to such distraction. His eyes became reflective. *Except one* . . . he amended resentfully. And that particular woman was someone Marc preferred not to remember. His chest rose and fell in quick breaths as he strove to contain the bitter pain that memory elicited.

What kind of power did McKenzie hold over him? Marc didn't believe in magic, but he had never before felt himself drawn by some intangible force to another human being, either. It would not be wise to let her get close to him, his subconscious warned. He didn't know anything about her beyond her work credentials.

Very soon I'll find out, Marc assured himself confidently. Much wiser now, there was no way he could be fooled by another woman's charms. He vowed to stay as far away from McKenzie as possible. The last thing he needed was to get involved with another deceiving woman. With the discovery of his mother's betrayal, he'd had enough to last him a lifetime.

He had only been in love once, and that had been enough. After Margie, Marc had never allowed himself to become emotionally involved with another woman. It hurt too much. In the beginning, he simply trifled with them until he lost interest or exposed their lies, whichever came first. But as he matured, he no longer bothered with the games. Using women brought him no joy. Instead, he was left with remorse. He wondered if McKenzie would prove to be different from the other women.

Marc was bothered about the way she'd left his office. He hadn't meant to embarrass her. He had gone down to her office earlier, but discovered she'd already left. Maybe it would be best to pretend the afternoon had never happened.

Eight

Two weeks later, The Angel Heart Foundation held its annual AIDS charity ball. With Carla being a board member and Chandler being the foundation's largest sponsor, McKenzie felt compelled to attend. She dreaded being around Marc in such a social setting. Since that day, the few times she had run into him Marc seemed overly polite, which only served to make her feel more uncomfortable. To add to her misery, she felt strange in her flowing silk gown. Carla had gone shopping with her and picked out the teal dress. It was Carla who'd helped McKenzie apply what little makeup she reluctantly agreed to wear.

McKenzie stood stiffly by the marble fireplace, patiently listening to Mrs. Dolly Fitzwater. Mrs. Fitzwater was an innocuous sort of woman, rather silly, and worth millions. She was one of the attendees who had donated thousands of dollars to AIDS research, and she wanted everyone to know. McKenzie didn't want to offend her, so she suffered through the conversation. It was a half hour later before she finally managed to escape, murmuring polite apologies as she fled.

McKenzie had to go to the bathroom. She'd sat through dinner and a boring speech, and just when she'd thought she'd made her escape she'd encountered Mrs. Fitzwater. Now she couldn't wait any longer. Not wanting to draw attention to herself, McKenzie headed toward a side door and up the stairs. Once there, she breathed a sigh of relief upon finding the ladies room empty.

* * *

Marc eyed McKenzie as she navigated her way toward the stairs. Tonight, dressed in a gown that fit as if made just for her, Marc thought her exquisite. She had even applied a touch of makeup—something she didn't need. McKenzie had a natural beauty. She was a proud black woman—proud of her Nubian features.

Seeing her nervously pulling at her dress on several occasions tonight, Marc surmised she was not comfortable. He preferred the comfort of more casual dress, and he had the feeling that that was something they shared.

Easing toward the entrance, Marc headed in the direction of the stairs. The rest rooms were located just to the right of the stairway. Now would be a good opportunity to freshen up.

A more relaxed McKenzie left the bathroom and headed toward the stairs. Suddenly she heard a woman's voice. She moved slowly toward the stairs she had come up, hoping to reach them unnoticed, but there were two people blocking her way—Marc and Glenda. McKenzie froze when she overheard part of their conversation.

"Why don't you come by my place tonight, Marc?" the woman pleaded. "I've missed you so much."

"Glenda, this is not the time or the place for this discussion," Marc stated flatly.

Standing in the shadows, McKenzie watched as Glenda wrapped her arms around Marc's waist. Feeling uncomfortable, she wanted to move away, but her feet were glued to the spot. Besides, they were standing just a few feet from the stairway. Glenda was making an outrageous play for Marc. McKenzie thought the woman needed her head examined. She swore inwardly that she would never be so clinging.

"You know how much I want you."

"I'm flattered, Glenda, but I can't do this. What we had is over," he said, removing her arms from around him.

McKenzie's eyes widened in shock when Glenda's hands traveled in search of the most male part of him.

"See?" she said in a triumphant voice, rubbing his arousal. "You still want me."

"No, I'm just too accustomed to having you." Clutching her wandering hands in his own, he said, "Glenda, don't lower yourself like this."

"It's Dr. Ashford. Isn't it? Don't bother denying it. I can tell you have the hots for her. I've seen the way you've been watching her all night long."

Marc stiffened slightly when he heard a faint gasp from the shadows. Then a smile came over his face. "She's not my type. Too skinny."

McKenzie clenched her fist. *The nerve of that man.* Why, she ought to go right out there and give him a piece of her mind.

But Glenda was not to be put off. Again she wrapped her arms around Marc, pulling his head down, kissing him.

Marc pushed her away. "I've tried to be nice about this, but you won't listen. I'm not interested," he said in exasperation. He turned his back to her.

"How can you be so cold?"

"I didn't want to hurt you, but you wouldn't listen."

"I hope you'll reconsider, Marc. You won't regret it."

Marc closed his eyes and shook his head. "You'd better head downstairs, Glenda. I'm sure your *date* is looking for you." He started to walk away.

Pulling at his arm, Glenda began, "Marc, you misunderstood—"

He whirled around, facing her. "Glenda, please. I know what I saw. Face it, you got caught with your pants down, literally."

Glenda said nothing. Without a backward glance, she disappeared down the stairs. McKenzie waited for Marc to leave.

"Didn't anyone teach you that it's poor manners to hide and

eavesdrop on private conversations?" he asked without turning around.

McKenzie stared, aghast. He had known all along she was there. Coming out of the shadows, she said, "The last thing I'd do is eavesdrop. Your conversation with your *friend* was certainly of no interest to me. I wanted to leave the two of you to your privacy, but you were blocking the stairs."

He turned around, inclining his head. "Well, you could've announced yourself."

McKenzie gave him a level stare. "Glenda had already made a fool of herself with you. I saw no need to embarrass her further."

"She probably wouldn't have seen it that way if the situation were reversed."

"Not a lot of people would, I suppose." McKenzie looked up into Marc's handsome face. "You certainly have a way with women." She clamped a hand over her mouth. She hadn't meant to say those words.

Marc threw back his head, laughing. "Why don't you tell me what you really think?"

"I shouldn't have said that. I'm sorry."

"Don't give it another thought." Marc stood for a long moment not saying anything, just studying her face as if trying to memorize it.

McKenzie grew uncomfortable under his intense scrutiny. Putting her hand to her face, she asked, "Okay, what is it? Do I have food on my face, or something?" Sighing, she said in a low voice, "That's why I hate these fancy dinners—"

He laughed deep in his throat. "No, you don't have anything on your face. I was just admiring your skin."

She self-consciously placed a hand on her face. "M-my skin?"

"You have a beautiful complexion."

"Thank you." McKenzie started to laugh.

"What's so funny?"

"It's . . . well, I've never been told that before."

"It's true." Marc looked away, then back at her.

They gazed at each other.

Marc looked away first. "I guess I should head downstairs. Are you coming?"

She shook her head. "No, I'll come down in a few minutes."

"Enjoy your evening, then."

"You, too," McKenzie whispered as he descended the stairs. She was glad to have this moment alone to gather her thoughts. In her mind, *she* had been kissing Marc not Glenda. It had seemed so real. She had almost felt him kissing her thoroughly, felt her body warm against his. McKenzie mentally shook herself. Shaken by the trail her thoughts had taken her on, she sank down on a nearby chair, taking deep breaths. *Where had that come from?*

Blinking hard, she was trying not to cry. Tears wouldn't solve anything, and she desperately needed some solutions.

Composing herself, McKenzie finally felt prepared to join the other guests downstairs.

Her eyes searched around the huge banquet room, looking for Carla. She wanted to go home. As she scanned the room once more, her eyes met Marc's. With a will of its own, her heart did a flip when he smiled and winked.

McKenzie spotted Carla talking to the Chief of Staff from St. Vincent's Hospital in Los Angeles. Waving to get Carla's attention, she held up her purse and keys. Carla soon made her way over to their table.

"I've been looking all over this room for you. Where did you disappear to?"

"I had to go to the bathroom. Are you ready to leave?" McKenzie glanced over at Marc, who stood a few feet away, silently watching them. "I've suddenly developed a headache."

"I'm ready if you are. Mrs. Fitzwater tried to talk my ear off. I felt so sorry for you when she had you cornered."

"She was okay. She made some good points, and she even liked my idea—"

"You mean, she actually let you get a word in?"

McKenzie laughed. "Not really, but she's just a lonely woman. If I hadn't had to run off to the bathroom, I would have stayed and talked . . . well, listened . . . to her more."

They made their way over to the door before someone called Carla over to their table. She looked at McKenzie, who said, "Go on, I'll wait here by the entrance."

Marc eased up beside her and whispered into her ear, saying, "You're not trying to sneak out, are you?"

"I wasn't sneaking out. It is still a free country, isn't it?"

"I'm sorry to hear you've developed a headache."

"Now who's eavesdropping?" McKenzie favored him with a look of mock annoyance.

Marc laughed. "I guess I deserved that. I wish you weren't leaving. I wanted to talk to you."

"About what, Marc?"

"About what happened in my office a few weeks ago—"

McKenzie cast her eyes down in shame. "Please don't remind me."

Marc leaned forward and lowered his voice. "I've given this a lot of thought. I know there's something between us, McKenzie. I know you feel it, too. It's not something I can explain, but it's there just the same. Maybe we should at least talk about it."

She shook her head. "I didn't mean to imply that I wanted anything other than dinner, Marc. I acted a bit hastily. I shouldn't have come up to your office like that."

"Why don't we—"

"Don't the two of you look cozy?" said Carla as she walked up. "I'm not interrupting anything, am I?"

Clearly amused, Marc downed the last of his wine. "No, I was just about to get myself another drink. You two ladies drive safely."

Gritting her teeth, McKenzie could have choked Carla at that particular moment. Marc had been on the verge of asking her something when she strolled up. She was now left with her own speculations as to what he was about to say.

"Good night, Marc," McKenzie said softly, easing by him.

Carla turned toward Marc and winked.

Glenda sidled up next to him. "Too skinny, huh? Looks to me like she's got your nose wide open."

"Where is your victim for tonight?" Marc asked.

"He's getting the car. Looks like you're going home alone." She patted his shoulder. "I hear a cold shower and a boring documentary are good ways to relieve sexual frustration."

"Good night, Glenda," Marc growled before stalking off.

She laughed. "You have a good evening, too."

McKenzie thought about what Marc said all night long and into the next day. He was wrong, she decided. There was nothing going on between them. Nothing at all. At least, not in the way he was thinking.

She searched through her pantry and the refrigerator, but found nothing to her liking. McKenzie decided to eat out.

She drove to a seafood restaurant in Marina Del Rey. While waiting to be seated, she felt a light tap on her shoulder.

"McKenzie?"

She turned around quickly. "Hi, Marc." He was dressed in a black suit, looking pretty much the same way he did in the office. From what she remembered, he had always been a dresser.

"Did you work today?" she asked.

"No—well, kind of. I had a meeting." Gesturing around the restaurant, Marc commented, "I guess we had the same idea."

McKenzie nodded. "Looks like it."

"I hate eating out alone. Why don't we sit together?"

She shook her head. "No, I don't think so."

"Why not?"

"Well, when I made a fool of myself by inviting you to dinner—it didn't go well."

"I'm really sorry about that. Let's call a truce for now. What do you say?" He grinned boyishly.

McKenzie relented. "That's fine. To be honest, I hate to eat by myself, too."

The hostess seated them quickly.

"Have you eaten here before?" Marc asked.

Peeking over her menu, McKenzie replied, "Just once. How about you?"

"This was my father's favorite restaurant. He loved seafood."

"So do I." McKenzie placed her menu on the table.

"Do I still make you uncomfortable?"

She shook her head. "No—well, actually you do."

He lowered his voice. "I never meant to embarrass you, Doc."

"We don't need—"

Marc interrupted her. *"Yes we do.* We need to talk about what's going on."

"There's nothing going on."

"From the day I met you, I intended to keep a professional distance between us, but I'm finding that I can't seem to keep you off my mind."

"Marc, please don't—"

"I believe in putting all my cards on the table. We are attracted to each other. You can't deny that. Can you?" He challenged her with his eyes.

She looked away, refusing to respond.

"I think we owe it to ourselves to investigate—"

"No," McKenzie interjected. "We don't need to do anything except ignore this . . . this whatever it is. I'm sure it'll pass."

The waiter arrived and took their orders.

"Doc, I don't think you're being very realistic."

"Marc, I think it's best if we just forget about this . . . this attraction. You're my employer, and I've always made it a practice not to play where I work. You can understand that, can't you?"

He nodded. "If only it were that simple."

"It can be. I really love my job at Chandler. I don't want to risk losing it over a failed attempt at a relationship."

Marc leaned in closer. "Do you think I'm not able to separate my business life from my personal life?"

"I don't know. But I'm not willing to take a chance."

"So where does that leave us?"

"An employer and his employee having dinner together." McKenzie couldn't call him a friend. She hoped Marc would not force the issue any longer. She tried to assess his unreadable features. "Marc?"

He smiled. "I was thinking we might try being friends. What do you think?"

A smile tugged at the corners of her mouth, and McKenzie smiled. Perhaps she should consider becoming his friend. Maybe she'd find out more of his secrets from the man himself. "Well, friend, any idea how much longer we have to wait for our food? I'm starved."

"It's on its way now." Marc nodded toward the approaching waiter.

Throughout dinner, McKenzie felt a certain sadness at knowing there could be nothing more between them. She also experienced a thread of guilt gently pulling at her. How could she feel this strange attraction toward a man she believed had a hand in her mother's death? All these years she'd been filled with hate for him. And now she felt an undeniable attraction. *How can this be?* she wondered.

"Doc?" Marc called her out of her reverie.

"Yes, what is it?"

"Aren't you going to eat? A moment ago, you could hardly wait for the food to arrive, and now you're letting it sit and get cold."

"I was thinking about something."

"Anything you want to talk about? I'm a good listener."

McKenzie shook her head. "Not yet." Picking up her knife and fork, she sliced off a piece of red snapper and put it in her mouth. *When the time is right, I'll tell you everything,* she added silently.

Marc found himself enjoying McKenzie. He didn't miss the way she attacked her food with gusto. Marc had never met anyone like her. McKenzie was good company, and seemed very grounded. In fact, she seemed perfect—too perfect.

Once again, warning bells sounded, but Marc refused to acknowledge them. He was having a good time. It was something he hadn't done in a long time.

"What's on your mind, Marc?"

He glanced up. "I was just thinking how much I've enjoyed talking to you."

She placed her napkin on the table. "I was the one doing most of the talking. I'm sorry I got so carried away about the vaccine."

"That's fine. I admire your dedication." Marc leaned back in his chair. "I think Carla made one of her best decisions in hiring you."

McKenzie smiled. "Thank you for saying that. But you're not off the hook, you know."

"What?"

"Tell me about Marc Chandler. I've told you my life story. I want to hear yours."

Marc hesitated, measuring her for a moment. "There's not much to tell. I was born in Miami, and we moved to California when I was a year old. I was a typical teenager—girl crazy. That is, until I got my heart broken. After that I got my priorities straight."

"You're a very secretive man, Mr. Chandler."

He smiled. "Not secretive—just cautious. I'm a very private person."

"I can respect that. But the truth of the matter is that you don't know me from Adam, and you're not quite sure you can trust me." McKenzie leaned forward. "What is it about me that makes you so distrustful?"

"It's not you, Doc. I'm like this by nature. Please don't take it personally."

"Well, if you're going to be my friend you're going to have to lighten up," she said with a slight smile of defiance.

His fingers ached to reach over and touch her. McKenzie

projected an energy and power that vitally attracted him to her. "I'll remember that."

When the check arrived, McKenzie reached for her purse. Marc stopped her with a gentle touch to her wrist. "Dinner is on me."

"Marc, you really—"

"What was it you said not too long ago? 'If you're going to be my friend—you have to lighten up'—was that it?"

She nodded. "But—"

"Dinner is on me. Understood?"

"Thank you, Mr. Chandler. It's been a wonderful evening."

"I enjoyed myself, too, and my name is Marc."

They stood up to leave.

"You know what, Marc? You're very bossy."

He threw back his head and laughed. "And you, Doc, are one of a kind."

"What are your plans for Labor Day, McKenzie?" Carla asked without looking up from her computer monitor.

Removing her glasses, McKenzie said, "I don't really have any. I thought about going to Florida, but changed my mind."

"Why don't you come over to my house? I'm planning to throw some steaks and burgers on the grill."

Are you having a lot of guests?"

Carla shook her head. "No, it's just going to be an intimate group."

"What should I bring?"

"Just yourself and a healthy appetite."

"Are you sure, Carla?"

"Positive." She swiveled around in her chair to face McKenzie. "Does this mean that you're definitely coming?"

"Yes, I'll be there." McKenzie chewed thoughtfully on the top of her pen. She wondered if Marc would be there. As much as she wanted to know, she refused to ask Carla.

"You know, I'm thinking about inviting Marc."

She kept her features composed. "Really? Think he'll come?"

Carla nodded. "You're still coming, right?"

"Why wouldn't I?"

"Well, I wasn't sure you wanted to be around Marc in a social setting. I don't want you to be uncomfortable."

So Marc had been talking to Carla. "Marc doesn't bother me in the least," McKenzie lied.

Nine

"McKenzie, you didn't have to bring anything."

"I didn't feel right coming over here empty-handed. It's just a sweet potato pie and a bottle of wine."

Carla embraced her. "It's very sweet of you." Holding the door open, she said, "Come on in and make yourself comfortable."

McKenzie glanced around the spacious one-story condo. "Am I the first to arrive?"

"No, Allie and her husband are on the patio. You can head out there through the den. I'm going to put the wine in the fridge."

McKenzie stepped out into the sunlight. Allie and her husband were sitting at a table shaded by a huge colorful umbrella.

"McKenzie, how are you? Enjoying your home?"

"Hi, Allie. I can't thank you enough for helping me find a place to live. I love the town house."

"I'm so glad to hear that." She introduced her husband to McKenzie."

Hearing male voices in the background, McKenzie turned around and saw Marc and two men she didn't know. She'd seen the heavyset man a few times roaming the halls of Chandler. As much as she hated to admit it, she was thrilled to see Marc. Her heart turned with unhappiness. She had to be crazy to be thinking along those lines. . . .

She said softly, "Hello, Marc."

"Doc, it's good to see you." He introduced her to Laine Ransom and Jim. "We all go way back. Laine and I used to play football together in high school. He lives in Washington, DC."

"It's very nice to meet you both. Jim, I've seen you a few times in the building."

"Yeah, I drift in every now and then." He leaned closer to her, asking in a loud whisper, "So, is the old man treating you good?"

She gazed at Marc, a mischievous glint in her dark brown eyes. "Yes, he's okay. He tries to be this big scary person, but I don't think it's really working. He's giving it his best shot, though. You have to admire him for that alone."

Jim let out a loud whoop of laughter. "I like this lady."

Marc shook his head. "Don't encourage him, Doc."

McKenzie laughed. "If you all will excuse me, I think I'll go see if I can help Carla with anything."

"She's got spirit," Jim observed. "And a great sense of humor."

Laine agreed. "I think you've finally met your match, Marc. She seems like a nice lady."

Watching McKenzie laughing and chatting with Carla and Allie, Marc nodded. "She's fun to be with."

Jim's eyes opened wide. "Really? Now how would you know that?"

"I had dinner with her a couple of weeks ago. And before you get carried away—it was a chance meeting. We were at Tango's Seafood restaurant. And since we were both there alone—we decided to eat together."

"Sounds like you two are really hitting it off. Haven't seen you so animated in a long time."

Marc stated simply, "We're friends, Laine, that's all."

Downing the last of his beer, Jim smashed the aluminum can with his hand, throwing it into Carla's recycle bin. "That's as good a start as any. Remember, old man, I've known you a real long time. You want that girl. You want her bad."

"I think I need a drink," Marc muttered. Deep within, he knew Jim was right, but he refused to acknowledge those emotions. He would not let lust rule his head. McKenzie was his employee, and he had to remember that.

"So, did you have a good time today?" Marc asked as he escorted McKenzie to her car.

"Yes, I did. How about you?"

He laughed. "Carla's a clown. I always enjoy being around her."

"You two are very close," she observed.

"She's the sister I never had."

McKenzie unlocked her door. Leaning back against her car, she said, "Thanks for walking me to my car. I'll see you tomorrow."

"I'm glad to see that you and Carla are becoming good friends. She really likes you, you know."

"I like her a lot, too." McKenzie slid into her car. "You don't have to worry, big brother. You know, I never would've pegged you as being so protective."

A probing query came into his eyes. "Just how do you have me pegged?"

McKenzie regarded him with a speculative gaze. "I'm not exactly sure," she admitted honestly. "But when I figure it out you'll be one of the first to know. Have a good evening."

"You, too." Marc shut her door.

McKenzie started her car, gave a final wave, and was gone.

"Are you still going to try to tell me that you feel nothing for McKenzie?" Carla asked as she joined him beside the curb. "She's been gone about ten minutes now."

"I'm not going to tell you *anything*." Marc glanced down at the petite woman. "Why don't you use your matchmaking skills for some good? Use them on yourself. Jim's in your house—probably looking pretty lonely. Take advantage of that."

"Fine," Carla snapped. "I'm through worrying about you. If you want to be alone for the rest of your life—then so be it."

"Do you really mean it this time?"

Carla whirled around, her full skirt flaring, and stomped back into her condo.

Marc shook with silent laughter. She was angry now, but he knew it wouldn't last.

He wasn't ready to admit his attraction to McKenzie. Not to anyone. There was still something about her that bothered him. She was entirely too cool and poised. He wanted to see real emotion, and not just about her work.

He had no intention of permitting himself to fall under McKenzie's spell. Marc could not let romantic notions distract him. He could not handle another disappointment.

McKenzie stared at the paper in front of her. It couldn't be, she thought, but a thorough check of her calculations brought no change. She leaned back in her chair, causing it to groan. Now, she would have to start over! McKenzie frowned. Her introspection turned to Marc. She would also have to start from scratch where Marc was concerned. She'd been at Chandler eight months now, and still she had nothing on him. Could he really be that squeaky clean?

The detective she'd hired months ago had turned up nothing she could use. The information he had given her simply did not add up. It was as if they were talking about two different people. Disappointed, she had fired him and paid him all monies due. Lately, there were times she questioned whether she had been wrong about what happened between her mother and Marc.

McKenzie was so engrossed in her musings that she didn't notice Marc standing in the door way. "Knock, knock."

McKenzie sat erect in her chair, taking in the expensive,

black, double-breasted suit, the crisp white shirt, and his paisley print tie. "Oh, Marc! I didn't know you were here." She viewed him suspiciously as he stood leaning against the door. McKenzie inhaled deeply, as if to give herself the strength to see him. As always, it was the look in his eyes that got her . . . they seemed to peer deep into her soul. "Is there something you want, Marc?"

"Yes. As a matter of fact, there is."

Recognizing the lustful gleam in his eyes, McKenzie immediately regretted her question.

"I heard you weren't coming to Chandler's annual Christmas party."

She had thought about not attending, but had changed her mind. Attending the Christmas party might be to her advantage. "I'll be there." If only he wouldn't keep staring at her. She could hardly think.

Marc smiled. "I'm glad to hear it. I insist on having all my *employees* attend company functions. Besides, I think you'll enjoy yourself."

"As I said, Marc, I'll be there." She refused to allow her feelings of disappointment to surface. Of course she was nothing more than an employee to him. The success of her plan depended on her gaining his complete trust, and that meant forging some type of friendship with him. She just needed to make sure she kept her emotions under wraps.

Clara appeared in the doorway. She acknowledged McKenzie briefly before turning her full attention to Marc. Apparently he was needed upstairs.

Relieved that he had to leave, McKenzie glanced up at the clock. Her new assistant would be arriving within the hour.

As she worked, McKenzie tried to deny the stirrings she felt in her being whenever she was around Marc. He was her enemy—nothing more. She couldn't lose sight of what she had to do. She shook her head, trying to clear her thoughts. Right now she didn't want to think of what would happen to the company she was beginning to love.

McKenzie gnawed on the eraser of her pencil. This was getting ridiculous. Why was she so afraid of the truth? She *was* attracted to Marc, but was too smart to make anything more of it.

Falling in love with Marc Chandler would not be wise. Not at all, her mind advised. She would simply become his friend to get the truth about her mother's death.

Her mother had always been dependent on men for her happiness, McKenzie thought with disgust. In the end, it had cost Barbara her life. McKenzie had stopped denying her feelings of resentment toward her mother for being such a needy person. It was that weakness that had led her mother on the path to self-destruction. She had never forgiven Barbara for being so insecure and needy. McKenzie vowed it would never happen to her.

She would let Marc believe they were becoming close, and then she would uncover the skeletons in his closet. This time he wouldn't be able to run.

Ten

"Welcome to Chandler Pharmaceuticals." McKenzie held out her hand to Sherrie Davis. She took an instant liking to the full-figured, blond young woman. Her Southern accent was charming, and she had a bubbly personality to match.

"Oh, I'm sure I'm going to love it here. I'm very grateful for the chance to work with you. I've followed your work with Mason Labs, and I think you're a brilliant scientist."

McKenzie scanned Sherrie's face. Finding nothing but sincerity, she said, "Thank you. I really appreciate your saying that. I've worked very hard."

She gave Sherrie a tour of the facilities. Just before returning to the lab they ran into Marc.

"Sherrie, this is Marc Chandler. He is the president and CEO—"

Sherrie rushed forward. "Oh, I'm well aware of who he is. It's a pleasure to finally meet you, Mr. Chandler. I saw your picture in *Ebony* magazine, a few years back. I must say you look exactly like your photograph."

He smiled politely. "Welcome to Chandler, and please call me Marc."

McKenzie watched as Sherrie batted her eyes prettily, tossing her honey blond mane. *She's practically drooling over the man. His ego can already fill this whole building. And just look at him. He's eating this up. What a flirt.* Having had enough, McKenzie said, "We don't want to keep you, Marc."

He raised an eyebrow. "You're not. I always enjoy meeting our new employees." Turning back to Sherrie, he said, "I have an open-door policy. If you ever have a problem, please feel free to come talk to me."

McKenzie rolled her eyes heavenward.

"I'll let you ladies get back to work."

"Why, thank you, Mr. Chandler. I mean, Marc. Thank you."

They headed back to the lab. When the door closed behind them, McKenzie found that her knees were shaking, and her hands trembled so violently that she shoved them into her lab coat pockets. She looked up to see Sherrie's curious gaze on her, and said faintly, "I guess we should get started."

Sherrie was still enthused over her introduction to Marc. "He seems like such a nice man. So easy to get along with, and humble. You know, most CEOs . . ."

McKenzie stared at Sherrie incredulously. She was still fawning over the man. Shaking her head in disbelief, McKenzie directed her assistant to a locker. Sherrie continued to rave about Marc, much to McKenzie's chagrin.

"He's quite handsome, don't you think?"

McKenzie shrugged. "I've never really noticed."

Sherrie' s blue eyes widened. "Honey, you've got to be kidding me! I've seen plenty of good-looking men before. This one beats them all."

"I'll have to take your word on that, I suppose."

Sherrie eyed her from head to toe. "If you don't know what a handsome man looks like, I think you need to get out of the laboratory more."

McKenzie's sense of humor took over, and she laughed in response. "I guess you're right. I detect a strong Southern accent. Where are you from?"

"Birmingham, Alabama."

McKenzie inclined her head. "So tell me, what brings you to California?"

Sherrie's expression was unreadable. Finally, she answered.

"I figured coming to California would provide me with better opportunities."

McKenzie was curious, having seen the change that came over Sherrie's face. Maybe she was being too nosy. "That's basically the same reason I moved out here, too. I still meet people who think the only reason people move to Los Angeles is to become an actress, or a singer."

Sherrie relaxed. "Well, I can't act my way out of a paper bag. As for singing, I can't do that, either."

On the way to McKenzie's office, Sherrie asked, "Where do you hail from? I can hear a faint Southern drawl coming from you, too."

McKenzie laughed. "Florida. Orlando, Florida."

"Do you like it out here?"

"It has taken some getting used to, but it's okay."

"Well, I think I'm gonna like it just fine. As a matter of fact, I'm gonna have a great future out here."

McKenzie wondered jealously if Sherrie planned to make Marc a part of her future. She told herself she didn't care who had him after she was through, but even to her own heart the words didn't sound true.

Sherrie rushed into the apartment, dropping her purse on a nearby coffee table. "Pierce, honey, are you home?"

"I'm in the kitchen." He stuck his head through the doorway. "Come in here and tell me about your day."

She planted a wet kiss on his cheek. "It was great! I met the great Marc Chandler." Placing an ample arm across her bosom, she said, "Honey, you wouldn't believe it. It's uncanny. I felt this weird feeling come over me."

Pierce continued to stir the pasta noodles instead of looking at Sherrie. "So, what do you think of him?"

"He seems very nice. I've heard he can be very abrupt when the mood strikes him, but he was real nice to me." She picked up a celery stalk and started chewing on it.

"Did you find out anything about him? Like about his family?"

Sherrie shook her head. "I was going to ask my boss, but I think she and Marc are attracted to each other. I didn't want her thinking I was after the man she wants. It would make working together hell."

"So then, Marc's not married?"

"Naw. I heard that he's never been."

"What about children?"

"No children."

"I see." Pierce took the boiling pasta over to the sink and drained it.

Sherrie surveyed the small kitchen. "Is there anything I can do to help? Dinner sure smells delicious."

"I've taken care of everything." He picked up the knife, preparing to slice mushrooms. "I just have to cut . . . *ouch.*"

"What happened, honey?" Sherrie rushed to his side. "Let me—"

"Get away," he ordered as he pushed her away from him.

"Pierce—"

"Please, just stay back. It's only a small cut. I can take care of it. Stay back," he implored her.

"Sure, honey."

Pierce turned and headed out of the kitchen. "Throw out the mushrooms I just cut. There's some more in the fridge."

"I don't think that—"

His tone was pleading. "Please, Sherrie, just do what I ask."

Watching him leave, she shrugged. "Whatever you say, honey." She knew he was only trying to protect her.

Marc's eyes kept darting across the room, toward the entrance, as if searching for someone.

Carla eased behind him. "I bet I know who you're looking for?"

Marc tugged on his bow tie. "What makes you think I'm looking for anyone in particular?"

Carla's eyes clung to his, as if analyzing his reaction. "I just thought you might be waiting for a certain spirited and captivating scientist—"

"I wouldn't call her——" He stopped short as McKenzie strolled into the room, her black velvet dress hugging her slender frame. She stood just outside the door, as if summoning the courage to enter.

Marc couldn't respond. Even from across the room, she looked exquisite in her calf-length snug-fitting dress. A shapely leg peeked out from a slit in the side of the dress as McKenzie circulated through the room, nodding at a few people.

He was vaguely aware of Carla touching his arm. "You were saying?"

"She may be every bit as captivating and spirited as you say, but she means trouble, Carla. I can feel it in my bones."

"Coward."

Before he could utter a response, Carla swiftly made her way over to McKenzie's side and carried her off in another direction.

Marc muttered a curse.

McKenzie moved around the huge room, completely in awe of the exquisite furnishings. When she arrived, she had been drawn to the Queen Anne mirror and lowboy that distinguished the foyer. Marc's house was extremely large, and had been decorated with the grandest elegance. Several large paintings hung in heavy ornate frames on opposite walls.

As she walked her heels made a soft clicking sound on the floor of gleaming rosewood with a thick, dark blue, Oriental carpet stretched across its center. A carpet runner of the same color and pattern hugged the center of the wide curving staircase that stood near the back of the entry. McKenzie observed the long garlands of fir, spruce, and artificial cypress that draped the stairway. They gave the house a definite Christmas-y feeling.

She smiled nervously when she spied Carla coming her way in a beautiful gown made of emerald green velvet. Alternating panels of red showed as she glided across the room.

Giving McKenzie the thumbs-up, she exclaimed, "Girl, you are looking good! I don't know why you hate dresses. You look so great in them. I'm so glad you decided to come."

"I thought it was a requirement," she commented dryly.

"Goodness, no." Carla looked perplexed. *"Who* gave you that idea?"

"Marc, of course." She noticed Marc, standing across the room, watching her intently. His gaze was riveted on her face, then moved over her body slowly. McKenzie didn't miss his obvious approval.

Carla didn't miss it, either. "Oh, I think he just wanted to make sure you'd come."

"But why?"

Carla gave a sly smile and shrugged. "You'll have to ask him what his motives are. Come on, let's go into the dining room. I'm starved."

Not having had a chance to grab a snack before getting ready for the party, McKenzie said, "Me, too."

In the dining room she admired the huge crystal chandelier that seemed to drip exquisitely from the white, intricately sculptured ceiling high above the center of the room. Lilies, roses, and Stars of Bethlehems filled tall vases while magnolia leaves, fresh fruits, and roses trimming greens served as table centerpieces.

"This house is really something."

"Uh huh. It was Marc's parent's house. He hates living here alone, but doesn't want to sell it. He says it's all he has left of his family. This house, and the company."

"Well, it is a big house. You know, I've always wanted to live in a place like this."

"Oh, really? How interesting." Carla's face took on a sly expression.

McKenzie sighed. "I didn't mean this one, exactly, Carla. I'm not stupid enough to think that'll ever happen."

Carla popped a shrimp puff into her mouth. "Well, you never know, McKenzie. Never say never. Marc might sell it to you one day."

McKenzie shook her head in dismay. "With the way he feels about me, I seriously doubt that. Besides, you just said he wants to keep it for sentimental reasons."

"Okay, okay! You don't have to jump down my throat. He may rent it to you, then."

McKenzie shot Carla a withering glance. "Why don't you stop playing matchmaker? And for that matter, I don't see *you* with a date. Instead of trying to match me up with—"

"For your information, I'm with Jim Rawlins tonight. See that man over there? He came with Marc to my house on Labor Day, remember?" Carla pointed to a man talking to Marc. When McKenzie nodded, she said, "That's my date. I gave up waiting on him to ask me out. I asked him. So there."

"You really go for muscular men, don't you? Goodness, that man has muscles everywhere. I'm surprised he was able to find a tux that fit."

Carla winked. "I do like a man with some meat on his bones." Gesturing toward Marc, she said, "Marc's looking good tonight, don't you think?"

"He looks nice." She shrugged as nonchalantly as possible. As if with a will of their own, McKenzie's eyes kept straying to where Marc and Jim stood talking. Facing Carla, she said, "Why don't we grab that bite to eat now, while you're waiting for Jim?"

"Sure."

They made their way over to the huge buffet. McKenzie had just stuck a Swedish meatball into her mouth when Marc walked up. Smiling sheepishly, she turned away from him. Swallowing, she composed herself before turning around to face him. "Hello, Marc." She dropped her eyes before his steady gaze.

"Hello, McKenzie."

Her eyes strayed to his. "You really have a beautiful house." McKenzie caught Carla as she eased away, grinning from ear to ear.

"Thank you. I'm glad you like it."

One of Chandler's employees joined them. While Marc and the man talked, McKenzie chose that moment to consume another meatball. Busy savoring the spicy sauce, she wasn't aware that Marc was once again standing beside her, near the banquet table, until she heard his husky voice near her ear.

"Would you care to dance?"

"Huh?" McKenzie turned to face him. Once again she was caught up in his hypnotic spell, feeling the powerful pull of his intense magnetic gaze.

"I asked if you would like to dance." He held out his arm to her.

"S-sure." She hesitated slightly before placing her hand on his proffered arm. "I have to warn you, I'm not a very good dancer."

"Neither am I."

He led her to the middle of the dance floor. McKenzie was acutely aware that all eyes were on them, especially Glenda's. She wondered briefly just how involved Glenda and Marc had been.

They danced to the sexy sounds of Keith Sweat, R Kelly, and Luther Vandross. McKenzie felt lighter than a feather as Marc held her tightly in his arms.

When the music stopped he pulled away from her, staring intensely into her face. "I don't think you've been honest with me, Dr. Ashford."

"W-what are y-you talking about?"

"Your not being a good dancer." He looked at her quizzically. "What did you think I meant?"

She laughed a nervous laugh. "I had no idea what you were

talking about." She glanced around, looking for Carla. Spying her, she turned back to Marc and said quickly, "Thanks for the dance, Marc. Please excuse me."

She was gone before he could protest.

McKenzie headed straight to where Carla and Jim were standing. "Jim, could you please excuse us? I need to borrow Carla for a moment, if you don't mind?"

"No problem. I need to talk to Marc, anyway."

McKenzie waited until Jim was beyond hearing range before speaking. "You can wipe that grin off your face."

Carla's smile became wider. "You two sure looked good out there dancing like that."

"It was just dancing, Carla. Nothing else." McKenzie caught herself glancing over her shoulder to where Marc and Jim were standing. She quickly looked away. "Sometimes I don't know what to expect. He's not an easy man to read."

"I don't know many men who are. But Marc, he just needs a loving woman to soften his sharp edges," Carla explained with a smile.

"Well, I certainly don't envy that poor woman," McKenzie said lightly, but she felt an odd catch in her heart.

She waved and smiled at Sherrie, who was walking by.

"Oh, there are a lot of them interested in taking on the job, to be sure, but Marc has spent a lifetime distancing himself from pain and heartache. It's going to take a special woman for him to ever become close to anyone. He's afraid of being hurt again."

McKenzie looked at Carla, her expression one of disbelief. "Why are you telling me this? It was just a dance. The owner of a company dancing with one of his employees."

"As I said before, it doesn't have to be just dancing. I've known Marc a very long time. I can tell he's attracted to you. Although I haven't known you all that long, I have a feeling you're attracted to him, also. I don't know why—"

A waiter interrupted them.

"Oops, duty calls. . . ." Carla was gone in a flash of green and red, leaving her alone.

"Hello, McKenzie."

She turned around to find David standing there. "Why, hello, David. You look so handsome in your suit. Almost like a different person."

He stood back, eyeing her from head to toe. "I could say the same thing about you. Look at you! Makeup and that dress . . . Mmm, girlfriend—"

"You need to quit, David." McKenzie glanced around. "I don't see Barry. Did you come alone?"

"Yup. I'm on my own tonight. It's usually that way for company functions." He grabbed her by the arm. "Come on, let's dance. We can show these people how to really party. Maybe start a rumor or two."

She was about to refuse, but out of the corner of her eye, she could see Marc heading her way. "Yes, I'd love to." McKenzie led the way to the dance floor. She wasn't ready to have another one-on-one with Marc—not right then.

After her dance with David ended, McKenzie felt a need to get some fresh air. She walked outside. What was it about Marc Chandler that kept her in turmoil? He had a way of looking at her that made her blood turn to fire in her veins. Perhaps that was the way he'd always affected all women—including her mother.

She could not let her emotions rule her head. Her mother was needy and had felt she had to have a man in order to be happy. She'd soon turned to alcohol and drugs. McKenzie did not intend to lose herself like that.

Eleven

Out the corner of his eye Marc watched McKenzie's every move as she made her way around the room. Her soft full lips could break the heart of a man . . . if that man had a heart to break. He'd always been able to retain control of his emotions—until recently. Until he'd met McKenzie, that is.

He believed her to be as faithless and scheming as all other women, and tonight that belief had been affirmed as he watched her dancing and flirting with David and several other male employees of Chandler. His smile changed into a sneer. Marc frowned as he watched her laughing as she and David danced. The two of them seemed very close. His distrust of women led him to believe she was no different than any other.

Seeing her with David had stirred something inside of him that he didn't understand, and didn't like. He tried to clear his mind, but every time his body started to relax he saw McKenzie's face.

He had to be losing it. In his opinion, there wasn't a woman on earth who could keep his interest for more than a week at a time—spoiled shallow women, women who had nothing better to do than flirt and tease, making promises they had no intention of keeping. Marc decided he'd seen enough. He headed toward the back door and ventured out into the cool night air.

The brisk weather did nothing for his disposition. Why was he feeling jealous? McKenzie was nothing to him. She was just another scheming female, on the make for a man with money.

His mind raced ahead to the upcoming holidays. Christmas. He remembered how much his mother used to love the holidays. She used to tell him those were very special family times.

He'd never thought she would keep secrets from him, but she had. Marc wanted to know why. Didn't she know how much he loved her? Did she realize how much she had hurt him by keeping secrets? When others sought to harm him, she had been his savior. She gave him love. Since her death, he'd often forgotten he'd once belonged in a warm and loving home.

Marc closed his eyes to block the sight of his mother, dying, begging for his forgiveness—something he should have given freely, but didn't. He had been too angry. He recalled all the times he'd hurt his mother, even made her downright angry, but she always forgave him. No matter how hard he tried to keep blaming his mother, he ended up blaming himself. Marc admitted that he could no longer hold on to his anger about her betrayal. Instead, he could not rid himself of the guilt he felt—guilt about not being able to give her what she had needed most: his forgiveness.

His thoughts were cut short by a noise. Someone was coming outside. It was McKenzie. Standing there, studying the way the gentle moon washed over her, Marc was caught by the picture she presented. She stood straight, her hair gleaming, her slender neck curved gracefully as she pulled her shawl closer around her. She obviously thought she was alone, because she was singing. He smiled as he listened to her sing "Silent Night" off-key. When she finished her solo, he clapped. "Encore."

McKenzie spun around quickly. "Marc! I wish you'd cough, or make some kind of noise when you're around. Are you trying to scare me to death?" she snapped. She was embarrassed that he'd caught her singing—if it could be called that.

He bit back his laughter. "I didn't mean to scare you."

"Well, you did." Gathering her wits about her, she added, "I'm sorry for snapping at you. I didn't mean to."

"Yes, you did," he said, his mouth twisting in a half-smile.

She was about to argue, but seemed to think better of it. "You're right. I did mean to snap. You scared me," she managed as a wave of heat washed over her. "And you caught me singing out of tune, so you can understand if I feel a bit humiliated."

He laughed. "You have quite a temper, Dr. Ashford. Don't you think you should work on that?"

She released a small chuckle. "What can I say? Maybe you bring out the worst in me."

Marc moved to stand in front of her. "Why do you think that is?" he asked, his voice husky. "For that matter, are you sure it's your worst that I bring out, or something else?"

"I don't know what it is. I can't put a name to it," she admitted honestly.

He glanced sideways in surprise. "I know what you mean. I feel the exactly same way. It's not going to go away, McKenzie."

She stepped backward but she did so proudly, wanting him to know she was not in retreat. Hugging her middle, McKenzie looked him straight in the eye. "And I suppose you think we should pursue this . . . thing, whatever we're feeling?"

"I think we should take each day as it comes," Marc said. As he gazed into her upturned eyes, wide and bright and thick-lashed, he experienced the hard twist of desire that was beginning to be natural whenever she was around. "Why don't we just see what happens?" Marc grinned.

McKenzie plastered a smile on her face. "Sure. I agree. We should take this very slowly. Who knows, we may end up hating each other."

His dark eyebrows arched mischievously. "Now, Dr. Ashford, why in the world would I hate you?" They faced each other, only half a dozen feet apart. Time stood still, and only Marc and McKenzie remained, locked in some strange vacuum of time and space.

She ran her hand nervously through her hair. "I haven't a clue, Mr. Chandler."

Marc laughed as if sincerely amused.

Some of her nervous energy vanished, and she couldn't keep herself from laughing. "I can't seem to figure you out, but I will."

"I'm not complicated, just very cautious." He moved closer. Now, I want to know why you're out here, and not inside enjoying the party."

"I just thought I'd come out for a breath of fresh air."

"I had the same idea." It was time to learn more about this woman, Marc thought. He knew the perfect opportunity. "McKenzie, what are your plans for Christmas?"

She looked out into the night. "I don't really have any family. I guess I'll stay home and catch up on some reading."

"You could spend it with me."

He said it so softly that she thought she'd imagined it.

Her mouth dropped open. "D-did you just ask me to spend Christmas with you?"

"Yes. I don't want to see you alone on such a joyous holiday. It's meant for people to be together."

"Then you should . . ." McKenzie halted, shocked to the core of her being. "Christmas is a day for families. You should ask some of your family to spend the holidays with you. Don't you have any brothers or sisters?"

Marc didn't respond.

McKenzie looked up to see a hardness in his eyes that he couldn't hide. "I'm . . ." she stopped. I'm sorry, Marc. I guess I've said something wrong. I really didn't mean to pry."

"It's okay. I don't have much family, that's all. Look, I need to check on things inside. If you like, I would enjoy having you spend Christmas with me. If not, I understand." He turned to leave.

"Marc!"

He turned when she called his name. "Yes?"

"I'd love to spend Christmas with you. Thank you for inviting me."

He nodded and left.

McKenzie did not miss the look of intense sadness that showed on his face when he'd spoken of family. For a short time she felt sad for him. Then she thought of herself. She was in the same situation, partly due to Marc. Why did she hurt for him?

What kind of person am I? she wondered. "You must feel so ashamed of me, Mama. I'm so sorry," she whispered before heading back to the party.

Two hours later, Marc was glad when the last of his guests went home. He was exhausted. Throwing off his clothes, he headed to the bathroom for a quick shower before dressing for bed.

In bed, he was unable to sleep because visions of McKenzie danced through his mind. He wondered what it would feel like to taste the sweetness of her lips. Just thinking about McKenzie sent waves of excitement through him.

Marc was irritated, more than a little, because he was allowing a woman to interfere with his sleep. His feelings for McKenzie had nothing to do with reason, he kept telling himself. He fluffed his pillows and lay back against them, trying to clear his mind.

Hours later, Marc muttered a curse and clasped his hands behind his head. No woman should disturb a man's peace of mind, let alone deprive him of his sleep. What exactly did he feel for McKenzie? Was it the most overwhelming desire he'd ever felt for any woman? Marc wasn't ready to answer that particular question.

Finally, he threw the covers off in frustration and rose to his feet. He might as well get up. It was obvious he wasn't going to get any sleep. Marc put on his robe and headed downstairs to the den. Once there, he positioned himself on the floor in front of the television, playing video games.

Morning found him sprawled on the sofa, controller still in hand, sleeping soundly.

* * *

Sherrie attempted to ease out of bed without waking the sleeping Pierce. As her body moved away from his, he turned over, pulling her close to him as if hungry for her warmth.

Groggily, he asked, "H-how . . . was the party? I tried to wait up, but I was exhausted."

"Very nice. Marc really knows how to entertain." She yawned. "I wish you could have gone with me."

"Maybe next time."

"Definitely." Sherrie turned to face Pierce. "I can't wait for you to see that house. Naw—that *mansion*. It's huge."

"Well, he *is* a rich man. Did you expect him to live in a shack?"

Sherrie shook her head. "Naw, I didn't know what to expect. You know, I hated leaving you here all alone, honey. I want you to meet Marc. It's been too long already. Ya'll need to see each other."

"I didn't mind staying by myself. I had some reading to catch up on. I'll meet Mr. Marc Chandler in due time." Pierce propped up on one elbow, facing Sherrie. "I know one thing for sure. When we see each other face-to-face, it's going to be something else."

Sherrie sat up then. "Honey, why do you want to keep putting this off? You and I both know that Marc won't be able to deny his relationship with you. Believe me, he'll know it, too."

"I'm probably the last person he wants to see."

She shook her head in dismay. "I don't see how you can say that. Go talk to the man! Let him tell you what he wants. It's futile to live with all these assumptions."

Pierce pulled her down to lie beside him. His finger stroked her arm sensuously. "Let's not argue about this right now. I *will* see Marc, but it has to be when I'm ready."

Sherrie reached out, lacing his fingers with her own. "Sure, honey. I won't mention it again."

"I love you, baby. And I appreciate all you've done for me," Pierce whispered into her hair.

"I know that." Burying her face in his neck, she breathed a

kiss there. She then kissed his chin. Sherrie pressed her lips to his, caressing his mouth more than kissing it.

"You deserve so much more—" Pierce murmured between kisses.

"Pierce—"

"I'm not going to say anything else. Right now I want to hold you. I—"

"Hold me, Pierce. Hold me and never let go." Sherrie drew his face to hers in a renewed embrace.

It wasn't until morning that McKenzie realized Marc had never answered her question about his family. She shivered, and a cold chill ran through her body. What in the world had she done by agreeing to spend Christmas with him? What had she been thinking? Wishing she understood what was happening to her, McKenzie did her best not to surrender to the peculiar sensations she was experiencing.

She remained determined to ignore any and all of the feelings Marc had awakened in her while she prayed fervently for a solution. She was losing control over the situation.

Her telephone rang, scaring her. McKenzie picked it up, saying, "Nancy's Chicken n' Fixins. We deliver."

"McKenzie? Is that you?"

"Who'd you expect, Carla? Yes, it's me."

"Well, the chicken and fixing thing threw me off. I thought I'd dialed the wrong number."

"That was the idea," McKenzie said dryly.

"Am I disturbing you?"

"No. I just wanted to give you a hard time." She managed a choking laugh. "I had a sneaking suspicion that it was you."

"I apologize for calling so early, but I knew you wouldn't be asleep. I just had to call."

"What's wrong? Did you and Jim have a fight?"

"Oh, no. It's nothing like that. When I didn't see you or Marc before I left last night, I couldn't help but wonder what happened to the two of you."

"Nothing *happened* to us. I hate to burst your bubble, but we didn't sneak off together. Marc was already outside when I walked out. If I'd known he was out there, I would've just stayed inside," she replied flippantly. McKenzie knew she was being defensive, but couldn't help it.

"Why? Was he rude to you or something?"

"No. No, he wasn't rude. He was quite nice, actually."

"Oh, really?"

"Wipe that pleased expression off your face, Carla."

"How do you know if I have a pleased expression or not?"

"Because I can tell from the sound of your voice. When are you going to stop playing matchmaker? In fact, shouldn't you be entertaining Jim, or did he just drop you off at your door last night?"

"Ha ha, that's really funny! For your information, Jim is in the shower."

"He's taking a shower at your house?"

"Yes. He stayed over," Carla said matter-of-factly. "Now quick, tell me, what are you doing for Christmas?"

McKenzie rolled her eyes and tapped her bare foot in irritation. "It appears you already know the answer to that question," she said dryly. "Why don't you ask Marc?"

"No, I want you to tell me."

"Carla, I'm going jogging. Since Jim is there, you might want to think about what you're going to cook for breakfast."

"I've already got that covered, dear heart. Anyway, you have a good weekend. I'll see you on Monday. Goodness, it's chilly in here."

"But I expect things will soon be heating up," McKenzie mused.

"You've got that right. I'll talk to you later, but before I go I want to say that it's good to see you and Marc getting along like this. I thought for a minute I was going to have to give you both boxing gloves for Christmas."

Her gentle laugh rippled through the air. "Now, now. You're fishing, but I'm not biting."

"Don't forget to wish Marc a Merry Christmas for me."

"You're hopeless, Carla. Christmas is still a week away. You have more than enough time to wish him a Merry Christmas yourself."

"Spoilsport."

Twelve

Marc arrived promptly at eight o'clock on Christmas morning to pick up McKenzie. Under his black leather jacket he wore a pair of black denim jeans and a black linen shirt. McKenzie was grateful that he'd chosen to dress casually.

"Merry Christmas, Marc."

"Merry Christmas to you, too." He scanned her critically and beamed approval. "I see you got my message last night."

"Yes. And I must admit I'm relieved. I'm casual when it comes to clothes."

"So am I."

She eyed him from head to toe. "I have to admit you look very nice in jeans. The suits make you look so stuffy."

He chuckled in response to her honesty. "I bet that compliment was hard for you to get out."

McKenzie laughed. "I guess I deserved that."

"Shall we get going?"

Holding up her purse, she announced, "I'm ready."

They drove in silence to a church located on San Vicente in Los Angeles.

"I'd promised to help out at the church today, serving Christmas dinner. I hope you don't mind." Marc had purposely left her in the dark about his plans for the day. He wanted to see what her reaction would be when she found out how they would be spending Christmas.

"Of course not. Why should I mind? As a matter of fact, I'd

like to volunteer my services. I'm sure they can use another set of hands." McKenzie threw the car door open, then rushed into the church hall. Not once did she look back to see if Marc followed.

Scratching his head thoughtfully, Marc was stunned. This was certainly not the reaction he had expected. He'd thought she would be angry, demanding to leave, or something else. Most women he knew probably would have accused him of tricking them, or trying to avoid an intimate setting. Spending a day feeding the homeless and the poor was not the way most women wanted to spend Christmas day. However, it didn't seem to bother McKenzie at all. She had already taken off her jacket, rolled up the sleeves of her sweatshirt, and had her arms elbow deep in dishwater.

He watched her out of the corner of his eye. Marc didn't want her to know how much of an effect she was having on him. Her laughter was clear, and could be heard throughout the dining hall at the church as she talked with the other women in the kitchen. She seemed to be enjoying herself immensely. Marc would not acknowledge how relieved he was to find she enjoyed volunteering as much as he.

A portly man in a dark suit strolled over to Marc. "It's good to see you, Mr. Chandler. How are you?"

The two men shook hands.

"Hello, Pastor Rivers. It's good to see you, too. I'm doing fine."

"It's been a while since I've seen you in church."

"You're right. It has been. Truth is, I have no excuse. I'll be there on Sunday, though."

"I'll be looking for you." Nodding toward McKenzie, Pastor Rivers whispered, "I see you brought a young lady with you. Does this mean—"

Marc shook his head violently. "Nooo, Pastor. She's a scientist at Chandler. New in town, and no family. I hated the thought of her spending Christmas alone, so I invited her here."

"She certainly has just jumped right in, hasn't she? Looks

like she's having a good time, too. Pretty little thing. Don't you think so?" He peered at Marc.

"Now, Pastor, don't you get started on me. I'm not looking for a wife. I'm happy with the way things are."

"Behind every good man is an even better woman."

Marc laughed. "If you say so. I'll have to take your word for it."

"I don't believe it's the Lord's plan for you to remain single. You should find yourself a wife."

Marc shook his head. "Thanks, but no thanks."

"I see I'm needed in the sanctuary. Ethel's over there signaling to me." Pastor Rivers stole another glance at McKenzie. Nodding in her direction, he said, "If things change, make sure you give me a call."

Marc chuckled. "If I ever decide to marry *anybody,* you'll be the first person I call."

He looked around for McKenzie. Marc found her with one of the ladies, placing red tablecloths on each row of tables. She and the woman were talking as if they were old friends. McKenzie seemed to make friends wherever she went. When she caught him looking at her, Marc winked and mouthed the words, "Remember me?"

She returned his smile and nodded.

McKenzie watched as Marc began to approach her, only to be halted by a dark-skinned little girl with ebony braids and colorful bows. McKenzie thought she looked like a little doll. White ruffles peeked from beneath her red velvet dress. Red patent leather shoes adorned her miniature feet. The wide toothy grin that she gave Marc was priceless.

"Hi, Mr. Chandler. I been waitin' fer you to git here."

Marc squatted until he was at eye level with the petite little girl. "Hi, baby. How have you been feeling?"

"I feel all right. Doctor says I doin' just fine." She peeked around him as if searching for something. "Didn't you bring me a present?"

"Now why should I bring you a present, Anya? It's not your birthday, is it?"

"Because it's Christmas, Mr. Chandler. Besides, I brought you one." Anya put her hands on her hips for emphasis.

Marc put his hand up to hide his smile. Pulling a large box from the table behind him, he handed it to the little girl.

McKenzie' s eyes watered seeing the pure joy that leapt into the little girl's eyes. Anya ripped the colorful wrapping off, squealing in absolute delight over finding a large beautiful brown doll inside. McKenzie brushed away a lone tear.

Marc excused himself for a moment, but soon returned with a large box of brightly wrapped gifts. He ended up making two trips, and McKenzie had to wonder exactly where he'd stored all those presents. He was soon surrounded by children. Patiently, he talked to them, answering their questions. He glanced at McKenzie, motioning for her to join him. Marc introduced her to the children, and together they handed out the rest of the gifts. She reluctantly admitted that Marc was good with children.

They were soon joined by a couple of policemen, who brought loads of toys with them. While they distributed the toys, Marc and McKenzie headed to the kitchen to assist with the final preparations for the Christmas dinner.

McKenzie eyed Marc as he moved about the kitchen. He talked and laughed with the other volunteers as if they were old friends. This was a side of Marc she had never seen. He seemed so human, and easy to be with. McKenzie felt the same tightening in her chest that she experienced every time she saw him, and she felt guilty. Marc was supposed to be the enemy, the man responsible for her mother's death. He was the one she'd sworn to hate, but found she could not. The more she grew to know him, the harder it became for her to believe he could be as callous as she had first thought.

But he *was* guilty. The day Barbara died, Marc had literally run into McKenzie, just as she was arriving home from school.

She would never forget the fear she saw in his face, no matter how hard she tried.

McKenzie knew she had no business being there with him, enjoying his company, but she was glad she hadn't refused.

She had originally hoped to learn something that might potentially be used against him. She certainly wouldn't find it there. He was some sort of hero to these people.

Marc and McKenzie worked hard and steadily. After serving dinner to the wandering mass that entered the church halls, they drove all over Los Angeles, delivering hot meals to AIDS patients and other terminally ill people.

Around six o'clock, they called it a day.

"I thought we'd go back to my place and have dinner," Marc said as he drove out of the church parking lot.

She inclined her head, and asked, "Did you have Christmas dinner catered?"

"I cooked it."

McKenzie looked surprised. "Did you really?"

"Why do you look so shocked? I've been cooking since I was sixteen."

"I don't know many men who can cook a complete Christmas dinner."

"What about you? Can you cook?"

"Yes. I'm a good cook, too," McKenzie said as if settling an argument.

Marc selected a CD and stuck it in the CD player. During the drive home, he and McKenzie sang along as they listened to Christmas songs by various artists.

Secretly, McKenzie was impressed. Marc had a wonderful singing voice. He was not the man she thought he was. It all puzzled her even more. Could he really be this Jekyll and Hyde type person that she assumed he was?

At his home, they enjoyed a quiet meal together of roast turkey, cornbread stuffing, steamed vegetables with a rich butter cream sauce, and homemade wheat rolls. For dessert, Marc produced a fresh baked apple pie, which he claimed to have made himself, and ice cream.

Afterward, McKenzie helped Marc wash dishes as they talked.

Putting a damp towel on the counter, McKenzie leaned against it with her arms folded across her chest. "Marc, tell me about Anya. I overheard her mention something about a doctor."

He took a deep breath. "Anya is HIV positive."

Tears filled McKenzie's eyes. "Oh, Marc, no!"

He nodded. She could see the sadness in his eyes. "Her mother was a drug addict. She abandoned Anya when she was just a baby—after finding out she was HIV positive."

"Who—"

"Pastor Rivers and his wife adopted her when she was six months old."

"Did they know she was HIV positive?"

"Yes, but it didn't matter to them. They still wanted to adopt her."

"She's a beautiful little girl. How old is she now?"

"She's seven. And such a sweetheart." His voice was filled with love for the little girl.

McKenzie was so touched by the emotion she saw in Marc's face. Without giving it a thought, she covered his hand with hers. "One day we're going to find a way to rid the world of this killer."

Marc looked at her then. "You really believe that, don't you? That we'll be able to get rid of HIV infection and AIDS?"

She sat up straight. "I take it you don't agree?"

Marc shrugged. "Hey, this is supposed to be a day of joy and celebration. So, why don't we change the subject?"

"Sure. I have to tell you something, Marc. I'm very impressed with your cooking skills. Dinner was wonderful!"

"Thank you. I'm glad you enjoyed it."

"I really love this house, too. It's what, about two hundred years old?"

Marc shook his head. "This place was completed in nineteen-ninety, not seventeen-ninety. My parents spared no pains to create their dream home. My mother always wanted to live in an eighteenth-century house." He grabbed her by the hand. "Come on, I'll give you the complete tour."

McKenzie was conscious of where his warm flesh touched hers. Her body tingled from the contact, and she felt blood coursing through her veins like an awakened river.

He guided her into the living room. McKenzie immediately noticed a hand-carved tripod table standing by the sofa.

"That is absolutely gorgeous. Where did your mother find this table?"

"Would you believe at a garage sale? She refinished it herself."

"Incredible." McKenzie surveyed the room, her keen eyes picking up the fact that the mantel garland, with red ribbon and gold cord, echoed the pattern in the window swags. "Did you decorate this house for Christmas all by yourself?"

"No. I had Carla come over. Come on, let's resume our tour." As they walked, Marc added, "One wing houses the master bedroom, five guest rooms and three bathrooms; in another wing there's a library, the kitchen, dining room, three-car garage and the laundry room. When I moved in, I added a media room, an office and an exercise room."

They walked through the dining room as they headed to the library. McKenzie noted how the richly carved molding and mantel enriched the dining area, giving it a rich flavor. When they entered the mahogany-paneled library, she thought she'd died and gone to heaven.

"This is so beautiful, Marc. I love this room. I could stay here forever. I've only dreamed of having an office similar to this."

"I'm glad you like it. It's my favorite room in the house."

His eyes held hers as intimately as if he were touching her. She turned her back to him, pretending to be interested in the books on the shelf. "Eh . . . maybe we should head back into the den." She moved to leave.

"Not just yet. I want to show you something." He led her to a set of photographs. "This is my mother and father."

She studied the pictures, then looked up at him. "You look like your mother. You didn't take after your father at all."

"That's because he's actually my stepfather. I never knew my real father. Charles Chandler adopted me when I was fifteen. He was a good father, but we had our ups and downs."

"How so?"

"Well, I was fourteen when he married my mother. At that time I thought I was a man. I felt she didn't need him. I thought she loved him more than she loved me. So I set out to make their lives miserable."

Her mouth parted in surprise at his statement. "And he still adopted you?"

"Yes. Why does that seem so surprising to you?"

"If I were he, and you'd treated me that way, I think I would've run the other way."

"Hmm, I can't imagine you as the type who would back down from a fight. My dad wasn't, either. He even kicked me out when I dared to raise my hand to him. I was sixteen at the time."

"What did you do?"

"After two nights on the street, I begged to come back home. I straightened out after that. He put me through college, and after I graduated he offered me a job with Chandler, but I refused. I met a young lady, fell in love, and moved to Florida to be with her. I went a little wild."

"In what way?"

Marc guided her over to a navy-and-white striped sofa in the room. They sat down side by side. "Well, I was head over heels in love with this particular young lady. I did whatever she wanted me to do. I mean, she had my nose wide open. I loved her so much . . ." He paused as if caught up in memories.

McKenzie gently urged him to continue. He shook his head.

"Anyway, she damn near ruined my life. I almost lost my mind. I ended up in jail. My dad bailed me out with the understanding that it would be the first and last time he'd do it."

"Your father sounds like he really loved you, in spite of the fact that he was hard on you."

"He did."

"Marc?"

"Yes."

"How did you end up in jail? What did you do?"

"Do you really want to hear this?"

Although not at all sure she really did, McKenzie nodded.

"This same lady was also messing around with a drug dealer. Margie always traded cars with me, saying she liked mine better. I later found out that the only reason she wanted to borrow my car was so she could make drug runs for this dealer. One night Margie called and said she'd left her briefcase in the trunk of my car. She asked if I could bring it to her. I immediately said I would. Anyway, I was stopped by the police. I thought it was for some routine traffic violation. During a search of my car, they found the briefcase. After forcing it open, they found cocaine. A lot of it." Marc paused, taking a deep breath. "I was shocked, but the cops knew all along what would be in that briefcase."

"They carted me off to jail and booked me for drug trafficking. When I was allowed my one phone call, I called Margie. She assured me that she must have somehow picked up the wrong briefcase. She said she would come right down with a lawyer and straighten everything out. After spending a day and a half in jail, I realized she wasn't coming, so I begged them to let me call my dad."

"What did Margie have to say after your father got you out?"

"Nothing. By then she had disappeared without a trace. With her went all of my money, furniture, everything. I did run into her ten months later. Like a fool, I still confessed my love for her, but that time she laughed. Margie delighted in telling me she never cared anything about me. It was all about the money. She even bragged how she and her lover set me up."

"Were you ever convicted?" McKenzie struggled to steady her voice.

"No. Thank God. My lawyer was able to convince the district attorney of my innocence, but it was too close for comfort."

"Did they ever get caught?"

"One week later, Margie and her lover were found dead in the trunk of a stolen car, with bullets in their brains. Apparently, she had driven up to Jacksonville on a drug run. The newspapers labeled it as a drug deal gone bad."

"How terrible! Did you leave Florida after that?"

"No, I stayed for another year. I experimented with drugs for a while. Then something . . ."

McKenzie released the breath she was holding. "What?"

"I saw what happened to a friend of mine. My friend . . . died of a drug overdose. That's when I decided to straighten up for good. I called my parents and told them I wanted to come home. My dad offered me a job at Chandler, a second time. I quickly accepted, and I've been here ever since."

Inside McKenzie's head, a whirlwind of thoughts consumed her. Was he talking about what happened to her mother?

"You're so quiet. What are you thinking about?"

McKenzie turned away. She hoped none of the bitterness she felt showed on her face. "You have such painful memories."

Marc shrugged. "It's the past."

She gave a nervous laugh. "Well, what about your next relationship? Surely that one was much better."

Marc laughed. "She wasn't a criminal, but she was just as manipulative as Margie."

"How do you mean?"

"She tried to convince me she was carrying my child."

"How do you know she wasn't?"

"The nine-pound bouncing boy was born two months early."

"Oh." She was quiet for a moment. "Didn't you have any good relationships?" When he shook his head, she continued.

"I suppose that's why you're so hard on women, now. Because of what happened."

"Enough about me. Tell me about your relationships."

"Well, um . . . I haven't really had many. I spent most of my time concentrating on school."

"You have been out on a date, haven't you?"

McKenzie laughed. "Of course I've dated. I've always tried to maintain friendships. I think that's a very important part of any relationship. I don't think you ever got to know any of the women you dated as friends, did you?"

"No, I didn't. I was young, I had raging hormones—"

"That's no excuse."

"It's the truth. Since you have all the answers, Dr. Ashford, why is it you're not married? Are you looking for Mr. Right?"

"Yes, I guess I am. I've always felt that I'd know him on sight. I just haven't met him yet."

"You may have already met him—you're just too stubborn to admit it." Before she could respond, he stood up and grabbed her hand. Together, they returned to the den. He left her standing in the middle of the huge room and strode over to the bar.

"Would you like something to drink? Perhaps a brandy?"

"Sure, I'll try a glass of brandy." Though she never drank, McKenzie hoped this one time it would help her relax.

"Here you are." After giving her the glass, he led her to a chair before the fire.

Watching the flames, in vivid colors of red and orange, McKenzie was caught up in a whirlwind of memories. Her mother had been arrested one night, after the cops found drugs in one of her boyfriend's cars. She still remembered how angry her grandmother had been. Granny Mae had threatened to take her from Barbara. McKenzie downed the brandy as if it were water, then gasped and choked.

"Are you okay? Brandy should be sipped."

"I . . . I normally don't drink. I'm fine."

"I don't think it has anything to do with the brandy. It's

something more. I can see the sadness in your eyes. Why won't you talk to me?"

She said nothing. Instead, she stared at him as if she didn't know him, her eyes shadowed with pain and guilt.

"Talk to me, McKenzie. Tell me what you're feeling," he encouraged.

"I really miss my mother," she whispered, tears filling her eyes. "It's always hard for me around the holidays. The day she died, we had an argument." She looked at Marc then, through eyes filled with guilt. "I said some terrible things to her. Things I never had the chance to take back . . ." McKenzie couldn't go on. The words froze in her throat, and tears blinded her. She felt his arms go around her.

"I'm sorry, McKenzie. I'm so sorry, sweetheart."

In pain, she felt tears come spilling over her cheeks. She clung to him, and his hold tightened around her.

"It will be all right. Everything will be all right." The side he showed her was gentle and compassionate. The timbre of his deep rich voice sent tingles racing up and down her spine.

He reached up and gently cupped her face. McKenzie flinched at the sudden contact. His touch seemed to burn.

The only light in the room came from the fireplace, and they silently listened to the crackle of the fire. She could feel her tense body begin to relax against him.

The heat from his body seemed to undulate from him in warm waves. Once again, she had fallen under his hypnotic spell. She felt the heady sensation of his lips against her neck. The caress of his lips along her jawline and her mouth set her aflame. Marc's lips pressed against hers, then gently covered her mouth. His tongue sent shivers of desire coursing through her veins. Raising his mouth from hers, he gazed into her eyes.

"You are so beautiful."

Between each word he planted kisses on her lips, cheek, and forehead. McKenzie quivered at the sweet tenderness of his kisses. Their mouths locked once more. Marc scooped her in his arms and put her back down on the sofa. Leaning over her,

her eyes absorbed the beauty—of the moment, of the setting, of the woman.

"You want this as much as I do, don't you?" Marc whispered in her ear.

When McKenzie's body sank into the cushiony sofa, her brain revolted. Suddenly her mother's face loomed before her. This man was in some way connected to her mother's death.

She was about to make the same mistake her mother made. Bolting upright, McKenzie butted his chin with her head. Marc jumped back. Instead of rising, she clutched her face and sat back on the sofa, weeping into her hands.

"McKenzie?" When he tried to embrace her, she pulled back. "What's wrong?"

"I can't, Marc."

His heart still beat to the rhythm of passion. His body ached with it; his voice was weakened by it.

"Can't?"

McKenzie sobbed into her cupped hands.

Confused, he pulled her hands away. "What's wrong, sweetheart?"

Her sobs intensified, blurring her words. "I'm not s-sure. I just know that I can't do this." McKenzie gulped, trying to slow her palpitating heart. The musky fragrance of his cologne was slowly but surely warping her senses, clouding her brain. Forbidden desire and denial warred in her. "I'm sorry I gave you the wrong idea. I hope you understand." She no longer sobbed, but an unending river of tears rolled down her cheeks.

Marc struggled to keep himself from reaching to brush them away. "You don't have to do anything you're not ready for. We agreed to take things slow."

McKenzie's tears stopped then. "Thank you for understanding, Marc." She stood and headed toward the door. Just as she neared the front door he reached her, then pulled her back into the den.

"Do I scare you, McKenzie?"

She squared her shoulders and stood facing him. "No. I think I scare myself."

"Are you sure you want to go home?"

McKenzie nodded, afraid that if she spoke her words would indicate otherwise. "I can call a taxi."

"You don't have to do that. I'll take you."

"That's not necessary, Marc."

He held up his hand. "Just give me a minute to grab my jacket."

McKenzie said nothing during the short trip to her home. Just as he parked the car, she jumped out. Marc got out too, much to her surprise.

"You don't have to walk me to the door, Marc. I'll be all right."

"I'm walking you."

Marc stood on the step below her. They stood head to head, staring at each other. He reached for her, then, and planted a kiss on her lips. Pulling her closer in his arms, he whispered in her ear, "Merry Christmas, Dr. Ashford." Without looking back, he left.

Thirteen

McKenzie could not control the trembling in her body. Unable to move, she stood rooted to the spot, watching Marc drive away without a backward glance.

McKenzie closed her door and tried to pull her thoughts together. She was glad to be home—home, where she would be safe from Marc. She needed time to think. What had started out as revenge had turned into something more.

His kiss had awakened something in her that went far deeper than mere anger. *Stop this,* she ordered her rebellious thoughts. What on earth was wrong with her? She would not allow herself to fall for his charm. He was just another of the many men she'd met all her life.

As she readied for bed, McKenzie continued to chide herself for her behavior. How could a reasonably intelligent woman manage to twist her life into such a tangled mess? How could she kiss him back like that? The searing heat of humiliation spread throughout her body. *I'm so sorry, Mama. I didn't mean to let you down. I just don't think I can do this.* Leaving her clothing in a heap on the floor, she sat on the side of her bed.

McKenzie cursed herself a dozen times over as she replayed the events that had happened earlier in her mind. Shame splashed across her cheeks in various shades of red. Covering her face with her hands, she tried to stop the tears that seemed determined to flow.

Although she was ashamed of the way she'd carried on,

McKenzie admitted that she'd enjoyed his kisses. One evening with Marc, and her world had gone up in smoke. Her desire for him was so strong that she'd wanted him to make love to her. Balling her left hand into a fist, she pummeled her pillow several times and then flung it across the floor. *How could I be so stupid?*

McKenzie no longer tried to stop the tears that streamed down her cheeks. For the first time since setting out on her path of revenge she began to doubt her reasons. She gave in to heart-rending sobs, praying as she cried that the water from her tears would cleanse away the blot on her soul.

After dropping McKenzie off, Marc went home and decided to take down the decorations. Christmas was over. He looked around the gaily decorated house sadly. How his mother had loved it here. *Now she had just . . .* Marc let the thought drift as he suddenly remembered what she'd said the day they moved in: *Now I have just about everything I could possibly want. There is only one thing I want now.* He had wondered at the time what she meant.

Why hadn't she told him then? It was pointless to continue asking questions. He would never get the answers.

Marc quickly packed up all of the Christmas ornaments, carefully wrapping each one in tissue as his mother used to do. When he was finished, he picked up the box and headed to a closet in the hall. As he lifted the box, preparing to put it on the shelf, he was barraged by a colorful waterfall of boxes, papers, and hats.

"What the hell?" He bent to see what had fallen. It was some of his mother's possessions. Hardly anyone had ever used this closet except his mother. Marc had forgotten about it until it was time to decorate the house for Christmas. It was the first time in three years he'd bothered to decorate.

The medium-size box that had fallen, hitting him on the head, was gift wrapped. After further examination, Marc realized with a heavy heart that it was a gift to him from his mother. His heart knotted as he realized that his mother, believing that she wouldn't live to see Christmas, must have bought his gift early. She'd had no idea he wouldn't find it until three years later.

Laying the gift aside, he began to pick up his mother's collection of Sunday hats, colored tissues, and gift wrap. As he was about to pick up the last of the papers, he spied a large manila envelope. Curious, Marc turned it over. He recognized his mother's handwriting. It was addressed to him.

Opening it, he examined the contents. In it, he found a note detailing instructions to him, and another envelope. Marc sank down on the floor, his whole body trembling. When he felt in control once more, he reread the note. Tomorrow he would call the detective and Jim. They now had the information they needed.

Marc glanced at the gift, summoning the strength to open it. As he did, he could feel the warmth of his mother's love circulating. Pain clutched his heart as he called to mind the way he'd treated her as she lay dying. "I was an awful son to you. I wish I could make it up to you, but it's too late," he whispered.

Tears rolled down his cheeks when Marc pulled a beautiful sweater from the box. It had been knitted by his mother's loving hands. Pressing it to his cheek, he could almost feel her gentle caress. He sat there holding the sweater close to his heart and wishing he could change the past.

"Are you sure, Sherrie? Maybe they just didn't want to advertise that he was adopted. That's not always somethin' you go round telling people."

"Well, honey, that's what I was told. Carla said that Charles Chandler was Marc's stepfather, but that Lillian Blue-Chandler was his natural mother. I even saw a picture. There's a strong resemblance."

Pierce walked over to the window, his shoulders slumping. He didn't say a word, just stared straight out. Sherrie wondered if he really saw anything at all. Her heart went out to him, and she wished she could make the pain he was feeling go away. *Hell,* she wished she could take away everything that was wrong. He deserved so much better. Sometimes life could be so cruel. She sighed.

She turned to leave Pierce alone with his thoughts, but he called her name softly.

"Sherrie."

"I'm here, baby." She walked briskly over to join him at the window. Putting her arms around him, she held him close.

"I love you more than my own life, Pierce. Just you remember that. Don't jump to any conclusions right now. Let's just wait and find out the whole story." She kissed his cheek, noting that it felt damp.

"It's not about the money—"

"I know, honey. I know."

"Why? That's a-all I want to know." His voice broke.

Sherrie held him tighter, tears gathering in her eyes. She could feel his pain.

After the Christmas holidays, Marc seemed to distance himself from her. Whenever they passed each other in the hallways, he simply smiled and waved. McKenzie surmised she wouldn't be able to proceed with her plan unless she allowed Marc to get close. She resolved to become more approachable where he was concerned. Marc, however, seemed to have other ideas. He treated her like any other employee.

Two weeks went by, and McKenzie decided she would have to be the one to make the next move. Her chance came later that afternoon. She ran into Marc as he was leaving Carla's office. McKenzie removed her glasses, placing them into the pocket of her lab coat. "Hello, Marc."

He looked her over seductively. "McKenzie."

"Would you mind coming into my office? I would like to talk to you."

Marc stopped midstride. "Is there a problem?"

She shook her head. "No, not really. I just think we should talk, that's all."

"After you, then, Dr. Ashford."

He whistled softly as they headed to her office. After Marc settled in one of the chairs facing her desk, McKenzie took a calming breath. "I want to apologize for Christmas. I—"

He spoke in a soft gentle tone. "There's no need to apologize. I've been doing a lot of thinking. And I think it would be best if we kept our relationship professional."

"I see," McKenzie managed to say through trembling lips. "Have I done something?"

"No. Why would you think that?" He smiled, then. "Feeling a little guilty about something?"

McKenzie's breath caught. "N-no." She cleared her throat. "I have nothing to fe-feel guilty about. I was just wondering why you're acting so cool lately."

"I'm not looking for anything serious, but I know you enough to realize that you are. You don't seem like the type to play around."

McKenzie stood up, squaring her shoulders. "I'm not looking for a husband, Marc." When he raised his eyebrows she smiled and added, "I'm not looking for a lover, either."

Marc leaned closer to her, asking in a lower huskier tone, "Then tell me, Dr. Ashford, what are you looking for?"

"How about good old friendship? I don't think it's ever hurt anybody. Besides, that's what we agreed on in the beginning."

He laughed. "You have a point."

McKenzie stood and moved over toward the window in her office. Without looking back at Marc, she said, "We're intelligent people. Can we manage being friends?"

Marc joined her. "I'd like to think so." When he took a step toward her, she flinched.

His expression grew worried. "What's wrong? I'm not going to attack you, McKenzie."

She felt a shudder of embarrassment. "I know that, Marc,"

Her tone was apologetic. "I—" Her telephone rang, interrupting their conversation. "Excuse me for a minute." She sat down to take her phone call. "This shouldn't take long."

Marc nodded. He stood surveying her choices of paintings.

"Calvin! I'm so glad to hear from you. I've missed you so much." So delighted over her call, McKenzie missed Marc's frown.

"You're coming to California? That's great! Yes, we'll have the whole weekend together. I can't wait to see you. Of course you're staying with me. I wouldn't have it any other way."

McKenzie was not aware of Marc quietly easing out of her office.

When she hung up she was dumbfounded to see that Marc was gone. McKenzie was about to go after him, but Sherrie needed her in the lab. Reluctantly, she went to see what Sherrie wanted.

She didn't see Marc again for the rest of the day.

Finally, at around six-thirty, McKenzie grabbed her briefcase and rushed to her car. It was time to head to the airport. Calvin would be arriving in less than one hour.

McKenzie didn't notice Marc watching her from the window in his office.

Calvin. Calvin had to be the man in McKenzie's life. No wonder she said she didn't want anything more than friendship. Yet, her body language told him something else. Marc could even see it in her eyes. He admired her lean athletic torso as she practically ran the short distance to her car.

"Wouldn't want to be late picking up *Calvin,*" he muttered sarcastically.

Turning away from the window, he wondered why in hell the thought of her with this Calvin person filled him with rage. *Because you're jealous,* said a little voice in his head. "I am not. McKenzie means nothing to me!" he whispered to the empty office. Marc sank down in his leather chair, preparing to call it a day.

The telephone rang.

Knowing Clara had already left for the day, he answered on the sixth ring. "Chandler Pharmaceuticals."

"Marc?"

"Yes. Who is this?"

"It's Glenda, silly. I'm so glad I caught you before you left the office. I was wondering if you'd like to have dinner this evening. It'll be my treat, Marc."

"Don't tell me you're alone?" he said mockingly.

"What's wrong, Marc? McKenzie's not giving you the time of day?"

"Why don't I meet you around seven o'clock at The Olive Garden?" he barked.

Laughing, she said, "Great. I'll see you then."

Marc hung up, his dark brows rising slightly at his own actions. It bothered him that McKenzie had another man staying with her this weekend.

A much slimmer Calvin disembarked from the plane. McKenzie could hardly believe her eyes. He looked so handsome. Running to him, she threw her arms around him, hugging him tightly. "I've missed you so much. Ooh, Calvin, you look so good. Why didn't you tell me you were on a diet?"

"I wanted to surprise you." He twirled McKenzie around. "You don't look too shabby yourself. Uh-huh, girl, you look like a million bucks."

On the way to the car, they talked about his job, Orlando, and some of their mutual friends. McKenzie drove to CoCo's, where they had dinner.

"So, tell me, Calvin—what brought about this change?"

"Nothing. I just decided it was something I wanted to do. I've been wanting to lose weight for a long time now."

"You really look good. Are you exercising, too?"

"Yeah. I work out three times a week. How are things at Chandler?"

"They're okay."

Calvin arched an eyebrow. "Just okay?"

"My job is great. I really love what I'm doing."

"So, what's it like working with Marc Chandler?"

"He's okay, I guess. Not much different from any other employer. He's a very private man."

"And that bothers you?"

"Yes. Wouldn't it bother you?"

"I guess it depends on the type of relationship you have." He eyed McKenzie closely. "Just what kind are we talking about here?"

"It's not what you're thinking, Calvin. I'm just trying to be his friend."

"But how do you feel about him? Be honest with me, Mack."

"Honestly, I don't know, Calvin. I really don't know."

"You're attracted to him." It was a statement, not a question. McKenzie nodded, not able to confirm it aloud.

"I see."

"Calvin—"

He smiled sadly. "It's okay, Mack. You've always been honest with me about your feelings. I just hope everything works out for you. I really do." He bit into his sandwich, chewing slowly.

"Everything is so messed up, Calvin." She placed a slender hand over his. "I never meant to hurt you. Believe me, I don't want to be attracted to Marc. I'm not ready to get all emotional over a man."

"You have no control over that. Girl, you're going to meet somebody and fall head over heels for him—"

"See! That's exactly what I don't want to happen. My mom was so needy when it came to men, Calvin. She started doing drugs after my dad dumped her."

"You are not your mother, Mack. Remember that. It's okay to fall in love." Calvin looked down at his plate. "I believe you've already fallen in love with this Marc person. You're just afraid to admit it to yourself."

McKenzie snorted. "Huh! I think you've lost your mind. The last thing I'd ever feel for Marc Chandler is love."

"Mack—"

She waved her fork at him. "I don't want to talk about my boss anymore. For the record, I am not, nor will I ever be, in love with Marc Chandler. Do we understand each other?"

Calvin leaned toward her. "Don't you get an attitude with me, girl. You want to convince me that you have no feelings for your *boss,* as you call him? Well, then you might as well not waste your time. I don't believe you for one minute."

They finished their meals, scowling at each other. After leaving the restaurant, McKenzie drove to her town house. She made it to the door, then turned around to face Calvin. "I am not in love with Marc!" she sniped.

"Whatever." Calvin chuckled and eased around her to enter the house.

That night McKenzie lay in her bed, thinking about what Calvin had said. He was wrong. She was not in love with Marc Chandler. Yes, she was attracted to him, but it could not be what most would consider love. It was lust, pure and simple, that was it. She lusted after him. Satisfied, she turned on her side and drifted off to sleep.

Fourteen

The persistent ringing of the alarm clock finally penetrated through the fog of McKenzie's brain, still clouded with sleep. She was bone-weary after an exhausting weekend with Calvin. They'd spent Saturday sightseeing and shopping, then taken in a movie. On Sunday, they drove along the coast, returning in time for Calvin to catch his plane back to Florida.

McKenzie glanced at her calendar as she dressed for work. She had been with Chandler Pharmaceuticals for nine months and still hadn't found anything incriminating against Marc Chandler. He had really covered his tracks well. Or had he?

She had not been able to find out any more than what Marc had told her about his time in Florida. She checked for any information on his alias. Nothing turned up there, either. Marc Chandler did not have a criminal record. She knew now, too, she had been mistaken about him being a drug dealer. McKenzie was beginning to think that maybe she had been wrong about a lot of things. Nothing added up.

Why had he left her mother like that? Especially if it had been an accident. Why wouldn't he have tried to save her? She knew she could not give up before she had all the answers she needed.

Something her Granny Mae told her years ago came to mind. When McKenzie had vowed to get the man responsible for her mother's death, her grandmother had stopped her right then and there. She said that no one killed Barbara—no one but Barbara, herself. She alone was responsible for her destruction. Granny Mae had urged McKenzie to give up her mission for revenge.

She remembered how angry she had become at her grandmother. McKenzie could not understand how Granny Mae could say such things. She had lost her only daughter. Although she longed to ask Granny Mae about her comments, she dared not. Her grandmother would not tell her any more until she was good and ready. *Only she died before that time came,* McKenzie thought bitterly.

She quit her musings and quickly drained the last of her tepid chocolate raspberry-truffle drink. Grabbing her purse, McKenzie rushed out the door to her car. If she didn't hurry she would be caught in traffic. The last thing she needed was to be late for a staff meeting. McKenzie didn't want to give Marc any cause to jump all over her. Before she left on Friday, Marc had shut himself up in his office. She knew him well enough to know he acted like that when he wasn't in the best of moods. For some reason, she felt today would be no better.

When she arrived at the office, McKenzie sadly discovered that her intuition had been correct. She could tell Marc wasn't in a good mood when she entered the conference room. On top of that, she was late due to traffic. McKenzie prayed all was fine when he didn't even glance up when she entered the conference room. Walking swiftly, she eased into a chair at the opposite end of the table.

As soon as she was seated, Marc spoke. "I received a call from Melanie Thompson, of the AIDS Research Consortium in Atlanta. She is of the opinion that more research is needed on designing HIV vaccines before advocating any treatment to patients. What do you think, McKenzie?"

"I don't agree. I think it should be left up to the patient. Some are more willing to participate now, while others are waiting for more information before starting treatment."

His eyes challenged her. "What about the implications directly upon the AIDS virus itself? My concern is whether or not the patients will develop a resistance to the drugs."

McKenzie found herself concentrating on his mouth. What heat he aroused in her. Maybe if she didn't look into his eyes she could keep from melting.

"Well?" Marc prodded.

Embarrassed, McKenzie cleared her throat. "Er . . . our initial informal studies are very exciting and promising. They were conducted on patients with advanced HIV. None of them have developed any form of resistance so far." McKenzie then pulled her notes from her briefcase and passed around sheets of paper. "Here are comparison charts on more than forty HIV vaccines that are currently in clinical trials."

Marc looked over the charts. "I see you're well prepared even though you were late, Dr. Ashford."

McKenzie glared at him, wishing she knew why he fascinated her so much. She couldn't wait for the meeting to end. When it did, she was the first one to leave, wanting to escape his penetrating stare.

McKenzie spent the rest of her day alternately wishing Marc Chandler would fall off the face of the earth forever and longing to see his rare smile. Her telephone rang. It was Marc. Her body tensed like a tightrope.

"Can you please come to my office? I need to speak with you."

"Sure. I'll be right there."

She arrived ten minutes later, carrying her notebook and mentally preparing herself for a fight. She gathered all her strength to keep her nerves in check. McKenzie took a seat, pushing her glasses up the bridge of her nose. "Well, here I am. What is it?"

"You must have had some weekend. You could barely make it to work this morning."

"I was late because of traffic. It won't happen—"

"Relax, Dr. Ashford. I didn't call you here to berate you for being late. What you do, and with whom you do it, is none of my business." He pointed a finger toward her. "Unless it starts to interfere with your job here."

"So." She folded her hands across her chest. "Why did you call me? Have I done something that was not to your satisfaction?"

"I overheard you telling Carla how much you like basketball. I happen to have two tickets to the game on Sunday. Would you like to go with me?"

McKenzie was flabbergasted. "I'd love to. Thank you for asking."

"I'll pick you up around noon. I thought we'd have brunch first."

"That's fine. Thank you again, Marc."

"I hope I didn't offend you this morning, Doc. It was not my intention."

"It's okay. Personally, I thought it was obvious to everyone that I was late, but those who weren't aware of it certainly were after you announced it to the whole room."

Marc's eyes flashed in amusement. "I think I've kept you away from your work long enough." He waited for her to depart. When she made no move to leave, he inquired, "McKenzie, is there something else?"

Turn away. The words screamed through her mind, but she couldn't do it. She spoke softly. "No."

"So, it's a date, then?"

She knew she should refuse but she couldn't. Her heart pounding in her ears, she answered slowly, "It's a date, Marc.

"Doc, sit down. If you don't quit yelling at that referee security's going to have us moved. I think the next time I'm going to spring for tickets in the nosebleed section."

"If the man needs glasses, he should get some. It's obvious he's blind as a bat." Putting her hands to her mouth, she yelled, "Didn't you just see what Michael Jordan did? He double dribbled, you idiot!"

Marc shook his head, his body quivering with laughter. He

was glad to see McKenzie enjoying herself. When she jumped up, he pulled her back down into her seat. "Doc, calm down."

When the Lakers won, Marc was relieved. He had the feeling McKenzie would've taken on the whole team and the referee if they hadn't.

Walking out in the massive crowd at the Great Western Forum, Marc grabbed McKenzie by the hand. "I don't want to lose you."

His words had a heating effect on her. "You won't," was her soft response.

"I had no idea you were such a basketball fan."

"That's an understatement. It was a dream of mine to play pro basketball."

"What happened?"

"I guess the call to the medical field was greater."

Marc smiled. "Any regrets?"

McKenzie shook her head. "No, not any."

"You know, I've noticed you have a quite an appetite. Would you like to go get something to eat?"

"Thanks so much for mentioning that, Marc."

Marc squeezed her hand gently. "Doc, I didn't mean to make you uncomfortable. I like a woman who isn't ashamed to enjoy her food. It pisses me off when I take someone out and she just picks."

She felt better after hearing him say that, although it bothered her to think of him dating.

As they neared the car, Marc said, "So, tell me about Calvin."

Gazing up at him, she asked, "Calvin? Why?"

"Well, you seemed so excited over having him visit for the weekend. I assumed he must mean a great deal to you."

"He does. He's a very good friend, not to mention one of the sweetest men I know. How do you know about Calvin?"

"I was in your office when he called you on Friday. Are you in love with him?"

Grinning, McKenzie pointed out, "I don't know if that's any of your business, Mr. Chandler." Why was he acting like a suspicious lover? she wondered, yet it thrilled her to see him acting jealous.

"It isn't. But I still want to know. Are you?"

"I love him." She watched a myriad of emotions flash across his face. McKenzie bit back a smile. "But not in the way you mean. He's a very good friend."

"I see." Marc opened the car door for McKenzie. "Does he feel the same way about you?"

"No. He feels differently."

"He's *in* love with you. Is that what you're saying?"

"Yes," she said quietly.

Marc shook his head sadly. "Poor man. I can sympathize with him."

McKenzie's head snapped up. "What do you mean by that?"

"I know what it's like to love someone with your whole being, and have that love rejected. I'll never go through that again. *Not ever."*

"I've been honest with him, Marc."

"I'm not sure that makes him feel a hell of a lot better."

"Maybe not, but I felt I owed him the truth. Sometimes it hurts more to be honest."

Marc nodded. "I have no right interfering in your life. I'm sorry if I crossed that line."

"I think you're just nosy."

Marc knew she was teasing him. He threw back his head and laughed.

"So, what does this Calvin do? If you don't mind my asking."

"He's a stockbroker. Why?"

"I was just curious."

"No. Tell me the truth. You're just being nosy." She giggled. "Marc, I have a question for you. Why do you try so hard to push women away? I know you've been very hurt, but don't you ever get lonely?"

"I don't have the time or the energy to play mind games. Today's woman wants to stay at home, sitting on her butt watching soaps all day long. She wants to shop, drive expensive cars, live in a mansion—"

"Some women may feel that way, Marc. Personally, I don't think there's anything wrong with that. But there are women, like me, who have worked damn hard to get an education and secure a job that will provide them with the financial freedom they need to maintain their desired lifestyles—without depending on men. I might add that there are men who are doing the very same thing you just accused us women of."

Marc looked a bit sheepish, to McKenzie's delight. "You're right, of course. I guess I never really thought of it in those terms."

She grinned wickedly. "Most men wouldn't."

"This time I'll pay for dinner, Marc."

"You don't—"

"I wouldn't want you to think I'm after your money." She flashed a bright smile as Marc pulled his Mercedes into the restaurant parking lot.

Marc followed McKenzie into her town house. They sat side by side on the plush sofa.

McKenzie looked down at her folded hands, then up at Marc. His look was so galvanizing it sent a tremor through her. She cleared her throat, pretending not to be affected by him. "I really had a nice time tonight. Thank you."

"I have to admit I had a nice time, too. I've enjoyed your company. I'd like to see more of you."

McKenzie said nothing. Her mind told her to resist, but her body refused. She reasoned that this was all part of her plan.

"Well?"

"I'd like that, too, Marc. I really would."

He bent and kissed her lightly on the lips. Their eyes locked as their breathing came in unison. "I'll see you in the morning, Dr. Ashford."

Smiling, she watched him until he drove away.

As McKenzie readied for bed, she reflected on her dinner with Marc. It had been an enjoyable evening. She'd never thought the day would come when she would think something like that. Perhaps Marc had changed over time.

Her hunger for revenge lessened the more she grew to know Marc. Carla had been right about him. Marc had been hurt so much in the past that he wore a shield of armor around his heart.

She crawled into her bed, propped herself up with pillows, and proceeded to write in her journal. She wondered, too, in the midst of her own turmoil, why Marc's troubled soul moved her in ways that Calvin's goodness never had.

Fifteen

On the second day of February, Jim rushed into Marc's office. He seemed so excited that he looked ready to do back flips across the room.

"What has you in such a great mood?" Marc asked.

"You're going to get riled up too, when you read this." Jim handed Marc a folder.

Reading it, his face lit up like a Christmas tree. "Oh my God! I can't believe it. We've found him."

Jim nodded. "I think we should leave right away."

"You mean you're going with me?"

"You're damn right! I've been with you through all this. You think I'd abandon you now, old man?"

McKenzie rapped lightly on the door before entering. "Do you have a moment, Marc?" Seeing Jim, she smiled. "Hi, Jim. How are you?"

"Just fine. And you, Doctor?"

"I'm fine." She turned to Marc and asked, "Should I come back later this afternoon?"

"No. We can talk now. I won't be here this afternoon. Jim and I have to fly to Birmingham tonight." Marc thought he saw the barest hint of disappointment wash over her face. It thrilled him to the core. "I'll be gone at least a week."

"Oh . . . well, I wish you both a safe trip." She handed him a report. "This is what we spoke about earlier. These are the figures to back up my theory."

"I still disagree, McKenzie."

Jim settled back, watching the two debate, amusement written all over his face. Marc glanced over at Jim and winked.

"I'll tell you what, McKenzie. We'll talk about this some more when I get back."

"That's fine with me."

Marc thought he detected an underlying tone of anger in her response. He wondered why she seemed upset. Maybe it was because he was going out of town.

Jim shook his head. "That girl sure is pretty, and no bigger than a minute. But she's very independent. Going to be hard to tame her."

Marc laughed. "I don't want to tame her. I like her just the way she is. It keeps our relationship very interesting." He had Clara make the necessary arrangements while he and Jim left to pack. He was in such a good mood that he whistled as he drove down the highway, heading home. *It's about time.* His search was over. As soon as he reached Birmingham, Alabama, he would find the man he'd been searching for.

Marc and Jim had arrived in Birmingham with high hopes, which were quickly dashed. The man they were looking for had disappeared without a trace. For the first time in a long time, Marc felt defeated. All roads had led to a dead end. Maybe it was time to give up the search, his brain told him, but his heart wouldn't let him.

Defeated, they returned home. After dropping Jim off, Marc stopped by Chandler. He worked for about an hour in his office before deciding to leave.

As an afterthought he headed to Carla's office, somewhat surprised to see her there.

"Carla, what are you still doing here? It's almost eight o'clock."

"I needed to finish up my notes. How was your trip?"

Marc shook his head. "I couldn't find him. He left Birmingham months ago."

"I'm sorry, Marc. I know how much this means to you."

"I'm not giving up—not yet."

She smiled. "I'm glad to hear that."

"Well, I thought I'd just check to see if the building was still standing. I'm tired. Why don't you call it a day? I'll walk you to your car."

"Wait one more minute. This is the last of it. By the way, there's something I think you should know."

McKenzie gave one final stretch before getting up from the floor. She had done enough exercising for one night. She bent, rubbing her sore muscles. Marc had been gone for a week, and she missed him terribly. She thought of him with tender yearning.

McKenzie had decided to abandon her quest for revenge—it was time to bury the past. When she thought of Barbara she still felt a twinge of guilt. However, she could no longer deny her feelings for Marc. Her attraction for him was more than fleeting passion; it was fondness, kinship.

She sighed again. Curiosity ate at her. Why on earth did Marc fly off to Alabama?

"Still working as hard as ever, I see."

McKenzie whirled around, shocked to see Marc standing in her doorway. "How . . . where . . ."

"Your door was ajar. You really should keep it locked."

"I didn't know you were back from your trip." She noticed he kept one hand behind his back.

"I arrived a few hours ago."

"You don't have to stand in the doorway." She motioned toward the sofa. "Why don't you have a seat?"

Marc moved forward. In his hand he held a beautifully wrapped gift. "Happy belated birthday, McKenzie."

She was touched beyond words. "How did you know?"

"Carla. Need I say more? Why didn't you tell me last week it was your birthday? I wouldn't have flown out that night."

"Well, I was under the impression that your trip was extremely important. I certainly didn't want to interfere."

"I could have left the next morning."

She kissed him on his cheek. "Thank you for being so thoughtful. Can I open it now?"

Marc laughed. "Go for it."

McKenzie ripped through the paper, box, and tissue to find a intricately designed porcelain box. Opening it, she discovered it was actually a musical jewelry case. "Oooh, Marc! This is beautiful. Where did you get this?"

"It used to belong to my mother."

Her eyes shot up. "I—I can't keep this—"

"I want you to have it. It's my gift to you."

"Thank you, Marc." This time she kissed him fully on the lips, lingering for a moment. She slowly pulled away.

"Carla tells me CP-281 is ready for Phase I clinical trials."

"That's right." McKenzie put her glasses on as she talked. "Patients will take CP-281 orally for up to twelve weeks."

"I'm glad to hear it. That's great news."

"Oh, Marc, I want to show you something while you're here." She led him over to her computer monitor. "I want you to look at this." McKenzie moved aside to give Marc visibility and pointed to the screen. "This shows an all-atom view of the uncomplexed protein. Note the symmetry between the two subunits." The keys on her keyboard clicked under her slender fingers.

"And this gives you an idea of the overall structure. This is what I've been trying to tell you. Those who remain clinically asymptomatic and maintain a T-cell count greater than two hundred for at least ten years following infection will provide ample evidence that some people appear better able to resist progression of the HIV infection *or* the development of AIDS."

Marc could not contain his whoop of joy. "I have to hand it to you. You're brilliant."

"So you and Carla keep telling me," McKenzie said dryly, and she turned to walk away.

Marc turned McKenzie around to face him. "You know, I missed you. You were on my mind the whole time I was gone."

Her face lit up like candles on a birthday cake. "Really?"

He leaned down to kiss her passionately. "What do you think?"

She smiled. "You've been on my mind, too."

"I was thinking we could do something later on."

"What did you have in mind, Marc?"

"I thought we could take in a movie. What do you say?"

She smiled. "What time should I be ready?"

Marc glanced at his watch. "Is eight o'clock too late for a movie? It would give us a chance to get a bite to eat before the movie, say around six-thirty or seven?"

"Sounds good."

"I need to go by my office for a couple of hours. I'll be back shortly." Marc lowered his head, kissing her on the forehead.

McKenzie's lusty state of mind made her weak with both guilt and desire. Marc was a temptation that she could not afford. She knew she did not have a future with him, so she would have to be content with her fantasies of him.

A few days later, with a plan formulating in his mind, Marc knew exactly what he would do. He quickly called Clara into his office and dictated instructions. They had a lot to do, but Marc's goal was to have all tasks completed, thereby leaving his evening free.

Although he worked steadily, the rest of the day dragged as he anticipated spending time with McKenzie. Glancing up at the huge wall clock, Marc realized he still had a couple of hours to go.

Finally, Marc was through. Checking the time once more, he knew McKenzie would be leaving within the hour, so he snatched up his briefcase and hurried to his car.

Marc was waiting for McKenzie outside her door when she arrived home. He was dressed in a pair of navy sweats, and juggled a basketball from hand to hand.

"What are you doing here?" Surprise was written all over her face.

He thrust the ball at her, and was only mildly surprised when she caught it and dribbled it up and down. "I thought I'd take you down to the park and we'd play a little one-on-one."

Smiling, McKenzie stood with her back against her front door. "And what happens if I win?"

"I'll take you to the restaurant of your choice."

Her eyes narrowed suspiciously. "And if you win?"

"I get to have dinner here at your cute little house tonight. Homemade. No catered affair."

McKenzie couldn't help laughing. "You have some nerve. You know that, don't you?" She tossed the ball back to him before turning to unlock the door.

"That's how I've gotten as far as I have."

She opened her door, holding it open for him. "Well? Don't just stand there. Come on in while I get ready. You're on."

"Like you really know how to play ball." Marc put his hand up to his mouth in an effort to hide his chuckle.

McKenzie folded her arms across her chest. "Oh, you think I don't? Didn't I ever tell you that I've been playing basketball since I was able to walk?"

"Hurry up. I can't wait to get you out on the court."

"I guess you're in serious need of a butt whipping." McKenzie brushed her fingers across his chest. "I hope you brought a suit with you."

"Why?"

"Because when you lose, you're going to take me to the most expensive restaurant in Los Angeles."

Marc chuckled. "Which is?"

"I don't know, but I'm sure you must have some idea. Give me a minute to change, and I'll be right out to teach you a few things about basketball."

Marc broke into laughter.

McKenzie came out of her room ten minutes later. They continued to boast of their talents as they headed downstairs to Marc's car.

Marc won two games out of three, much to McKenzie's chagrin. She'd wanted to knock the cocky grin off his face.

"You cheated, Marc." McKenzie threw the ball at him and missed.

Marc ran after the ball, shouting, "And you're a sore loser, Dr. Ashford."

"Prove it! Prove you didn't cheat. Let's make it four out of five."

Marc shook his head. "No deal. We made a bet and I won. Let's go back to your place so you can make me dinner. I'm starving."

McKenzie smirked. "It wasn't a real deal. We never shook on it."

"I didn't think we had to. I took your word as a lady."

McKenzie clenched her teeth together so tightly that Marc burst out laughing.

He placed a muscled arm around her waist. "Come on, sore loser. Your kitchen's waiting." He held the car door for her.

McKenzie threw the ball, aiming at Marc's head. "Oh, hush!"

Marc laughed and ducked as a flash of orange whizzed by his head.

"What's on the menu?" he asked as he pulled into McKenzie's garage half an hour later.

"How does peanut butter sandwiches sound?" McKenzie suggested, still peeved about losing.

Marc was aghast. "You're kidding, right? I hate peanut butter!

"Of course I'm kidding. I was actually thinking of serving grilled cheese sandwiches . . . with mayonnaise. Yummy."

"Like hell!"

McKenzie doubled over in laughter. Still giggling, she made two attempts to insert her door key.

"What's so funny?" Marc took the key from McKenzie and unlocked her front door.

"You should see your face, Marc. You actually look green—something very hard for a black man to do."

Marc glared at her.

"Oh relax. I'm just teasing you. I'll make us a great dinner. I promise."

"I don't know if I should trust you in the kitchen."

"You can trust me anywhere." She peeked out of the kitchen and asked, "By the way, you never said anything about your trip. How did it go?"

"Birmingham turned out to be very disappointing, but I'll tell you about it another time."

McKenzie noticed a strange expression wash over his face. She wondered about it, but chose to ignore it. They were having a good time, and she didn't want to ruin it. "There's some brandy in the liquor cabinet. You're welcome to it."

"Thanks. Can I fix you a glass?" he called from the living room.

"No, thanks. Remember, I don't drink."

"That's right. I sometimes forget that." Marc poured himself a drink. Walking over to the couch, he sat down and settled back.

The savory smells from the kitchen wafted to his nostrils, interrupting his musings. Marc stood and headed to the kitchen.

Standing in the portal of the doorway, he watched McKenzie as she cooked. She worked diligently, unaware of his perusal.

"Whatever you're cooking smells delicious."

McKenzie smiled. "Maybe you should reserve your comments until you've eaten. I don't know that it'll be as good as yours. I honestly thought you had ordered the dinner," she said softly. "I loved the stuffing especially. It was great. Everything was. I'm one of those people who uses their dishwasher until the death, but I even enjoyed washing dishes with you."

For a long moment they stared into each other's eyes. Struggling to find his voice, Marc finally spoke. "I'm glad to hear you say that. I've always been proud of my cooking skills."

Marc leaned in to kiss her full lips, but McKenzie eased away from him, laughing. "Since you're so talented in the kitchen, impress me again." She handed him a pan. "You can make the muffins."

"Blueberry, strawberry, or apple cinnamon?" Marc asked, rubbing his hands together.

"Apple cinnamon."

Forty-five minutes later, they sat down together to eat. Soft jazz played in the background, but neither one paid much attention to it. McKenzie took a bite of her muffin. "Mmmm, this is delicious. You certainly do have a way with bread."

Marc laughed. "Your stuffed pork chops aren't bad, either. This is good."

After dinner McKenzie placed the dishes into the dishwasher. Marc moved toward her saying, "Thanks for being such a good sport."

McKenzie stared up into his face, trying to find words. "I . . . I didn't mind, Marc. I enjoyed your company," she said, still mesmerized by his piercing amber eyes.

Marc smiled down at her. "That's good to hear. Especially since I came here uninvited."

"You're always welcome here, Marc."

He captured her face between his strong hands, studying her face for a moment as if to memorize it. Then his mouth slowly descended on hers, sending a flame throughout her body that burned sweetly and languorously, consuming in its blaze all protests, all fear. She gave herself up completely to his ardent kisses, moaning with pleasure as his hand caressed her back, forcing her closer to his hard body.

"McKenzie, McKenzie, you are so sexy," he whispered

against her mouth. "Do you have any idea what being this close to you does to me?"

She smiled and pulled away reluctantly. "Maybe we should head into the den."

Marc looked down into her dark brown eyes. "Lead the way, sweetheart," he said softly.

McKenzie took his hand and led him from the kitchen. Sliding beside him on the couch, she asked, "Do you play video games?"

"Yes. Do you?"

McKenzie grinned. "I sure do. And I'm extremely good at it. What do you say about a game or two?"

"You're on."

McKenzie and Marc sat on the floor manipulating the controls as they warred against one another on video.

She watched Marc out of the corner of her eye. There were so many facets to the man. This evening he was just an oversize kid. McKenzie liked this side of him. It was refreshing.

Two hours later, Marc winced when McKenzie won again. She leaped up, laughing and jumping up and down. "I won. I beat you. Now what do you have to say about that?"

"I think you cheated." Marc was laughing.

McKenzie stopped jumping, and pretended to be angry. "I did not! You were the one cheating."

Marc held his hands up. "Okay. Okay. I'll give you this one. You won fair and square." He pulled her down on the floor beside him, and into his arms. His eyes locked with hers, inviting. Marc moaned before touching his lips to hers, gently at first, then demanding that McKenzie melt against him, returning his drugging kisses, letting his tongue explore, teaching her the exquisite sensations it could evoke.

McKenzie pulled away. "I think we had better put a rein on our passions, Marc."

"You're driving me crazy, McKenzie."

She realized she could hear his heart beating rapidly, and his speech was rough with emotion.

"Marc, please understand. I want you, I really do, but I'm not ready to take that next step."

"I understand, sweetheart. You know, I haven't met any old-fashioned girls in a long time. I have to admit I like it."

McKenzie inclined her head. "I thought you were upset with me Christmas because I wouldn't—"

"No, I was just frustrated. I wanted you so much, and I thought you felt the same way, too."

"I did. Only I didn't want to rush into something that I might later regret. I take making love very seriously."

"You're the type of woman who wants a commitment."

She looked up into deep piercing eyes. "Yes, I am."

He nodded. "I'm a very cautious man."

McKenzie kissed him on the cheek. "I won't hurt you, Marc. I promise."

"I really believe you mean that." Marc stood up then, trying to hide his desire from her. "I guess I should head on home."

She followed him to the door. "Marc—"

"We are going to make love, McKenzie. You can't keep running away from it. Maybe not tonight, but it's going to happen."

McKenzie had to use the wall for support as she felt her knees go weak with desire. She knew he was right.

Sixteen

"Why do you think they went to Birmingham?" Pierce removed the stack of still-warm towels from Sherrie and placed them carefully into the empty laundry basket. Digging into his pockets, Pierce pulled out a roll of quarters, handing them to Sherrie. He watched as she stuck them one by one into the coin-operated dryer.

Sherrie closed the door and turned toward Pierce. "Honey, I don't know. I just happened to overhear Carla mentioning it to McKenzie."

Pierce silently carried the laundry basket as they made their way to the elevators. Shifting the basket from side to side, he finally spoke when they were in the elevators, heading up to their floor. "Do you think he could have been looking for me?"

Sherrie shook her head. "I honestly don't know. Nobody seemed to know anything about his trip. Except that it was all of a sudden." Seeing Pierce's crestfallen expression, she wrapped her arms around him. "I'll tell you what. I'm going to find out everything I can for you, okay?"

He stopped and set the basket on a nearby table. Breathing heavily, he leaned against it. "I'd appreciate that." Pierce looked up into the mirror, and stood staring at his reflection. His medium brown eyes teared.

Sherrie came behind him, putting her arms around him. "You know something? I just love that cute li'l mole of yours." Just above your lip. Oooh, that's so sexy!"

He smiled, his eyes shining brightly. "And here I was thinking it was my charming personality that drove you wild."

Sherrie picked up the basket. When he tried to take it from her, she pulled away. "Honey, I can handle it from here. You need to take it easy." Kissing his cheek, Sherrie whispered, "I'll tell you a secret—everything about you drives me wild."

Pierce fumbled with the door until he unlocked it. "You deserve so much better."

"Pierce, honey, I hate when you talk like that—"

He held the door open for her. "I wouldn't hate you if you decided to find yourself a real man—"

"I have a real man!" Rare anger coursed through her. "I love you, Pierce. I don't want another man. So please stop trying to be so damned noble!" Sherrie dropped the basket on the floor in their bedroom. As she ran a brush through her waist-length hair, she glared at Pierce.

Pierce stared at her angry reflection. "I'm sorry, baby. I just don't want you to miss out on a wonderful life."

"I have a wonderful life—with you. Just because you have an illness, don't think you have to be alone. We're together in this."

"In all honesty, I would be afraid to lose you."

"I'm glad to hear you say that. You know, you really should make an honest woman out of me."

"Sherrie . . . we've been through this before—"

"Why won't you marry me? We love each other."

"It's because I love you." Pierce reached for Sherrie, but she pushed away from him.

"Baby, don't act like this. Please."

Sherrie brushed away a tear. "I'm sorry, honey. I know you think you are protecting me, but you're not. I love you so much . . ."

Pierce pulled her back into his arms. This time she did not resist him, instead leaning into the security of his body.

"Sherrie, I love you, too," he murmured in her hair. "I want you to believe me. I love you more than my own life."

"I know you do."

They stood in the middle of the room, just holding each other.

Finally Pierce spoke up. "Hey! Why don't we catch a movie, maybe grab something to eat?"

Sherrie shook her head. "I really don't feel like it. Maybe tomorrow, okay?"

"Sure, whatever you say, baby." Pierce walked over to the couch and sat down. Using the remote control, he clicked through the channels on the television.

Sherrie watched him, tears rolling down her cheeks. Sighing heavily, she walked out of the bedroom, closing the door behind her softly.

"You deserve so much more, baby," Pierce whispered. "It kills me that I can't be the one to give you the world."

"I'm sorry, Tarla. I tan't tum in. I feel terrible."

"I can tell. You sound so stuffed up. Stay in bed and get plenty of rest. Do you have anything to take?"

McKenzie sneezed. "Excuse me. I have some tode medicine somewhere around here."

"With the flu going around, maybe you should go to the doctor. I'll come pick you up at noon."

"You don't habe to do that. I'll be fine, really. All I need is bed rest. In a touple of days, I'll be dood as new."

"Are you sure? I really don't mind."

"Thanks, but I'll be fine. Don't worry. I'll stay put for the next touple of days."

"Promise?"

"I promise." McKenzie hung up the phone and crawled back under the covers. She had never felt so awful in her life. Raising herself on weak arms, she popped two Tylenol capsules in her mouth, followed by water. She fell back onto the plump pillows with a groan. Her body hurt all over!

McKenzie tossed about under the covers, not able to get comfortable. Eventually she lay still, welcoming the sleep that took her into its arms.

"Morning, Carla." Marc strolled into Carla's corner office. Removing her briefcase from a nearby visitor's chair, he took a seat. "Where's McKenzie? I though she would be in by now. It's not like her to be this late."

Carla sipped her coffee. "She's not late, she's sick. She has a cold."

Flipping through a magazine, he murmured, "I hope she's okay. I've heard that we're in for one of the worst flu epidemics ever."

"She's going to be out for a couple of days, but Sherrie and David should be able to handle the workload by themselves." Carla settled back into her comfortable black leather chair.

"I'm not worried about that." He was clearly concerned about McKenzie. "Do you think she'll see a doctor?"

"Who? McKenzie?"

"Yes. Maybe someone should take her to the doctor."

She smiled knowingly. "Why don't you go by her place and check on her, Marc? You know she doesn't have any family here."

He grinned. "I think I'll take your advice this time. I'll do that."

Marc rang the doorbell twice, and when he didn't receive a response he proceeded to knock soundly. Still no response. Getting more and more worried by the minute, Marc was about to attempt to bash the door in when McKenzie opened it. Her pale and sickly appearance worried him.

"Marc! What are you doing here? I wasn't expecting anyone." Her voice sounded terrible. Marc thought she sounded like a frog. "Come on in."

She stepped back to let him enter. Wrapping her terry cloth robe tighter, she made a self-conscious sweep with her hands at her hair. It was apparent that she was embarrassed about her appearance.

Marc was concerned by her unhealthy pallor. "I know. Carla told me you had the flu, so I thought I'd bring you something to eat." He held up a white paper bag. "I brought you chicken soup."

"Thanks, Marc. That was very sweet of you."

"Have you had anything at all to eat today?"

She shook her head no. "I don't have an appetite."

"You know you have to eat in order to keep your strength. I want you to eat this soup."

"Marc—"

"If I have to, I'll feed you."

"I'll eat."

McKenzie put a spoonful of soup in her mouth. It was clear to Marc that she was in pain.

"Is your throat that sore?"

She nodded.

"I'll go pick up some spray for your throat, as well as lozenges."

"Marc, you don't have—"

"I know. But you're sick, and I'm going to take care of you. Now I don't want to hear another word about it. Understood?"

"Understood."

McKenzie ate a spoonful of soup, squeezing her eyes shut in an effort to block out the pain of her sore throat. She suffered through two more spoonfuls before pushing the soup away from her. "I can't eat this right now. My throat hurts too much."

Marc removed the tray from the bed; "I'll take it down. You try to get some rest." He made sure she was comfortable

"I'm going run out now and get the things for your throat. I'll be back in a few."

"Marc, there's a spare key over there." McKenzie pointed to her dresser. "In my jewelry box. The second drawer. Take it. I don't know if I can make it back downstairs again."

When Marc returned from the pharmacy, McKenzie had already fallen asleep. He watched her for a moment before settling back into a chair near the bed to watch TV.

A few hours later, Marc jerked his head up at the sound of McKenzie's voice. He reached over to take her hand. She didn't open her eyes, but she seemed to calm down. When her breathing was steady once more, he sat back in the chair and watched her. McKenzie had slept fitfully throughout the rest of the day, and now she had a fever. He had tried to get her to drink water earlier, but she'd barely sipped it. Marc felt her forehead again. She was still hot. He went to the bathroom and quickly returned with a cool wet washcloth, applying it to her forehead.

McKenzie moved her head on the pillow, but she didn't open her eyes. "Marc," she mumbled, turning over to her right side. She slowly opened her eyes. With a great deal of effort, McKenzie forced herself to roll onto her back. Marc was sitting in a chair next to the bed, his feet propped on the edge, his hands against the chair back, and he was snoring softly.

Her heart ached when she looked at him. McKenzie watched him as he slept, taking in every part of him—his long muscular body, the strength that was evident in his arms, and the set of his mouth as he slept. When Marc suddenly opened his eyes McKenzie felt embarrassed, and she quickly averted her eyes.

"You're awake," he said, putting his feet on the floor and sitting up. Quickly he rubbed his hands over his face. "I didn't mean to fall asleep."

"Thank you for staying with me, Marc. I really appreciate it."

"You had a fever. I didn't want to leave you alone." Marc reached forward and placed his hand on her forehead. "Feels as if the fever's broken."

McKenzie grimaced. "I wish I could get my body to stop hurting."

"I'll get you some Tylenol," Marc offered. "Are you hungry?"

"No. I don't feel like eating. Maybe later."

Marc sat next to her on the bed. "You're going to have to eat, sweetheart. You want to regain your strength, don't you?"

"I'll eat later. I promise."

"I'm going to hold you to that. Let me get your medicine."

McKenzie watched Marc walk into the bathroom. He soon returned with a glass of water and two small capsules.

"Here you go."

"Thanks." As McKenzie reached for the glass of water, her hand began to shake. She tried to set the glass on the nightstand, but she missed. It dropped to the hardwood floor and broke. "Oh, no!"

"Why don't you lie back and let me clean this up? I'll get you some more water."

When he returned with the water she said, "I'm so sorry, Marc."

"Don't be," Marc said gently. "Everything's okay."

McKenzie lay on her side, her knees bent toward her chest. She felt helpless. Her back and head throbbed madly. She prayed the pain would soon stop.

Seventeen

A few days later, McKenzie's throat felt better, but she still had a lot of pain in her shoulders, back, and head. She despised being sick. She had heard somewhere that whiskey and lemon helped to rid the body of a cold. She was restless, and willing to try anything to get rid of this nagging cold. McKenzie went downstairs to retrieve a lemon from the kitchen and a bottle of Jack Daniels from her bar. Although McKenzie didn't drink, she kept bottles of liquor stored for entertaining purposes.

As she headed back to her bedroom she started having second thoughts, but after a coughing attack and agonizing chest pains at the top of the stairs, she decided that she would have just a sip. Surely one sip wouldn't hurt, would it?

Pouring the amber liquid into a glass, McKenzie took a sip, and immediately regretted it. It was like swallowing fire. She sneezed and coughed and choked until tears ran down her cheeks. When she regained her breath, she realized she felt warm. She took a second sip. And a third.

McKenzie, dressed in a pair of faded blue jeans and a denim shirt, lounged on her bed, amazed at the numbing effect the whiskey had on her body. Wrapped in her cumbrous knit cover, she began to perspire. Her nose tingled, and her legs felt noticeably heavy. She was so relaxed that sitting upright seemed to require tremendous effort. The half-empty bottle of Jack Daniels lay next to her.

She lost herself in fantasizing about Marc. He was such a

sexy man. His firm buttocks had hugged his jeans like a second skin. Just thinking about him in them made her body flush with heat. No man had ever made her feel that way. She wanted Marc in a way she'd never wanted any man.

McKenzie hungered for his firm lips on hers. Her nipples hardened at the thought of him kissing her, touching her everywhere. She wanted him to make love to her. It was all she could think about.

Shaking her head as if trying to rid herself of her lustful thoughts, McKenzie reached for the bottle of Jack Daniel's. Pouring some in her glass, the lemon forgotten, she quickly drained the contents. She had to find a way to make the visions of Marc, dancing naked in her head, disappear.

When Marc entered the bedroom, he stopped dead in his tracks.

McKenzie looked up and gave him a lopsided smile. "Hull, Marc. I—I didn't know you were here."

Her words were slurred. Marc spied the bottle of Jack Daniels on the nightstand and a glass in her left hand. Shaking his head, he removed the glass from her fingers. "I think you've had enough. You're drunk."

"Wha?" she said, and then frowned at her inability to form the proper pronunciation of words over her thick tongue. She had to concentrate to enunciate clearly. "I . . . I'm not drunk."

"I believe you're misinformed. You, sweetness, are drunk as a skunk."

Another frown knitted her delicately arched brows. Her words were growing more slurred by the minute. "Marc," McKenzie said tipsily. "You know wha', Marc? You, yer far too handsome fer your own good," she said, the whiskey working like a truth serum.

"Am I?" Marc grinned.

McKenzie nodded affirmatively. "And yer a very good kisser."

"So are you."

One delicate brow slid to a quizzical angle, even though the excessive consumption of whiskey made it impossible for her facial muscles to hold an expression for too long. "You think so?"

"Yes."

Marc eyed the rise and fall of her chest as she breathed. He strolled to the bathroom, returning quickly with a damp washcloth. He unzipped her now damp shirt, revealing the luscious swells of her breasts beneath the silken fabric of her bra. He blinked twice when her hands nimbly opened her shirt and eased it off her shoulders. Suddenly he lost all interest in the conversation, even though it might be the only time in his life that he received compliments from this feisty woman.

"You wanna kiss me, Marc?"

"You know I do." He chuckled, delighted by her brazen mood.

"Kiss me," McKenzie requested in a throaty whisper.

"McKenzie, I don't think—"

"Don't think. Ah, come on, Marc, gimme a kiss. You know you want to."

Before he could respond, she impulsively pulled him down onto the bed and raised tempting lips to his.

Marc's lips rolled over hers. She melted in his arms, and instinctively arched toward him. A muffled groan rattled in his palpitating chest when leaping flames blazed through every nerve and muscle in his masculine body.

Marc wanted to savor and devour her all in the same moment.

McKenzie wanted to explore his body as if he were the eighth wonder of the world. Her numb fingertips fumbled with the buttons of his shirt, and she divested him of the garment. Tossing his shirt aside, he gripped her waist and held her close. In wonderment, she traced her hand over the padded muscles and dark matting of hair that carpeted his broad chest.

"Magnificent . . . you are so fine." She breathed, then pressed her lips to his tawny skin to taste what she had touched.

When her brazen caress coasted down his belly to undo his pants, Marc completely forgot to breathe, and why he needed to. The feel of her moist lips skimming over his ribs put tiny bonfires in his bloodstream. Inexperienced though McKenzie was, she somehow knew how to drive a man over the edge and send him tumbling into the most sensual dimensions of desire.

With each breathless second that ticked by she became bolder and even more inquisitive. She discovered all the ultrasensitive places he liked to be touched. She marveled at Marc's reactions to her exploring caresses, reveled in the pleasure she received from memorizing the muscled planes and contours of his virile body. McKenzie yearned for more.

Her hand folded around him, stroking him until he groaned in torment.

Marc twisted away to work his skillful magic on her. Her body seemed to beg for his heated touch, for his soul-shattering kisses. Clumsily, McKenzie managed to take her shirt off. The thin straps of her bra slipped off her shoulders as she lay back against the plump pillows. Marc's experienced fingers unsnapped her bra, baring the tips of her swollen breasts.

He groaned and whispered, "I love your breasts." He pulled at her jeans. When she raised her hips just high enough to let him slide the jeans from her hips and then her panties, Marc's brain malfunctioned. He was all eyes and strangled breath.

He caressed her everywhere. His mouth came down on hers in a hot explosive kiss. Greedy kisses flooded over her. Red-hot flames leaped across every nerve ending until her entire body was on fire with wanting. He set her ablaze with fiery passion. His free hand and moist lips teased the dusky tipped peaks, and she craved more, begging for all he could offer. His body covered hers, crushing her into the mattress.

McKenzie rubbed her nipples against him. Pleasure shot from her breasts to her stomach, and her muscles turned to melted wax. Gently, his hand outlined the circle of her breasts. Her head reeled and every muscle tensed. Just when she thought she could take no more, he changed to her other breast. He traced the outline of her breasts with his tongue until his mouth found their hardened peaks. His tongue caressed one before going to the next. McKenzie searched for his hand and placed it on the breast he had just left. Heat washed over her. Her back arched, and a low moan escaped her parted lips. She groaned when he left the bed to undress.

When he was as naked as she, he rejoined her on the bed. Cradling her close to him, Marc ran a hand down her side, across her buttocks, lingering in her most private part until McKenzie thought she would go mad. Lost to instinctive urges, McKenzie raised her hips to him, impatient for what she'd heard so much about. She felt a soaring of spirit that was nothing less than joy.

Marc parted her thighs and lay on top of her, his mouth covering hers once again. His name was a whisper on her lips, so soft he thought he must be imagining it. He positioned himself between her legs and lifted her hips so he could have an easy entry. With a forceful thrust, he drove deeply inside her.

Marc felt her stiffen as a gasp of surprise and pain escaped her lips when he pushed through the slim barrier of her maidenhead. Her hands grabbed the firm flesh of his sides, her nails raking into his skin as the piercing pain chased away the earlier pleasure.

My God, how can that be? A virgin, Marc's mind called out in warning, but it was too late. He was the first man ever to make love to her. He had been so sure she had been with other men. Happiness flooded his soul. She had chosen him to be her first.

All the earlier pain had fled, and in its place a pulsing filled her, sending rapturous delight stirring within her core as he moved in and out. Slowly her body began to undulate, her hips rising with his and keeping a steady movement that was breathtakingly pleasurable. Her hands were clutched lightly on his back, her legs wrapped around his hips to receive all of him and to taste the full depth of the unbelievable feeling. Her eyes seemed to enlarge, and moans of passion escaped her lips as wave after wave of ecstasy shuddered over her.

McKenzie was wild and breathless with wanting him. Her body cried out to his. They were like two starving creatures who could not get enough of each other, could not bear for the splendorous moment to end, frantic to appease the tormenting needs that consumed them.

How could a woman touch him so deeply, drawing out feelings that he'd vowed to keep dead and buried? Marc had felt the same sense of vulnerability when he thought himself in love with Margie. And yet, with McKenzie, it was vastly different. It was worse, he realized with a start.

After pulling the sheet over himself and McKenzie, Marc cuddled her against him. He should get up and get dressed, he knew, but he couldn't leave her just yet. He wanted to go on holding her forever.

In a few hours he would get up, get dressed, and leave quietly. Expelling a weary sigh, Marc closed his eyes and nuzzled against McKenzie's neck.

Eighteen

McKenzie's stomach pitched and rolled like a storm-tossed ship on an angry sea. A thundering headache plowed through her skull to puncture her pickled brain. Her mouth was as dry as cotton. Even her eyebrows hurt!

Fully awakening to the feeling of being entrapped by something strong and unyielding, McKenzie opened her eyes to find herself surrounded by Marc's body, his powerful arms wrapped about her. Instantly the dream came to mind. But this was no dream. She could feel his heart beating against her breasts. This was real. A gasp escaped her lips. What had she done?

In desperation she pulled herself out of his arms and away from the heat of his large naked body.

"What are you doing here?" she gasped, fighting for a portion of the sheet as she discovered she was stark naked.

In a tender tone, Marc said calmly, "Holding you until you awoke."

"How dare you? How could you take advantage of me like that?" McKenzie hit Marc in his relaxed belly with all the fury she felt.

"Hey!" Marc leaped out of bed. She was not acting at all as he expected; she was furious with him. She was treating him as if he were the worst sort of person. "What the hell are you talking about?" He hurriedly put his pants on.

"You took advantage of me!" McKenzie spat.

He felt a small spark of anger. Did she intend to blame him

for everything that had happened? "I did no more than you desired. I guess you don't remember begging me to kiss you?" he muttered as he buttoned up his shirt. "Or the way you begged me to make love to you? Or—I know!—when you moved under me like a wild woman while I was inside of you." His tone was harder than it had been earlier as he defended what had taken place. "I guess I should have known all those moans and cries of pleasure were really sounds of protest," he went on, grumbling.

"I-I didn't . . ." McKenzie's voice rose higher. "I didn't know . . . I was . . . I was . . ." She couldn't even form the words to explain her behavior.

"Are you planning to accuse me of rape?" His eyes were now cold as hers, his disbelief evident in his tone. "Is this some sort of blackmail scheme? Is that what this is all about?"

"Stop tripping, Marc!" McKenzie grimaced when she glanced down to see the telltale signs of her lost virginity on the sheet. Flashbacks from the previous hours began to whack their way through the tangled jungle of her mind. Fragments of disjointed memories leaped at her, giving her a worse headache than she already had. Ever so slowly, the hazy picture materialized. Her face flushed red. "I'm not planning to blackmail you. I do know what happened now. I'm remembering everything. I . . . was a more than willing participant."

The remorse in her voice caused Marc's heart to twist in his chest. Damn her! She had seduced him. "Good. The last thing I need is for you to start playing the part of the injured maiden. For the record, I've no intention of getting married, or playing daddy."

McKenzie looked stricken, holding her throbbing head in her hands. Did he truly think she'd consider marrying him, or trying to trap him with an unwanted pregnancy? *He must be totally insane,* she thought.

Raising her chin proudly, she looked directly at him. "You have nothing to fear in either regard."

Marc glanced at her, his amber eyes dangerously bright. He

should have been heartened by her words, he told himself, but her quick adamant refusal served only to heighten his displeasure. Thinking of nothing else to say, he turned on his heel and left.

McKenzie stood staring at the door long after he'd left.

She groaned disparagingly. Damn her foolishness. Damn, damn, *damn*. Damn Marc! He had taken what a woman could give only once in her life. She'd made love to the man connected to her mother's death. And she didn't even know if he'd used protection. Recalling Marc's comments about playing daddy, McKenzie sadly surmised that they must not have. How could she have been so careless? After all, she was actively searching for a way to rid the world of a disease that was the result of having unprotected sex.

It was still dark outside, but—feeling as if the walls were closing in on her—McKenzie threw on the pair of earlier discarded jeans and decided to take a short walk. Pulling her jacket closed, she stepped outside her home. As her foot neared the bottom step, McKenzie heard someone whisper her name.

Marc's voice came out of the darkness, startling her. Turning her head, McKenzie saw him standing a few feet away, leaning against his car.

"Are you okay?"

She swallowed hard, afraid to meet his gaze. "I'm fine."

"Come here." He beckoned.

McKenzie hesitated. Her heart pounded. She took a couple of steps toward him, then hesitated again. Tears burned in her eyes, to her astonishment. No longer feeling hatred toward Marc, she felt lost, not knowing herself anymore. She knew if he touched her again, and kissed her, she would welcome him with open arms.

As she neared, he pulled her into his arms. Together they stood holding each other, watching the stars, saying nothing.

The cold night air had the needed affect on her as she stood staring up at the stars. What was she going to do about him? He was driving her insane.

"I'm so sorry, sweetheart—"

"Marc, I need to ask you a question. Something is really bothering me."

"What is it?"

She pulled out of his arms. "When we . . . when . . . er, did we—"

"We were protected."

She was visibly relieved. "I'm so glad to hear that, Marc."

"I didn't know you were a virgin. I was surprised, to say the least."

"It's not something I'd include on my resumé," she said quietly. She would have thought that he would be pleased. "I told you that I take making love very seriously."

"Sweetheart, I didn't mean anything by it. I just didn't expect you to be a virgin. Most women your age have some experience—"

"I'm sorry I wasn't more to your liking!" She turned away and ran up the stairs, wanting to get as far away from him as possible.

"That's not what I meant," Marc called after her. "McKenzie, come back here! We need to talk about this—"

Blocking out the sound of his voice, McKenzie ran as fast as she could. She didn't stop running until she reached the safety of her bedroom. She stood with her back against the door. Closing her eyes for a moment, she thought about Marc. She felt her stomach tighten, while her heart actually beat faster. The very thought of the way his hands touched her, the way his lips pressed against hers made her feel giddy. But more than that, more than his physical presence, was the way he looked at her adoringly. She wondered if he could ever love her.

Marc couldn't get his mind off the wide-eyed passionate woman. The more he thought about McKenzie, the more he wanted her.

Before he realized what was happening Marc found himself

in his car, heading back to McKenzie's house. He had to know what was going on between them. It was time for the truth. He knew what she wanted. McKenzie wanted a committed relationship. And what did he want? He wanted her. Only her.

He had barely knocked when McKenzie answered. For a minute she just stood there gazing at him, before saying, "Marc, I-I just tried to call you. I—"

Marc pushed the door shut with his foot.

McKenzie felt the familiar tightening in her loins. Standing there, he made quite a picture. She couldn't shift her eyes away. Suddenly feeling fluttery inside, McKenzie quickly glanced away. *No, no, no. I can't allow this to happen again.* Clenching her fists, she gritted her teeth to keep from responding to him.

Stepping in front of her, Marc moved closer, leaving scant inches between them. She could smell the intoxicating scent of him, could still feel the heat of his body coursing through her own. The anxiousness swelling in her abdomen reached unbearable proportions, and McKenzie was lost beyond all reason.

Marc's eyes held the smile that was on his lips. Trouble lay behind that smile, trouble for her. He lifted her hand and kissed the fingers one at a time. McKenzie was unable to hold a rational thought, and she eagerly gave herself over to her senses completely.

Marc raised up his eyes to look into her wide dark brown eyes. "I want you, sweetheart. I want to make love to you."

Her thick lashes lifted, and she groaned. Standing on tiptoe, she pulled his head down, moving her lips under his, and forgot all the reasons that it was wrong. Nothing could be wrong with fighting the loneliness. Nothing at all could be wrong, when everything felt so right. She kissed him, lingering, savoring every moment. Looking into his amber eyes, she whispered, "I want you, too."

"Are you sure, McKenzie? I want no misunderstandings between us this time." He held her face in his hands.

"I've never been more sure of anything in my life."

Tugging at her robe, Marc pulled it apart and filled his hands with her full breasts. There was no stopping the inevitable. Pure instinct ruled their actions now. McKenzie no longer wanted to remember why she'd called him her enemy. With hands frantic to feel their naked flesh united, they quickly removed their clothes.

Marc caught the back of McKenzie' s neck, and she leaned into him, rubbing the aroused tips of her breasts erotically against the hair-roughened muscles of his chest. He led her over to the sofa, pulling her down with him.

McKenzie straddled his hips, bringing the center of her womanhood to rest over his burning hardness. She moved against him mindlessly, the need to be filled with him guiding her.

Placing his hands on her hips, Marc lifted her upward. With one swift sure plunge, he filled her aching emptiness with his strength, and McKenzie was unable to hold back the cry of rapture that escaped in a long groan of abandon.

Moving slowly, tentatively at first, her hips rose and fell, over and over, faster and faster, until he was deep inside her, filling her to capacity. It was difficult to breathe. She lost all concept of time and place as he surged into her. They traveled higher and higher, until at last they were hurled wildly into the heavens, to float helplessly back to earth on a cloud of contentment.

McKenzie collapsed on Marc's chest. She sighed happily, all their differences forgotten for the moment.

"Now isn't this better than fighting?" Marc murmured, his voice hoarse and sending a warm rush of response spreading along her veins.

"Mmm," McKenzie moaned, bringing her mouth to his in an effort to fuel the hunger of the ever-growing fire raging through her.

Upstairs in bed, as Marc lay sleeping next to her, the sudden realization of how she'd succumbed a second time to a man who might be responsible for her mother's death assaulted her thoughts. Disgust and self-loathing for her weakness tore at her insides.

McKenzie struggled to remove herself from his embrace, not able to bear his closeness another minute without proving herself to be a liar. She was still burning to feel him inside her again, to have him make love to her over and over.

McKenzie gulped, trying to quiet her palpitating heart, and then a tormenting realization plowed through her mind: *I love him. I love Marc,* she mused disparagingly. *Damn.* She had vowed not to fall in love with him. She had allowed her foolish heart to rule her head—just like her mother.

McKenzie felt tears of regret trickle down her flushed cheeks. It seemed so unfair that she found herself in love with a man she could never have. Secretly she admitted that she hoped Marc would confess to love her in return. But those words would never form on his lips. He wanted her, desired her, yet lust was a world away from love.

Carla jogged down the street to her house. She had been out all morning, exercising. As she rounded the corner, a couple caught her eye. It was Marc. *He was with Sherrie!* Carla hid behind a nearby tree before they could spot her. She chewed on her lower lip and stole another look at them. She stood rooted to the spot, watching them enter an apartment building two blocks from her house.

Carla rushed into her house and up the stairs. She picked up the phone several times to call McKenzie, but realized she couldn't. There was no way she could betray her oldest and dearest friend. But she didn't want to see McKenzie hurt, either.

She had no idea what to do. Before she said or did anything, Carla decided to wait and see if Marc would come to her first. She hoped he would confide in her. Even if he didn't, it was obvious that there was something going on between him and Sherrie.

Still troubled, Carla stepped into her shower. She only had twenty minutes before Jim arrived. They were going to catch an early movie, then have dinner.

Jim arrived promptly at three o'clock. Carla, garbed only in her bathrobe, ushered him into the living room. As they stood toe to toe, she kissed him devouringly. His mouth grazed her earlobe, and she giggled and said, "If we plan on making that movie you'd better let me get dressed. It will only take a few minutes."

"Take your time, Carla. I'm in no hurry. The way you look in that robe . . . we don't even have to go out. We can make our own movie right here."

"Jim."

"Aw, come on, woman. Don't you go acting like a virgin bride."

Carla backed away from Jim, pointing. "Just march yourself over to that sofa, and behave." She was about to walk away, but stopped. "Jim, have you talked to Marc, by any chance?"

Jim nodded. "Yeah. Right before I came here."

Carla was stunned. "You did? Was he at home? I tried to call him earlier."

"No, he wasn't home. He called me from that car phone he has. I invited him and McKenzie to join us, but he said that they had separate plans for tonight."

I just bet they did, Carl thought. She knew McKenzie planned to do some research at the library.

"What's wrong, sugar?"

Carla was quiet.

Jim called her name once more.

"Huh? Oh, I guess I'd better get dressed."

"What's the matter, Carla? You look as if something's bothering you."

"Nothing's the matter, Jim. I was just thinking about something."

"Now, you know we can just stay here and enjoy each other's company. Maybe work on that mov—"

"Don't you start that again. Getting out of the house will do me a world of good, sweetie."

"You're sure, now?"

"I'm sure."

"Then what are you waitin' for? Go get dressed, woman."

"Yes, dear heart."

Carla could not concentrate on the movie. Her mind was on what she'd seen earlier—Marc and Sherrie together. It just didn't make sense. But whatever was going on didn't concern her. She and Marc had always made it a point to never interfere in each other's lives. She decided to let Marc and McKenzie work it out.

Nineteen

The next day at work, McKenzie noticed Carla's quiet demeanor. She had barely said two words since coming to the lab. "Carla. Is something wrong?"

"Huh? Oh, no. Nothing's wrong. I was just thinking about something."

McKenzie searched her friend's face. "I've never seen you this quiet. I was worried. I didn't mean to pry."

"You weren't prying. But I'm about to. How do you feel about Marc, McKenzie?"

"I-I like him. Why?"

"Are you in love with him?"

"Yes." She wondered if that was what was bothering her. Was it possible that she was jealous? She had to know. "Carla, do you love Marc? I mean, are you in love with him?"

"Oh, no! That's not why I'm asking you about your feelings. I was curious as to how things are going with the two of you. I know it's not my business—"

"Are you afraid that I'm going to hurt him?" McKenzie interrupted.

"I don't want to see either one of you hurt." She glanced down at her watch. "Goodness! I have got to go. I didn't realize it was this late! I have an appointment in one hour, and traffic is backed up during this time of day."

"But—"

"We'll talk later. I've got to run . . ."

Carla left McKenzie curious as to what had just transpired.

"Hi, Marc. Clara said it was okay to come in."

Marc glanced up to find Sherrie standing in the doorway of his office. "Come right on in. I wanted to speak with you. Close the door behind you, please." He then buzzed Clara.

"Yes, Marc." Claire's scratchy voice came over the intercom.

"We're not to be disturbed."

Sherrie twisted her hands nervously in her lap. When she spoke, her voice trembled slightly. "Am I in trouble, Marc?"

Marc smiled. "Of course not. I wanted to ask you some questions about Birmingham."

"B-Birmingham?"

Marc watched the play of emotions on her face. "As you probably know, I've made a couple of trips to Alabama. Birmingham, especially."

"I-I heard something about it. I don't know why, though."

"There are only a couple of people who know my reason. This is to be held in strict confidence. I'm looking for someone, and I'm hoping you might know him."

"I grew up in Birmingham, so I might. Is this person someone special to you?"

"Yes and no. You see, I've never met him."

"So then, this is someone you want to meet, then?"

"For now, let's just say I want to learn everything I can about this person."

Sherrie nodded. "Okay. What's his name?"

As he told her the name of the person he'd been searching for, Marc surveyed her face for a reaction. Sherrie's expression was unreadable.

Finally she presented him with a quick smile. "I'm sorry, Marc. I wouldn't be any help."

"Will you at least ask among your friends and relatives back in Birmingham?"

"I sure will. I'd better get back to the lab." Pausing midstride, she turned around. "Marc, this person is very important to you, isn't he?"

Marc nodded sadly. "Very important." Sherrie seemed ready to say more, but she apparently changed her mind. This time he saw something more in her eyes. Hope sprang into his heart. Maybe she did know something. Before he could question her, she was gone.

Rubbing the side of his head, Marc concluded that it had probably been his imagination.

"Hello, Clara. Is Marc in his office?" McKenzie walked in with two cans of soda and two wrapped sandwiches.

"He's in there, honey, but he can't be disturbed right now. He's with Sherrie."

McKenzie looked confused. "They're in a meeting?"

"I assume so. Shouldn't be long, though. Why don't you take a seat?"

Settling back onto one of the maroon chairs, McKenzie wondered what Marc and Sherrie could be talking about behind closed doors. There weren't any problems with her work performance. Maybe Sherrie was having problems. But why wouldn't she come to her?

Just then, the door opened, and Marc escorted Sherrie out. He spotted McKenzie and smiled. She stood up, looking from one to the other. Sherrie appeared uncomfortable, and quickly headed to the elevators.

McKenzie turned back to Marc, saying, "Is there something wrong?"

"No, there's nothing wrong. I just needed to talk to her."

"Oh." Holding up the soda and the sandwiches, she said, "I brought lunch. Are you hungry?"

"Yes I am, but it's not for food," he whispered huskily.

"Marc!"

"Come on, let's go into my office. Clara's going to fall flat on her face if she leans any further trying to hear our conversation."

Pulling him by the arm, she whispered, "Hush, Marc. She might have heard you."

"I don't doubt it. She's a nosy woman."

"Will you lower your voice?" McKenzie opened the door and entered. They both burst into laughter as soon as they were behind closed doors. She stifled her giggles. "I can't believe you did that."

Marc wrapped loving arms around her. Placing a gentle kiss on her forehead, he murmured, "What did I do? Besides state the truth. Clara *is* nosy."

McKenzie gave a small laugh as she pulled away. "She's a sweetheart. Stop picking on her."

"I'm not. I was just making an observation."

"Here. Sit down and eat your sandwich."

"Thanks. I wasn't sure if I'd get a chance to eat at all."

McKenzie nodded. "I thought that might be the case. I know you've got several meetings lined up today."

"I'm glad Mike canceled."

"Is he the rep from Med-Tech?"

"Yes." He stopped chewing. "Why? How do you know him?"

"He ran into me one day downstairs. He asked for my phone number."

"Did you give it to him?"

McKenzie stopped eating. Staring Marc straight in the face, she asked, "And if I did, what of it?"

"You're supposed to be my lady."

"Marc, don't take that tone with me. I'm my own person, but I am dating you. *Only you.*"

He removed her sandwich from her hands, and placed it on a napkin on a nearby table. Pulling her up, he started to remove her shirt.

"What do you think you're doing?"

"I'm undressing you."

"Marc!"

"Ssssh, honey."

"We can't, Marc. You've got a meeting in about thirty minutes."

"You really know how to excite a guy, don't you?"

"I didn't schedule your appointments this way. You did."

"Don't remind me." He kissed her once more. "I want a rain check. *For tonight.*"

McKenzie slowly buttoned her shirt. "I'll see you tonight."

A week later, McKenzie sat tapping her fingers on her kitchen counter as she waited for Calvin to answer at the other end of the phone line. Marc had left town on business, and she was feeling lonely. She was just about to hang up when she heard someone pick up.

"Hello, Calvin. I'm glad you picked up."

"Hey, Mack! It's good to hear your voice. What's going on?"

"Nothing much. But why don't you tell me what's going on with you? I've been trying to reach you for a while. You're hardly ever home anymore. Are you traveling more with your job?"

He laughed. "No, it's nothing like that. I do have a social life outside of work, Mack. I've been seeing someone. Her name is Ellen. She's a wonderful, beautiful lady."

"I guess so. You sound very happy."

"I am, Mack. I was going to call you this weekend, anyway. I have some good news."

"What is it? I could sure use some right now."

"I asked Ellen to marry me, and she accepted."

McKenzie couldn't keep the surprise out of her voice. "Y-you're getting married?"

"Yes, and I want you to be my best person."

"Your *what?*"

"You're my best friend, Mack. I want you to be my best man, er . . . person. What do you say?"

Still stunned by his announcement, McKenzie was quiet for a moment. When he prompted her, she said, "Sure, Calvin. But I do have one question. Do I have to wear a tuxedo? I know with my short hair and all, I could pass for a man . . ."

Calvin laughed. "No, girl. You could never pass for a man. You don't need to wear a tux, at least not the kind a man would wear."

"What other kind is there?"

"Mom found this sharp tuxedo dress."

"What? Oh, wait a minute. You mean a long black skirt with the satin tux stripes on the sides and a double-breasted blazer?"

"Yeah, yeah, it's something like that. It would look good on you."

"Are you sure you want me to be your best—what did you call it? Your best person?"

"Yes. Now tell me, how are things with you and your boss man? I hope you haven't killed the poor man with that sharp tongue of yours."

"I haven't killed him *yet*. We are seeing each other. He's out of town right now."

"That's great! Not about him being out of town, I mean. You did the right thing, Mack. You're not a vengeful person."

"You think you know me so well."

"I do."

"Then why did you agree to help me, Calvin?"

"Because I care a great deal for you, and I'm your friend. I never believed for one minute that you'd go through with it."

"You're a good friend."

"I know. So, tell me, was I right, or was I right? You're in love with the guy, right?"

McKenzie giggled. "You're a crazy one, Calvin. All I said was—"

"Will you quit hedging, girl? Go on and tell me the truth. You're in love with boss man. Just say it. Come on."

"Okay, okay. Yes, Calvin. I'm in love with Marc."

"See, that wasn't so bad, now was it?"

"No. It feels good actually, except—"

"What?"

"Except when I think about my mom. I feel like I'm betraying her."

"How is that?"

"Remember the man I told you about? The one who left my mother to die?"

"Yeah, I remember. But what's that got to do with anything?"

"Calvin, that man was Marc Chandler."

"What?"

"You heard me. He's the man."

"Naw, I don't believe that, McKenzie. I think you're way off base there. Besides, that man's name was—"

"It was an alias, Calvin."

"I don't believe that," he repeated. "I think you're wrong."

"I have a photograph of the two of them. Marc and my mother."

"You can't see nothing on that picture. It's so old and faded."

"It's him," McKenzie argued. "I know it is."

"Well, maybe it's time for the two of you to sit down and talk about that night. Find out what exactly happened between the two of them."

"I plan to, but I'm waiting for the right time, when I can handle the answers."

"Do you think your relationship will lead to something serious?"

"You mean like marriage? No, I don't think so."

"Aw, Mack. You never know. I never thought I would be marrying Ellen. I always thought it would be yo—" Calvin cleared his throat. "Anyway, Ellen is right for me. She loves me, and treats me like a king."

"You deserve nothing less, Calvin. I'm so happy for you. Everything seems to be working out for you. I know one thing though—she had *better* treat you right! She'd better not trip, or she'll have to answer to me."

Calvin laughed in a deep jovial way. "You don't have to

worry about that. Ellen's cool people. I can't wait for the two of you to meet. Mack, you're going to like her. I know you will. As for you, don't drive that man away with that hot head of yours. Give Marc a chance to explain."

"Hey, let's hope he can."

"Hey, nothing. Keep an open mind. But temper or not, I love you, girl."

"I love you too, Calvin."

As she hung up the phone McKenzie swallowed hard, feeling a lump of painful emotion. In her happiness for Calvin, she discovered the sadness of her own situation.

A desolate feeling overwhelmed her. McKenzie still felt a strong sense of guilt when she thought about Barbara, She was in love -with the same man her mother had loved. He was the last one to see her alive. There was still the remote possibility that he was responsible in some way for her death. *If only things were different,* she wished desperately. She would eventually have to confront him. She needed to know what really happened.

Marc had taught her to feel, to want, to love. Something had been between them from the beginning. Although she tried to deny it, she could not. It was something that could not be defined within the ordinary bounds of love or hate; it was too passionate, too contradictory. . . .

Her troubled thoughts were cut short by the insistent ringing of the doorbell. McKenzie jumped off the stool and ran to the door. When she opened it, the despair in her heart soon turned to happiness at finding Marc standing there. Impulsively, she threw her arms around his neck. "I'm so glad you're back," McKenzie exclaimed, tears bright in her eyes.

Marc smiled at her. "Hello to you, too, sweetheart. Were you busy? It took a while for you to answer the door."

McKenzie shook her head. "No. I just got off the phone with a friend." Reluctantly, she released him and led him into the house. "I didn't know you were coming by. I would have made you dinner or something."

He turned her to face him, grinning seductively. "I think I'd like the *or something.*"

"Marc!"

"What?" he mimicked in the same tone she had used.

McKenzie pushed him down on the sofa, then slumped down beside him. "Why didn't you tell me you were coming home today? I could have at least made myself a little more presentable." She ran a slender hand through her short wavy hair.

"I think you look beautiful." He kissed her forehead. "Actually, I hadn't planned to stop by. I was heading home from the airport, but before I knew it I found myself here." He glanced down into her eyes. "I hope you don't mind my coming by. Without calling first."

"I don't mind, Marc. I'm actually very glad you stopped by."

"Why? Is something wrong?"

McKenzie snuggled next to him. "No. I just wanted to see you."

Marc kissed her gently on the lips, then. "Are you sure you're okay? You seem a little sad."

"I'm fine. Really," she assured him. "I'm just glad you're here." McKenzie snuggled closer to him, placing her head against his chest. She sat listening to the steady thumping of his heart. The rhythmic beating was like sweet music to her ears.

Twenty

A few days later, McKenzie decided to splurge on clothing. In Nordstrom's she stood holding a Jones New York jacket. It would look great with taupe pants she already owned. "Oh, what the hell! If I don't buy it now, I'll just regret it," she muttered.

While McKenzie waited in line to pay for her items, she surveyed the store. She took notice of a couple coming toward her. They looked familiar. McKenzie gasped. It was Marc and Sherrie! What were they doing there—and together? As they neared, she forced herself to move. McKenzie placed the jacket on the nearest rack in her haste to leave the store.

Tears clouded her vision, but she kept walking, faster and faster. She just wanted to put as much distance between Marc and her as possible. How could she have been so foolish?

McKenzie was breathless. Not only was she jealous, she was angry. *How dare he treat her like that?* McKenzie whirled around and headed back into the store. She planned to confront the two, give them a piece of her mind. If Marc wanted Sherrie, he could have her! Glancing up one aisle and down the next, McKenzie couldn't find them. She scanned the store once more. Where could they have disappeared to? After checking near all of the entrances, she decided to give up her search.

McKenzie sighed. She tried to believe it was just as well, that she had no right to be angry. Marc could do what he wanted. And so could she. No matter how much she tried to reason about it, though, she was still hurt. She could not get Marc and Sherrie off her mind. Marc's betrayal hurt.

Tears blinded her as she fumbled around in her purse for her keys. Wrapping her fingers around them, she pulled them out and unlocked her car door. Before getting in, McKenzie could not resist taking another look around the parking lot.

As soon as McKenzie entered her house she collapsed on her living room sofa. Marc and Sherrie? Were they seeing each other? They had to be. There was no other reason for them to be together. And in Nordstrom's. Well it wasn't as if she and Marc were committed to each other, she reasoned. She had no right to be jealous.

McKenzie found the light on her answering machine blinking when she walked inside. With trembling fingers, she pushed the *play* button. It was a message from Marc.

"Hi, sweetheart. I'm in Los Angeles for a meeting. It started late, so I'm going to have to cancel dinner tonight. I'll try to give you a call later. Sorry about tonight."

McKenzie could have spit nails, she was so angry. He had lied to her.

The next day, she turned the answering machine off. She didn't want to hear from Marc. He had already called twice the night before, but McKenzie refused to pick up. Right now she was still too hurt and angry to talk to him.

She flipped through the pages of the magazine she had been reading. Her eyes found an attractive advertisement for the Cayman Islands. Dropping the magazine on the sofa, she reached for the telephone. McKenzie quickly made reservations to fly out that evening. She needed to get away. She wanted to be alone in order to think about her relationship with Marc.

After all travel arrangements were made, McKenzie called Chandler. "Hello, Carla. I'm sorry this is last minute, but I need to take some time off. I really need to get away."

"That's no problem, McKenzie, but what's the matter?"

"Nothing."

"Are you sure you're okay?"

"I'm fine. Really."

"Then why don't I believe you?"

"If I tell you something, will you keep it between us?"

"Sure. What is it?"

McKenzie took a deep breath. "It's Marc. I think he's involved with Sherrie."

"Why . . . do you say that?"

"Because I saw them together. Yesterday, at Nordstrom's."

"I see."

"You don't seem shocked." Realization washed over her. "That's because you *knew*. My Lord, you knew about them, and you didn't tell me. You let me make a fool of myself. I thought you were my friend."

"I am your friend. But I'm also Marc's friend, McKenzie. It's not my place to get involved."

"If the shoe were on the other foot, I bet you wouldn't have the same attitude," McKenzie said sarcastically.

"McKenzie, look—"

"Forget it, Carla! I have to go. I have a plane to catch."

"When will you be back?"

"Next weekend. I'll be back Sunday morning."

"McKenzie, I know you're angry with me. I'm sorry, but I'm in a bad situation. You're both my friends. I think the two of you need to sit down and talk—"

"Marc and I have nothing to talk about!" McKenzie snapped.

"You love him, McKenzie. Don't you think he's worth fighting for?"

McKenzie sighed. "Yes, I love him, but I want a man I can trust! Marc lied to me about where he was. He wasn't even man enough to be honest with me."

"Please call him," Carla pleaded. "Talk to him."

"Maybe when I get back. I just can't right now."

"Where are you going? I may need to reach you."

"To Miami for one day, and from there, the Cayman Islands."

"Oooh, how nice. I've always wanted to go there."

"Want to join me?" McKenzie teased.

Carla sighed loudly. "How I wish I could. Do you know where you'll be staying?"

"At the Sunset House, Grand Cayman Island." McKenzie quickly gave Carla the number.

"Have fun, McKenzie. And think about what I said. You and Marc need to sit down and iron out the kinks in your relationship."

"Thanks. I will think about what you said." McKenzie hung up and hastily packed a suitcase. She had to be at the airport in three hours.

Two hours later, Marc called just as she was about to walk out the door. Annoyed that she had turned her machine back on, she paused, listening to his deep-timbred voice. A pain squeezed her heart as she thought of what they had shared over the past few months. It had been a game to him. McKenzie sadly acknowledged that she had been as gullible as her mother where Marc was concerned.

She struggled to keep from running to the phone. In spite of everything, she still loved Marc. McKenzie was disgusted with her weakness. Shaking her head in loathing, she rushed out of the house.

Marc stood waiting patiently for Carla to finish her instructions to David. As soon as David left her office, Carla drew her attention to Marc.

"Were you waiting to talk to me?"

"Yes, I was. Do you have any idea where McKenzie is? I called her place all weekend, but I didn't get an answer."

Carla eased into a chair and turned on her computer. Without turning around, she said, "That's because she's on vacation, Marc. I'm not *surprised* she didn't tell you, though. Not after the way you've treated her. I can't believe you!"

"What are you talking about, Carla?"

She kept her eyes glued to the computer screen. "I'm not stupid, Marc. I know what you're doing."

Marc strode angrily to the door, closing it. His voice was cold when he asked again, "What are you talking about?"

"Marc, how can you be so blind? McKenzie is good for you, and look how you treat her. You go and cheat on her—"

He shot her a cold look. "Have you lost your mind? I haven't cheated on her."

Carla's accusing voice stabbed the air. "What do you call it, then? I've seen you with Sherrie myself."

Marc's angry gaze swung over her. "And that qualifies as an affair?"

"What other reason would you have for being with her?"

"She's my employee, Carla. And she's from *Birmingham*. I've talked with her on several occasions . . . regarding certain people in her hometown."

Comprehension dawned. "Oh dear. I didn't make the connection. I guess I wasn't thinking. Does she know anything about him?" Carla's tone was apologetic.

"She says she doesn't, but I have the feeling she knows more than she told me. It's as if she's hiding something." He sat down and shrugged. "I don't really know what to make of it."

"But surely she would've been able to make the connection. I'm sure she would have said something sooner. If she knew anything, that is."

"I thought so, too, but apparently not."

Carla stood up and walked to where he was sitting. She eased down beside him, placing his hand in hers. "I'm so sorry, Marc. I guess I jumped to the wrong conclusion when I saw you two together."

"Apology accepted." He laughed. "You know, I didn't realize you were so protective of McKenzie."

"She saw you with Sherrie at Nordstrom's, and it really hurt her. She sounded so sad when I talked to her. I hated hearing her sound that way. McKenzie decided she needed to take some time off. She wanted to go away and think about things."

"She saw us where?"

"At Nordstrom's."

"I wasn't at Nordstrom's with Sherrie. I've only talked to her here at work . . ." His voice trailed off.

Carla was thoroughly confused. She had seen them together near her house. "Marc, I saw—"

"Excuse me," David interrupted. "Carla, you really need to see this." He handed her a computer printout.

"I think I know what's going on. How long will McKenzie be gone?" Marc wanted to know.

"A week," Carla answered without looking up.

"Any idea where she went? Back to Florida?"

"She went to the Cayman Islands. Marc what *is* going on?"

"I can't tell you right now. But soon, I promise." Marc picked up a piece of paper from Carla's desk. "Is this where she can be reached?"

Carla nodded.

"Do you mind if I use your phone?"

She shook her head no. Pointing to her computer screen, she said to David, "Why don't we change that to this? See? That works."

Marc looked at his watch, then called Clara. "Clara, please call the travel agent and book a flight for me to the Grand Cayman Islands. I want to leave this afternoon."

Replacing the phone on its cradle, he said to Carla, "Think you can manage without me for a few days?"

She gave him a sly smile and nodded. "I'm sure of it."

Marc clasped his hands together. "Good. Well, I'm out of here. I've got to go home and pack. If McKenzie calls, don't tell her that I'm on my way to join her. I want it to be a surprise."

"Don't worry. I won't say a word. I hope the two of you can work things out."

"We will, Carla. We will."

Carla and David looked at each other, grins plastered on their faces.

Twenty-one

McKenzie tried to enjoy the surrounding calm, tourmaline waters, and healthy reefs of the Cayman Islands. That morning, she had begun her day with a walk at dawn along Seven Mile Beach. After that, McKenzie rented a Jeep and drove around, discovering the charming districts of North Side, East End, Bodden town, and West Bay as she went in search of souvenirs.

Returning to the hotel, McKenzie stopped to take pictures of the tropical garden setting that surrounded Sunset House, where she was staying. Then she walked slowly back to her room, to the loneliness. Although exhausted, she intended to enjoy every single minute of her vacation. She tried to stay busy, to keep from moping over Marc. He simply wasn't worth it. As soon as McKenzie opened her door, she rushed straight to the bathroom. She intended to take a long soak in the tub.

Thirty minutes later, she felt better. After putting on a black silk sheath, she settled down to read a novel she'd purchased months ago. McKenzie found she couldn't concentrate on reading. Her mind kept straying to Marc. *What a fool I've been. How could I let this happen?*

"I've got to get out of here. I refuse to sit and think about that arrogant womanizer," McKenzie mumbled as she grabbed her purse and made her way to the door.

When she flung the door open, McKenzie collided with Marc, who had just arrived and was about to knock. Shock spread throughout her body. "W-what are you doing here?"

He frowned, his eyes level under drawn brows. "I was jus
about to ask you the same thing."

Anger soon replaced the shock over seeing him at her door
"I *am* entitled to take a few days off," she snapped.

"There is nothing going on between me and Sherrie. I know
that's why you left."

McKenzie kept her features deceptively composed. "I never
realized you were so conceited. Did it ever occur to you tha
maybe I'm not alone on this trip?"

Marc checked out the room. "Doesn't look like there's any
one here with you. Are you trying to tell me that you aren'
alone?"

"No. But I could have been. Tell me, Marc, do you alway
go chasing down your *employees?*"

"You are more than just my employee. You know that."

McKenzie flushed, but remained silent.

"I swear to you there's nothing between me and Sherrie. I'n
looking for someone, and I thought that maybe she could hel
me."

"Then why is it such a big secret, Marc? Every time I asl
you about your trip to Birmingham, you clam up. Then you li
about being in Los Angeles, when you weren't."

His expression became a mask of stone. "I haven't lied t
you about anything. As far as Birmingham goes, there are som
things going on in my life that you don't know about. As soo
as I have everything figured out, I'll tell you."

"I see." She turned away from him.

Marc turned her to face him. "Look, McKenzie. I'm nc
committed to you or anyone else. I can do what I damn we
please. I don't have any reason to lie to you. I'm just not read
to confide in you yet."

"But you can confide in Sherrie."

"I haven't confided in Sherrie. I just asked if she knew th
person I'm looking for."

"Why are you here, Marc?"

"I wanted to see you. Since you decided to run off, I thought we might as well spend some time together."

"Did it ever occur to you that I might not want you to be here? Am I not entitled to some privacy?"

"Do you want me to leave?"

She said nothing.

"Well?"

"No." At that moment, she despised her weakness.

When he reached for her, McKenzie summoned up all her strength to push away from him.

Marc shrugged. "I won't apologize for my bluntness, McKenzie. I think it alleviates any misunderstandings that might otherwise occur. Are you angry with me?"

"No. What good would it do me to be angry? Would it change anything?"

"Not a thing. I'll tell you everything, but in my own time. Now, I'm very hungry. Have you eaten?"

"No."

"Well, have you overcome your jealousy enough to have lunch with me?"

"I wasn't jealous."

"Yes, you were. Now, do you have any suggestions for a restaurant?"

"Yes. The Whitehall Bay Restaurant is excellent. It has a beautiful view of the harbor in Georgetown."

"Sounds good. Are you ready?"

She grabbed her purse once again. I'm ready if you are." McKenzie then noticed the black leather garment bag he'd left by the door. "Do you need to put your bag in your room?"

"No. I'll just leave it in here." He headed over to the closet.

"You haven't checked in yet?"

"No. I didn't think there was a need to. I planned to stay here with you."

McKenzie thought she couldn't have heard him correctly. "You planned to do what?"

"I'm staying in your room. I want to spend every single moment with you."

"We can spend time together, Marc, but we won't be sleeping together. We're going to have separate rooms."

He chuckled. "Who said anything about sleeping?" Marc walked out the door, leaving a stunned McKenzie with her mouth open.

She followed him outside.

Marc turned to her. "What's on your mind, McKenzie? You haven't said a word since we left your room. Did I shock you that much?"

"What kind of woman do you think I am, Marc?"

"A very hot, passionate woman. I know you want me as much as I want you. Don't try to deny it. I can see it every time you look at me."

McKenzie knew she was lost, but still she had to fight him and her own body's betrayal. "No!" she insisted, adamantly shaking her head from side to side. "We can't do this, Marc. I can't just fall into bed with you. And you're not looking for anything serious. . . ."

"You say that now. Before the week is out, we will make love, sweetheart. We will."

She tried to control her conflicting emotions as she drove to the restaurant. She was glad when Marc seemed to be taken with the tropical scenery. It gave her time to assess her emotions.

At the restaurant, Marc pulled out a chair for McKenzie before taking the one across from her. He attempted to draw her into conversation. "So, have you enjoyed yourself so far?"

"Yes. It's a beautiful place. It's just kind of strange having to share the sidewalks with boldly strutting chickens."

Marc laughed. "I've heard that they're harmless."

"I wouldn't know. I don't give them a chance to get that close to me. I go out of my way to avoid them." She scowled at Marc for laughing.

He stopped suddenly, his expression turning serious. "Why

didn't you come to me about Sherrie? Do you actually think I would try to date two women in the very same department, in the very same company? I'm not a glutton for punishment!"

McKenzie stiffened. "Is that supposed to be reassuring?"

"I didn't mean that the way it sounded. I care for you, McKenzie. I wouldn't hurt you like that."

"But you can't—no, won't—confide in me?"

"I can't right now, sweetheart. I don't understand all of it myself."

"I don't understand you, Marc. I'm not sure I ever will."

"Be patient."

"Marc, why did you say you were in Los Angeles when you weren't?"

He laid his menu down on the table. "That's the second time you've said that. Why do you think I've lied?"

"Because I saw you with Sherrie . . . at Nordstrom's."

"Carla mentioned that to me. McKenzie, it wasn't me you saw."

"Yes, it was. I saw you as plain as day."

Marc put both hands to his face. "McKenzie, when we get back home you, Sherrie, and I are going to sit down and have a talk."

"Why?"

"Because I want no misunderstandings between us. I can't explain right now, but as soon as we get home everything will become clear. To both of us, I hope. One thing I am sure of, and that's that I'm not involved with Sherrie." His heart implored hers to believe him.

Her eyes met his. "I believe you."

McKenzie was acutely aware of Marc watching her throughout their lunch. "Why are you doing that? Have I changed since you last saw me?"

He chuckled. "No, sweetheart. I just like looking at you. I happen to find you very pleasing to the eye."

"You're still not sleeping in my bed."

"We'll see," was all he replied.

When they arrived back at the hotel, McKenzie kept fighting the disturbing sensations Marc stirred within her by trying to bring forth her mother's image. All her efforts brought forth was a headache. Marc suggested she lie down for a while. McKenzie climbed into bed, to lie on her stomach. She closed her eyes to block out the pain.

She was aware of Marc sitting down gently beside her on the bed. Placing both hands on her back, he massaged the tense muscles. Her eyes drifted softly shut, and to her further dismay she felt herself actually starting to enjoy what Marc was doing.

Marc's hands slid over her hair and rested lightly against her neck. He stroked her from the back of her ear to the curve of her shoulder. His thumbs caressed the soft underside of her jaw. Marc bent down to kiss her on the cheek.

Whispering near her ear, he said, "Try to take a nap. I'll be here when you wake up. We can talk then." He eased up off the bed. McKenzie was not aware when he left the room, taking her key with him. She was fast asleep.

The room was dark when she opened her eyes. Her headache was gone. She looked around the room, but didn't see Marc. He was gone! Forcing herself not to panic, McKenzie raised up. "Marc."

The door to the bathroom opened. He came out with toothbrush in hand. "Did you call me?"

She was thrilled beyond words to find him there. "Y-yes. I thought you'd left."

Marc sat beside her. "I told you I would be right here. I went out awhile earlier. I went to check into the hotel. What's wrong? You look upset."

"No, I'm all right. Marc?"

"Yes, what is it?"

"I don't want you to get a separate room. I want you to stay here with me."

He kissed her, then. "I'm glad. They didn't have any rooms left."

She motioned for him to come closer. "Come here, Marc.

He settled next to her in the middle of the bed, enveloping her in his arms. "How's your headache?"

"It's gone." Smiling seductively, she said huskily, "It's my body that aches now."

Marc grinned. "I've got just what you need. Just follow the doctor's orders, okay?"

McKenzie nodded. "Whatever you say, *Doctor.*"

He slowly unbuttoned his shirt. "Touch me," he said. When he saw her hesitate, his hand circled her wrist and lifted her fingers to his chest.

Her fingers explored lightly at first, hesitantly but not reluctantly. McKenzie wanted to touch him. Her fingers slid along the edge of his jeans. Her hands disappeared behind his back and moved slowly over his skin. She felt the taut smoothness of him, the warmth and strength of him.

Marc's hands drifted over the neckline of her dress, his fingers sliding just beneath the material across her skin. McKenzie held her breath as he undid the first button. It made him smile. He began to widen the gap in the neckline. "Take off this dress. I want to see your breasts," he said huskily. "I want to see all of you."

While she undressed, Marc managed to kick off his pants. They cartwheeled in the air and landed in a heap on the floor. He picked her up and carried her over to the bed. His fingers sought her out, searching, stroking, giving pleasure.

The slow simmering warmth that had so easily taken over her body was really quite nice. He was nipping at her lips as McKenzie reached up and pulled his head down to her. Boldly she offered him her lips, an offer he readily accepted. His mouth burned hers with a passion so strong that McKenzie felt herself falling backward onto the bed. She thought she would die before he moved to lie beside her.

Desire exploded inside McKenzie's body, and as she arched toward the wonderful hands that caressed her breasts she smothered a cry. His lips moved down her neck, and his hot tongue circled around and around her nipples, causing them to tingle and swell.

Her heart filled with joy, because she loved this man. She loved him with all her heart.

Warm, wonderful, experienced hands moved down her naked form, touching, teasing, circling.

"You want me, don't you?" he growled against her lips. "Admit it."

"Yes," she whispered.

"Yes, what?"

"Yes, I want you."

Her hand was soft and satiny as she ran it down his back. He gritted his teeth as she moved her hips so his swollen shaft slid down her thigh to brush against her inner core.

Marc suddenly straddled her. With slow and deliberate movements, he pressed her thighs open and moved between them. He settled himself in place and entered her slowly.

McKenzie soon convulsed against him, whispering his name again and again, her fingers curled in his hair, as she rested her body in his strength. The suddenness of her satisfaction left her stunned. Tears sprang to her eyes, so she turned away from Marc. She didn't want him to see the tears.

He raised himself on one elbow. "What's the matter, sweetness? Why are you crying?"

"I love you, Marc."

He didn't reply. Instead, he let his fingertips stroke her wavy hair, feathering it away from her damp brow. His expression was inscrutable.

"You don't have to say it back. It's okay. I know you're afraid of falling in love with me. One day you'll see that I'm not going to hurt you. I promise."

Marc had just begun to sink into a splendid lethargy when he heard her say, "I love you." Then all traces of restfulness were gone. Those three words shook him to his soul. Marc found he couldn't meet her gaze. Glowing in her eyes was every evidence of a woman in love, and he didn't want to recognize it. Instead, he eased from her and cradled her close to his racing heart, trying to control his breathing and trying to calm the panicked notion raging inside that said he was in love with her, too. The unbidden words hit Marc like lightning, shaking every nerve in his body. Just as surely as the sun would rise in the morning, he'd fallen in love with McKenzie Ashford.

Because he'd sworn never to heed that vow, Marc knew better than to listen, but his heart had already heard, and was pounding a vigorous response. His jaw was clamped tight. He would never say those words. *Never.* He had made that mistake once, with Margie. Marc had sworn he would never again speak them and give a woman that kind of power over him, the kind of control that could destroy him.

Even though he loved her, a tender confusion settled in his heart. He wanted McKenzie in his life so fiercely it hurt. But having her meant trusting her. He questioned whether he was ready to let that final barrier down.

"Pierce, I think you should go see him. He's been looking for you!" Sherrie argued.

"But you don't know the reason behind it. Why is he looking for me?"

"I'm sure it's the same reason you're looking for him." Sherrie put her arms around Pierce's thin body. "Honey, we moved all the way out here so you could get to know him."

"I know, but—"

"No buts. Marc comes home tomorrow afternoon. We're going to go see him tomorrow evening."

"Sherrie—"

"No, Pierce. *This* time we're doing things my way. We are going to see Marc. You need to talk to him. It's time."

He looked down at Sherrie. "I know you're right. I . . . I just wish I knew what to expect."

"I wish I could make this easier for you, honey. But I really believe that once you two see each other it's going to be all right."

Twenty-two

Marc was bone tired by the time he returned home. Hell! He needed a vacation to rest up from spending a week with McKenzie. It had been five glorious days and four hot passionate nights. They had not been able to keep their hands off each other. Marc felt his excitement grow and himself hardening at the delicious memory of their lovemaking.

McKenzie would be arriving in a couple of hours, and Marc could hardly contain himself. He wanted her so much. He wanted to see the unclothed beauty of her smooth-as-silk skin, lying on his bed. Marc shook his head. He had to stop thinking like this. She was in his blood, and he knew it. He also knew without a doubt that he loved her. Even though he couldn't bring himself to say those words to her, he admitted it freely in his heart—something he had not been able to do since Margie. But then, it was time to forget what happened in the past.

He unpacked his overnight bag, dumping the contents on the bed. A small leather-bound book fell to the floor, landing with a soft thud.

"What is this?" he asked himself. It looked like a journal of sorts. Opening it, he recognized McKenzie's handwriting. Knowing how much he valued his own privacy, he knew he should not violate hers, but Marc couldn't resist reading a few entries. He hoped that maybe it would provide some insight into McKenzie.

What he read made him sick inside. Everything was a lie!

Here, in her own handwriting, McKenzie described how she'd planned to humiliate him by exposing him as a drug dealer. She'd even hired a detective to look into his past. Marc shook his head in disgust.

"So that's why you were so interested in working for Chandler." She blamed him for her mother's death. Marc was confused. He didn't know her mother.

He was hit by a barrage of emotions—outrage, fury, disbelief that he could be such a fool. The fury that burned in his heart was so strong that he wanted to strangle her with his bare hands. How she must have laughed at him. His wrath was boundless.

Marc realized what had caused him to fall victim to her charms. McKenzie had used her female wiles to capture his heart, and then left him floundering. She was beautiful and bewitching. How fortunate for her that treachery and deceitfulness did not show on her face. Marc had actually believed her lies. Therein lay her ability to be successful with her schemes. The love he'd felt for her suddenly turned to hatred so strong that it threatened to choke him.

He stood up slowly and walked to the window. Every step he took was like a hammer pounding in his head. Marc's eyes flamed, and he felt an anger so strong it consumed him. McKenzie had gone beyond making a fool of him. She had drawn on his deepest feelings, only to throw them back in his face. Marc felt sick inside because of his blind stupidity. Once again, he had been betrayed by a woman he loved.

McKenzie searched frantically through her suitcase, throwing clothes everywhere. *Where is it? Where is my journal?* In her mind, she tried to recall the last place she laid it. A tremor of fear ran down her spine. It had been laying next to Marc's bag. She sank down on her bed. Oh Lord! If Marc had her journal in his possession . . . McKenzie didn't want to think of that possibility. She reached for the phone. *Maybe he doesn't realize that he has it. Maybe . . .* The list of maybes could go on, she realized. There was only one way to find out. And that was to pay Marc a visit. Tonight she had planned to talk to him about Barbara, and what happened the day she died. McKenzie prayed she'd get there before he discovered the journal.

Marc was standing in the driveway when McKenzie pulled up. Before she could turn the ignition off, he had opened the door and pulled her out of the car. He was furious, she could tell. McKenzie tried to think of some way to make him understand she was not his enemy.

"Marc! Are you crazy? I'm not going anywhere. You don't have to manhandle me."

"I'll do what I damn well please." Marc's expression was bitter. He was thoroughly disgusted with himself for falling so swiftly under her spell. It was a mistake he'd not make again, not ever.

He practically dragged her through the house and to the den. Once there, he slammed the door shut. Turning, he walked over to her, glaring angrily. He waited for her to speak. When she didn't, he unleashed his fury.

"Did you really think I'd never find out? What?" he mocked, "No pleading a misunderstanding, no lies?"

McKenzie was silent. Her expression didn't waver, though her thoughts were filled with self-accusation.

Waving her journal around, he asked, "You know, I actually thought you cared something for me. Hell, I thought you were in love with me! Imagine my surprise when I read this. You were planning to expose me as a drug dealer. Well, did you get your evidence? Did your private detective find anything?"

Still McKenzie said nothing. Her eyes watered, then narrowed stubbornly.

Marc's finely shaped mouth curled into an accusing sneer. "Well, why don't you say something? Now is your chance."

McKenzie remained silent, and it sparked his anger into a flaming inferno. Before he realized what he was doing, he had grabbed her by the shoulders and was shaking her hard. "Damn you! You conniving little . . . say something. Deny it . . ."

"What do you want me to say?" Her husky voice came to

him. "If you want to hear me plead or beg, you'll have a long wait." Her voice was filled with mockery. Even trapped as she was, she managed to retain her dignity.

This was not what he expected from her. Marc wanted to see her humbled, broken and hurting like he was. He clenched his fist, fighting for control over his temper. He had never had a woman affect him the way this one did, he thought angrily. Not even Margie.

Marc had thought McKenzie was different, but she was like all the rest with their games and deceptions. He clenched and unclenched his fists.

Suddenly the heaviness of reality descended on McKenzie, and she reeled under its impact. She realized that she was entirely at Marc's mercy. She wouldn't beg, though. *Never.* She moved to walk around him but Marc reached out, swinging her around to face him. McKenzie pulled away from him. Seconds ticked away as they stared at each other.

"Why, McKenzie? Why me?"

She seethed with mounting rage. *"Why you?* Why my mother? You just ran off and left her to die," she cried with an anguished sob as she looked into his face. All her unshed tears began to flow uncontrollably.

Marc scoffed contemptuously. He had listened with rapt attention to her, and found himself thoroughly confused. Inclined to believe the worst, he snarled bitterly. "You're crazy! I don't know what the hell you're on, but I never knew your mother. If you'd ever bothered to ask me, I would have told you so."

McKenzie held up a photograph. "Are you going to tell me that this isn't you in this picture?"

Marc stared at the two people in the old photo, shock running through his body.

Sherrie pulled up into the driveway, parking behind McKenzie's car. "Looks like McKenzie is here. I hope we're not interrupting anything."

"We probably are. Maybe we should come back some other time."

"Pierce, we're not leaving. Marc has been looking for you. It's time the two of you met face-to-face."

He shook his head. "I don't know, baby. Marc may not be ready to see me."

Sherrie looked perplexed. "But why?"

Pierce only shrugged.

Placing her hand over his one, she leaned over and whispered, "Honey, I have such a good feeling about this. Don't put it off any longer. You need answers."

"But Marc may not have the answers, either."

Sherrie sighed. "Pierce, if you want to leave, we can. I'm not going to force you."

"No, we're here now." Pierce opened the door and got out.

Together, he and Sherrie stood before the massive oak door. Sherrie knocked. The door was opened quickly by the house-keeper.

She glanced at Sherrie, then Pierce. She looked back at Pierce, gasping loudly.

"Oh, my Lord!" She touched her hand to her bosom. "I . . . I don't believe . . ."

Holding out his hand, he said, "My name is Pierce Phillips. This is Sherrie. She works for Chandler Pharmaceuticals. We would like to see Marc Chandler, please."

"I . . . I . . . he's in the . . . den. Um, please come right in. Come on in. Follow me."

Sherrie stopped the stunned woman before she knocked on the door. "Could we please announce ourselves? Marc is expecting us."

The housekeeper could only nod.

They waited until she had disappeared down the hall. Just as they were about to knock, they heard voices raised in anger. When they heard McKenzie accuse Marc of leaving her mother to die, Pierce and Sherrie looked at one another, astonishment visible on both faces.

"Oh my God!" was all Pierce could say.

Before Marc could respond there was a light rap, and then the door opened. A slimmer version of Marc stood next to Sherrie.

"It's not you Kyla's talking about, Marc. It's me."

Marc was confused. He looked from Pierce to McKenzie. "It's you. I don't believe this." He stood shaking his head. "I don't believe it."

McKenzie whipped around to see the man who had spoken. He and Marc were identical in appearance except for the mole just above the man's top lip. *The mole. Oh, Lord, I should have realized it before. Marc doesn't have a mole.*

"Pierce." She looked from Marc to Pierce and from Pierce to Marc. The room started to spin, round and round, faster and faster. *This can't be happening,* she thought as the floor rushed up to meet her.

Sherrie rushed to McKenzie's side just as she crumpled to the floor.

"Oh my God. She's fainted. Do something, Marc," Sherrie cried.

Marc lifted McKenzie. "I'll be right back."

"What are you going to do with her?" Sherrie asked.

"I'm just going to put her on one of the beds in a guest room She's fainted from the shock. She'll be all right." As he carried her up the stairs, Marc wondered if he would ever be the same

Twenty-three

Marc returned after a few minutes. He and Pierce stared at each other for a moment, with Marc finally breaking contact. He motioned for them to sit down. "What did you call McKenzie?"

"Kyla. Kyla Reynolds is her name."

A swift shadow of pain swept across his face. "I can't believe this! She even lied about her name."

Sherrie tried to intercede. "Marc—"

"I don't want to talk about McKen—Kyla, whatever the hell her name is! I would rather talk about you, Pierce." There was a faint tremor in his voice as though some emotion had touched him. "I've been looking for you since my mo . . . Lillian died. I didn't know about you until then." Marc's tone was apologetic.

Pierce nodded. "I understand, Marc. It must have been quite a shock to you. I know how it was for me to find out I had a twin brother." His voice was low and smooth.

"She left a letter for us. I found it among her possessions this past Christmas. It's never been opened. She didn't want it opened until we found each other." Marc walked over to the desk and pulled out a small box. From it he retrieved a sealed envelope. He held it out to Pierce.

Pierce seemed unable to move forward. Sherrie prompted him by saying, "Honey, go on. Now's your chance to get the answers you need. Don't be afraid, sweetie pie."

He took a step, hesitated. Marc brought the letter to him, placing it in his hand.

"Read it, Pierce," he urged. Maybe we'll both get the answers we seek."

Everyone was quiet as Pierce read the letter. Tears formed in his eyes, and he could not continue. He handed the letter to Sherrie, who read the letter aloud.

Tears streaming down his cheeks, Pierce said softly, "She says she never stopped loving me."

"Knowing my mo . . . Lillian—as I do, she meant what she wrote to you. She was a young girl of fourteen who found herself pregnant and without a husband. I guess she was alone and very scared, so she did what she thought was best. According to what she wrote in the letter, she didn't want to give either one of us up, but knew she couldn't take care of two babies."

Sherrie placed her arms around Pierce. "It says that your mother thought she would get you back, Pierce." Wiping a tear from her eye, she continued. "Your mother never intended to give you up for adoption. Honey, she was tricked. A lot of that went on back then. She was just a kid, herself. She didn't know what she was signing."

Marc sighed. "Even so, she could have confided in Charles or me. We would have moved heaven and earth to find you. Hell, I did. I hired a private detective. But we kept ending up with dead ends. I didn't give up, though." Marc glared at Sherrie. "I even asked Sherrie if she knew you. She denied it, by the way."

Pierce sat up, then. "Don't be angry with Sherrie. She was just being protective of my feelings. She had no idea of your motives."

Marc looked into the face that mirrored his own. "She knew you were my twin, and that I was looking for you."

"That's why we're here now. I wanted to make sure Pierce could handle seeing you. I love him, and *his* feelings are my first concern."

Marc could only nod.

"You seem angry with our mother. Why?"

"Because she should have told me what happened a long

time ago. Not on her deathbed. If she didn't want to talk to me about it, she should have at least told her husband. Maybe something could have been done a lot sooner."

"We can't change the past, Marc. Don't agonize over it. As for me, I feel a little better knowing why she gave me away, though. She thought it was only temporary. She was lied to. It *could* have been because she never wanted me. That's what my adoptive parents used to tell me all the time. When I was a little boy, I used to dream that my real mother would one day find me."

"I thought we were a close family. I thought I could count on her to be honest. Then I found out that she didn't trust her own family enough to confide in us. I'm sorry, Pierce." Marc walked over and put out his hand. "I've always wanted a brother. I want you to know that. Welcome to the family."

Pierce stood up, and the two brothers embraced each other.

"I appreciate that. You can't imagine my shock at seeing your picture plastered in a magazine. It freaked me out."

Tears glistened in Marc's eyes. "I'm glad we found each other. I've always felt a part of me was missing."

"Me, too. Marc, don't be too hard on Kyla. She—"

"I know, she thought I was you. Somehow, that doesn't make me feel any better." His voice was cold and exact.

"You don't understand. She's been through a lot."

"But why? She keeps insisting I—you had something to do with her mother's death."

"I was involved."

"What do you have to do with her mother?"

"Barbara . . . Barbara and I were lovers. I was there when she died. I panicked, and did nothing to try to save her. She was heavily into drugs, and—during that time—so was I. We experimented with all types. One day, I bought some that turned out bad. I didn't know it until Barbara started without me. She needed a fix. Suddenly, she started convulsing, and it scared me. I just freaked. I took off running down the street, and I literally bumped into Kyla. I didn't tell her anything, just took off running again." Pierce wiped a lone tear that rolled slowly down his cheek. "I felt lower than a snake, man. I s-still do."

Sherrie rushed to his side. "Pierce sometimes has nightmares about that. Shortly after that, I met him. He had gone and gotten himself cleaned up. Barbara dying like that changed his life."

"The day Kyla's mother died I stopped selling drugs, and I stopped taking them. I never meant to take that girl's mother away from her."

Marc's thoughts went to his bedroom and the beauty in his bed; an angry scowl came over his handsome features. "McKenzie—Kyla—should have told me the truth up front. Hell, I didn't even know her real name. She shouldn't have played games with me." *Or my feelings,* he silently added. "I guess I'd better go check on her. While I'm gone, make yourselves at home. I would like the two of you to join me for dinner. We've got a lot of catching up to do."

A muffled moan tripped from McKenzie's lips as the beat of her own heart pounded heavily. She opened her eyes, momentarily wondering where she was. Memories of what had transpired before the black veil descended over her vision immediately assailed her. She sat up wearily. Her gaze locked with Marc's heated glare.

"You're awake," he said matter-of-factly.

She turned slowly. "Marc—"

"You thought I was my brother."

"Please—"

"I don't want to talk about this right now."

"I'm not leaving until you hear me out."

"I wish to God you'd been honest with me. You didn't have to play this game." Marc walked over to the window. Staring out, he asked, "Are you feeling okay?"

"I'm fine. Marc, please look at me."

When he continued to stare out of the window, McKenzie threw her hands up in defeat. "Well then, I think you've made your point, Marc. There's no point to my trying to explain anything to you. You're not going to listen." She eased off the bed and navigated her way toward the door. Straightening her back, she glided down the stairs, Marc on her heels. On the lower level, McKenzie tried one last time to apologize to Marc.

"Do you want me to drive you home?"

She shook her head. "I think I'll be fine. I'm sorry, Marc. I was wrong."

He was now very cold and distant. "I'd better get back to my guests. Drive carefully."

McKenzie, head held high, strolled purposely out of the door. She willed her body not to jump at the sound of the slamming door. Once it closed, she slumped, leaning her head against the portal. A single tear slid down her cheek as she wept quietly. "Oh, God, why did I have to fall in love with him?"

How she made it home, McKenzie had no idea. She sat in her car until she felt all cried out. Getting out of the car, she trudged sadly up the stairs. She picked up the phone several times to call Marc, but changed her mind. He would need some time to clear his head.

Upstairs, McKenzie lay on her bed. Her tears exhausted, she reflected on the turn her life had taken—from happy to dismal in a matter of hours.

Marc had a right to be angry, she admitted. She had made a grave mistake—one that would cost her the only man she ever loved, and a job that she enjoyed. McKenzie also reflected on her friendship with Carla. She was going to lose everything, all in the name of revenge, she thought bitterly—revenge against a man who had nothing to do with her mother's death. She knew Marc would never forgive her, but she had to try to get through to him. She loved him.

McKenzie found she couldn't sleep. All night long she pictured her confrontation with Marc, mulling it over and over in her mind. How on earth was she going to make him believe that she loved him dearly?

Seeing Pierce again had briefly whetted her appetite for revenge, but this time her heart wasn't in it. Seeking vengeance had caused her to lose the only man she would ever love. It had been a high price to pay. What was she going to do? How could she stand it if Marc never forgave her? Anxiety built to a roiling turmoil.

Shoulders sagging, Marc propped his elbows on the mantel and wearily rested his dark head on his forearms, gazing blindly into the glowing orange heart of the fire.

With a curse, he reached for the crystal snifter of brandy on the mantel, drained the contents in a single swallow, then hurled the glass into the fireplace.

Is that how a breaking heart sounds? he wondered bitterly as it smashed into a thousand pieces. *Like the tinkle of shattering crystal?*

"Are you okay, Marc?" Sherrie asked.

Marc turned to find Pierce and Sherrie standing in the doorway.

"I'm fine. Dinner should be ready in about ten minutes."

"Is there someplace we can wash our hands?"

He led the way to a guest bathroom. "You can use this one. When you're through, just head back up this hall. It'll bring you straight to the dining room."

When he thought enough time had passed for McKenzie to make it home, he called her.

"H-hello."

"I wanted to make sure you made it home okay."

"I'm fine."

They were silent.

"Marc?"

"I'm still here. Er. . . . I'm glad you're okay. I still have guest—"

"I l-love you, Marc. I never lied about that."

"I have to go. We'll talk later."

"Bye, Marc."

"Bye."

Marc was talking to the housekeeper when they came into

the dining room. He smiled and motioned for them to have a seat. As soon as everyone was seated, dinner was served.

Sherrie spoke up. "Marc, I want to apologize for not telling you about Pierce—"

Pierce interrupted. "It was really my idea. Don't be upset with Sherrie. We didn't want you to think we wanted money, or anything. I'm not here looking for a handout. I just wanted to get to know you. Be family. That's all. All I ever wanted, a family before I died."

"We *are* family, Pierce. I've searched for you ever since I found out the truth. You're my brother—"

"You don't know how good it makes me feel to hear you say that, man. I really needed to hear that. Especially now."

"Why especially now? You talk as if something's going on."

Marc caught the silent exchange between Pierce and Sherrie. "Is somebody going to tell me what's going on? Are you in some kind of trouble, Pierce?"

"No. It's . . ." Pierce took a deep breath. "Marc, I . . . I'm HIV positive."

Marc's fork fell to his plate. He couldn't believe what he'd just heard. "Y-you're what?"

"I'm HIV positive. If—"

Tears sprang to Marc's eyes. *"Damn.* I just found you!" He rose, and went to stand by the window. He wasn't aware of when Pierce joined him.

"It's okay, Marc. I'm learning to deal with it."

Marc turned to him then. "You have a great attitude. I don't know if I could be so positive. Me, I would most likely be mad as hell."

"Oh, there are times I'm very angry, to be sure. I wonder why I had to get it. Sometimes I wonder if this is just a bad dream, and I'll wake up one day. Other times, I know that this is so real. I don't want to die . . . but—"

Marc embraced him. "I couldn't have asked for a better brother. You're a brave man."

"Sometimes I wonder . . ." Pierce muttered softly.

Sherrie cleared her throat. "Are the two of you going to stay huddled over there by that window?"

Marc smiled. "We're not leaving you out. I just needed a moment alone with my brother." *My brother. It has a nice ring to it,* he thought. Marc didn't want to lose him. He prayed that his brother would be spared. They had just found one another. He and Pierce had a lifetime to make up for.

They joined Sherrie back at the table. Marc told Pierce about all the research and testing McKenzie had done. They discussed the advantages of protease inhibitors, and McKenzie's dream of developing a vaccine.

Long after Pierce and Sherrie left, Marc stared into the night sky. He had found his brother, and lost the one woman he deeply loved, all in one night.

McKenzie paced around her living room. She picked up the phone several times and dialed the Chandler's number, but hung up each time before someone answered. She was going stir-crazy just sitting around in her town house, but she was too embarrassed to set foot in Chandler. McKenzie was positive she'd been fired, especially since no one called to inquire when she planned to show up for work. Even David, her friend, had not bothered to call. As much as she dreaded it, McKenzie knew she would have to face them eventually, when she went in to pick up her belongings from the lab.

She wasn't sure what she was going to do now. McKenzie knew her career as a medical scientist was over. Marc would surely see to that. She climbed the stairs slowly, trying to fight the tears that threatened to spill. As soon as she set foot in her bedroom, the doorbell rang.

McKenzie rushed downstairs to answer her front door. As soon as she opened it, she immediately regretted her decision. Marc walked forward, not waiting for her to invite him in. She shrugged, closing the door, and followed him into the living room.

Marc faced her, then. "What in the hell is your real name? I don't even know what to call you." His tone was relatively civil in spite of his anger.

"My birth name is Kyla McKenzie Ashford Reynolds. I simply dropped my first and last name *legally* after my mother's death."

"Why? What did you have to hide?"

"Why are you here, Marc? To verbally abuse me?"

"I'm here to find out why you haven't been to work in three days. Are you too embarrassed to show your face?"

"No," she lied. "I really didn't think I still had a job. As a matter-of-fact, I'm very surprised."

Marc arched an eyebrow at her. "Why do you find that so surprising? This is business."

She straightened her back and folded her hands across her chest. "I see. Well, suppose I don't want to go back?"

"We have a contract, Dr. Ashford. Are you telling me you can't be trusted in your business dealings, as well?" His eyes issued a silent challenge. "Carla seems to think we can't manage without you."

Looking up at him, she asked, "And what if I refuse? Do you intend to drag me kicking and screaming into the office? Or am I allowed to walk?"

"Whichever you prefer," Marc replied coolly, but he did not release his grip on her. "Make no mistake about it, you *will* go into the office," he added when it looked as if she might balk. "You can go in upright, or thrown over my shoulder. It makes no difference to me."

"Somehow I didn't think it would," she said bitterly. Marc just shrugged.

"I wish you'd told me earlier—that you wanted me to continue working."

"I came by here last night. You weren't home."

"I was . . . I stepped out to get a bite to eat."

"You don't owe me any explanations."

"Marc, will you ever forgive me? I didn't know you and

Pierce were twins. You didn't even realize it until recently. Can't you understand?" Her question trailed into silence.

Marc cursed the sincerity in her voice, the unspoken plea. Why did he feel a grudging admiration for her as she faced him and dared to stand her ground?

"I don't want to talk about this anymore. Are you going to honor your contract, or not?"

"You hate me, Marc. Why would you want me in your face all day long?"

"This is business. And I don't hate you."

"I see. Can you forget what we had so easily, Marc?"

He ignored her question and asked one of his own instead. "Are you coming to work or not?"

She sighed. "I'll be there in an hour."

"Fine." Marc walked to the door.

"Marc."

Without turning, he asked, "What?"

"I—"

Just then the telephone rang.

"Are you going to answer your phone?"

"My machine will pick it up. Please talk to me, Marc."

Marc felt a burning emptiness inside. "You should probably get that. I don't think we have anything outside of business to talk about."

McKenzie's entire body seemed to wilt. Her dark brown eyes glistened with tears she barely managed to hold back. Realizing further pleading would be pointless when he was being so obstinate, McKenzie rose slowly to her feet. She spoke softly, turning away from him as she did. "I guess you'd better leave, Marc, so that I can get dressed. Thanks for letting me keep my job. I know you didn't have to do it," she said, stepping to the door.

"You should thank Carla," he returned in a raspy croak. "Nonetheless, I expect to see you at Chandler within the hour."

McKenzie managed to keep her controlled demeanor for as long as it took to walk up the stairs to her bedroom. Then the wavering dam on her reserve dissolved in a rushing torrent of tears, and she threw herself onto the satin-covered bed to cry out her misery.

An emotionally drained McKenzie arrived at Chandler forty-five minutes later. Seeing Marc, her face darkened, and she swallowed the tears forming a lump in her throat. How had she let herself imagine she meant anything to him?

Jutting her chin out stubbornly and setting her mouth in a tight smile, McKenzie gave a defiant toss of her head and crossed the room to the elevator.

She would not allow herself to become a whimpering mass of emotions. As far as she was concerned, she had survived the worst she could have imagined.

Twenty-four

McKenzie pounced on Sherrie as soon as she came through the door. "You knew, didn't you? You knew all along that Marc had a twin brother!" She glared at her with burning, reproachful eyes.

Sherrie calmly placed her purse in her locker. Her hands were trembling slightly. Not looking at McKenzie, she answered quietly, "Yes. I knew they were brothers."

"So, why didn't you say something? Didn't you think he had a right to know?"

"I wasn't sure how Marc would react when he found out. I wasn't even sure he would want to know. We didn't want him to think we were after money."

"With Pierce, I wouldn't blame him for being skeptical. I already know he's scum, and I'm going to make sure Marc knows."

Sherrie faced McKenzie, hands on her ample hips. "Don't you dare talk about Pierce like that! If you cared so much about Marc, then why weren't *you* honest with *him?*"

"I thought he *was* Pierce. And I wasn't dishonest with him."

"Oh really? What do you call it?"

McKenzie's eyes conveyed the fury within her. "I know you can't possibly understand. You're so wrapped up in Pierce—"

"Pierce is a kind, loving man! You think you know him so well, but I have a news flash for you. You don't know him at all. Yes, he did drugs and sold them. Yes, he and Barbara were lovers, and they enjoyed getting high together."

McKenzie turned to walk away. "I don't have to listen to this!" She couldn't bear hearing her mother talked about that way.

Sherrie moved to block her exit. "Oh no, *Missy.* You're going to listen to me. It's time you heard what really happened. Pierce didn't have to force her to do drugs. Your mother was an addict when he met her, McKenzie. And that was Barbara's choice. Pierce was young, too. He was looking for something, but he had no idea what. Your mother was, too. They found each other."

"You have no idea what happened! I found her, and she died in my arms, Sherrie." McKenzie's voice filled with tears. She lowered her voice to a hoarse whisper. "I was there when my grandmother died. I watched two people I loved more than my own life die right before my eyes. Have you any idea what that did to me?"

"I'm sure it had to be hard on you—"

"No, you don't have a clue. Why do you think I went into research instead of becoming a medical doctor? I'll tell you why. Because I couldn't handle people dying on me. I can't deal with it."

"He didn't mean to just leave her like that. He panicked. Pierce was scared to death. Do you know that even now he still has nightmares about that?"

"He should," McKenzie sputtered with indignation.

"You're not being fair," Sherrie replied in a low voice, taut with anger.

"I don't feel I *should* be fair where he's concerned. He wasn't thinking about being fair when it came down to my mother's life."

Sherrie shook her head. "I'm sorry you can't let go of the past, but Pierce *is* a good man, McKenzie. He's made some terrible mistakes in his life, and he's tried hard to atone for them. He even gave your grandmother the money to send you to school. Pierce paid for your first year of college."

Shock flooded through McKenzie's body in waves. *"What? Now I know you've completely lost your mind!"* She leaned onto the counter in the lab for support.

"I'm telling you the truth. He couldn't find you after she died. I suppose that's when you changed your name. Pierce tried to find you. He really did. He felt so bad for you."

"Did Pierce tell you this? If he did, then he's lying. Granny Mae said—"

"She told you that the money came from a life insurance policy she had on your mother."

"How do you know that?"

"Because I took the money to her. Pierce wanted you to have it for college."

McKenzie stared at Sherrie in astonishment. "Is this really the truth?"

"I wouldn't lie to you about something like that."

McKenzie could read the truth in her blue eyes. "I see. Well, I didn't know that."

"Of course you didn't."

"It doesn't change the fact that he left my mother to die."

"When you thought it was Marc, you were ready to forgive him. Why not Pierce?"

"I'm not sure I can explain it. With Marc, the puzzle pieces never seemed to fit. It was strange. I was ready to forget the past until Pierce came through those doors that night. All of a sudden the puzzle came together."

"Please consider everything I've told you, McKenzie. I'll be in the lab if you need me." Sherrie stood near the door watching her. "Did you hear me?"

McKenzie nodded.

"I'm really sorry about you and Marc. I hope the two of you can work things out."

McKenzie smiled ruefully as she looked down at her hands. Sherrie left, closing the door gently behind her.

* * *

"Dr. Ashford, may I have a word with you?"

McKenzie looked up to find Marc standing in her doorway. She experienced a brief panicky desire to crawl under her desk and hide until he was gone. But, knowing that running away wouldn't solve things, McKenzie took a deep cleansing breath and beckoned for him to enter.

She couldn't bring herself to meet his eyes. Taking another deep breath, she asked, "How are you, Marc?"

"How I am is none of your business. I only came by to remind you about the upcoming press conference. Please make sure that you're prepared."

McKenzie nodded. "I'll be ready." She had no right, she told herself, no right to want him so much, but the realization did not lessen the force of her desire.

McKenzie wanted to hug him tightly, to kiss him again and again and tell him how desperately she loved him, but she dared not speak a word. His greeting could not have been more insulting, and McKenzie knew that no matter how she felt about him he was obviously not in the least bit pleased to see her.

"Can we talk for a minute, Marc?"

"Is this business or personal?"

"P-personal," she stammered.

"We don't have anything to discuss outside of business. I thought we were clear on that." He remained standing near the door.

"Please, Marc." McKenzie hated herself for begging.

"You have two minutes."

"Would you please sit down? And close the door completely."

Marc seemed reluctant to do as she asked, but finally he acquiesced. After settling back into one of the chairs facing McKenzie, he waited for her to speak.

"I wanted to talk to you about y-your b-brother. He's n-not what you think he is—" She knew as soon as the words came out of her mouth that she had said the wrong thing. Marc pounced on them immediately.

Marc sat forward. "Pierce is not who he says he is?" He shook his head. "You're something else, I'll give you that."

"Marc—"

"My identical twin brother is not who I think he is? You, on the other hand, are exactly who I thought you were? Am I getting this right?"

"Will you please let me explain? What I meant to say is that even though he is your brother, he has done some terrible things. I'm just trying to tell you to be careful."

"I wish someone had warned me about *you*. But for the record, I don't need your concern. I know what happened between your mother and my brother. It was an accident, McKenzie. Now I suggest you give it a rest. My brother is sick, and I don't want you harassing him."

A warning cloud settled on his features, but McKenzie ignored it. She did not want to see him become a pawn in Pierce's schemes. "Harassing him? Sick? See, you are already falling into his trap. The man is not sick! What lies has he been feeding you? I suppose he needs you to pick up the tab on the medical bills—"

"That's enough!"

Marc's face was marked with loathing. McKenzie looked away swiftly at the sight of his fury. "I just don't want to see you get hurt, that's all."

"It's a little too late for your concern, Dr. Ashford. I've been searching for Pierce for a long time. I found out about him the night my mother died. Pierce told me everything, and I don't hold his past against him."

"Do you hold your mother's past against her?"

Marc didn't respond, but the tightness around his mouth gave McKenzie her answer.

"You hold your mother's betrayal against her, and mine against me. I love you, Marc. I didn't want to love you, but it happened, anyway."

"It no longer matters. In fact, it never mattered."

McKenzie dropped her lashes to quickly hide the hurt. Sh

sighed sadly, clasped her slender hands together, and stared at them. She looked up to find his piercing amber eyes on her. She felt like throwing something at him, but controlled her foolish urge. Instead she glared back at him. Without a backward glance, Marc got up and made his way out of her office.

McKenzie got up to search for a file. She fought to keep the tears in her eyes from falling. Trying to swallow the lump that had lingered in her throat, McKenzie leaned against her file cabinet for support. God, how was she going to bear working with him?

A couple of hours later, she heard Carla's voice coming from the lab. She knew that Carla, like Marc, was avoiding her, too. Although she had vowed not to let it bother her, it rankled her to the core. She refused to work in such tense conditions. McKenzie decided to have it out with Carla. She walked into the laboratory just as Sherrie was leaving.

"Hello, Carla."

"Hello." Carla looked up, then put her head back down, as if studying the results in her composition notebook.

"It's okay if you've decided to side with Marc. After all, the two of you are bosom buddies. But I thought you would at least be woman enough to tell me to my face, instead of avoiding me."

Slamming the notebook shut, Carla walked over to stand in front of McKenzie. "What the hell is *that* supposed to mean?"

McKenzie put up her hands in simple despair. "You know what, Carla? It doesn't matter. I just thought we were friends, too." Her eyes darkened with pain.

"Look, McKenzie, I'm still your friend, but you need to understand my position. Marc is my closest friend, and he's hurting right now. He's really hurting. I don't like seeing him this way." When McKenzie turned to walk away, Carla grabbed her by the arm. "Hold on a minute, will you? I don't like seeing you hurt, either, but it's not my place to get involved."

"I'm sorry, Carla. I made a huge mistake. I've tried to talk to Marc. I've apologized to him. I don't know what else I can do."

"What happened?"

"We talked."

"That's great. But why do you look so sad?"

McKenzie shook her head. She covered her face with trembling hands and gave vent to the agony of her heartbreak.

"I'm sorry about the way things have turned out." Carla guided McKenzie to a nearby chair. As she cried, Carla comforted her, patting her gently on the back. "Don't give up on Marc."

"I-it's my own fault, Carla. I r-ruined everything."

"Marc feels very hurt and betrayed right now. He doesn't take those emotions lightly. He's been through too much. He really cares about you, though. I believe he'll come around after a while."

McKenzie shook her head. Accepting a tissue from Carla, she said, "Let's face it. He's never going to forgive me, Carla. He thinks I lied to him about my feelings. He thinks I was planning to set him up—to ruin him."

"Weren't you?"

"Yes—no—it was Pierce. I wish I'd remembered his mole. It's always been there. Marc doesn't have one. I should have realized that was what was different about him."

"I don't see how you confused the two of them. They are as different as night and day."

"I didn't know he was a twin. I only saw him a couple of times. My mom didn't like to have her boyfriends hanging around when we were together. She said she didn't trust them that much."

"I need to know something. Did you really love Marc?"

McKenzie stiffened. She was clearly insulted. "Why would you ask me that? Of course I loved him. I still do. In the beginning, I felt terrible about loving him. I felt I was betraying my mother. He never read the sections of my journal where I wrote about my feelings of betrayal and guilt over loving him a man I thought had a part in my mother's death. It was extremely hard for me, until, finally, I decided to let go of the past. He didn't read that part either."

Tears streamed down McKenzie's cheeks. She sat down in a nearby chair, her hands to her face. Carla pulled another tissue out of her lab pocket and offered it to McKenzie. Dabbing at her eyes, McKenzie asked, "What am I going to do, Carla? I can't do this. I can't pretend that I've no feelings whatsoever for Marc. I love him too much."

"Put yourself in Marc's place, McKenzie. He's been hurt so much in the past. Can you understand how he must feel? Look what your mother's death turned you into. A woman on a quest for revenge."

"I'm not saying he doesn't deserve to be angry with me."

"Pierce is his brother. A brother he very much wanted to find. He's searched a long time for him. Can't you forgive Pierce? He didn't kill your mother. Your mother was already on the road to self-destruction. Can you admit that?"

"Pierce gave her the drugs that killed her."

"He didn't force her to take them. You want forgiveness, but you aren't willing to forgive Pierce. Seems to me that neither you nor Marc know how to let go of the pain, or to forgive. Think about it."

"I'm willing to do whatever it takes, Carla."

"Good. I'm rooting for the two of you." She headed toward the door. "I have a lunch date with Jim. I'll check on you when I get back."

"I'll be fine. Carla, I want to thank you for saving my job."

Carla stood in the doorway, smiling. "You're too valuable to lose. I simply pointed that out to Marc. He's a smart businessman."

Twenty-five

Marc, Jim, and Pierce waited to be escorted to their table. Jim made a cursory sweep of the dining area. His eyes fell on a certain couple talking as they ate lunch. He nudged Marc. "Well, well, well. What do we have here?"

Pierce followed Jim's eyes and said, "Looks like two employees from your company just having lunch together, right, Marc?"

Marc was not at all pleased to find McKenzie having lunch with David. It had been two months since their breakup. It was obvious to him that McKenzie had quickly found another man to replace him.

Pierce leaned over and whispered to Marc, "Man, why won't you at least talk to her? Go on over there and say hello or something."

"Hell, no! She made a damn fool out of me. I have nothing to say to her."

Marc was silent throughout their meal. Pierce and Jim discussed Pierce's childhood. They tried to draw Marc into the conversation, but failed. His eyes were constantly on McKenzie

Pierce watched him for a moment and shook his head. "Jim can't you talk some sense into him? He's in love with McKenzie but he's letting his pride get in the way."

Jim chewed thoughtfully. "Why are you treating her this way Marc? Your brother explained everything to you. Can't you find it in your heart to forgive her? Especially if the two of you really care about each other."

Marc snorted. "I only care that I've allowed myself to be fooled. I, of all people, should have known better."

Pierce's amber eyes stared into his brother's own identical ones. "Marc, you can't avoid living altogether because of the past. Hell, if I stayed in the past, with the kind of life I led, I might as well go somewhere and commit suicide. I used and sold drugs, I was a pimp—"

"But you realized those things were wrong. Besides, you were mistreated by your adoptive parents, and abandoned at the age of sixteen."

"It's no excuse for what I did. Those were choices I made. After I met Sherrie, everything changed."

Marc nodded. "She's very devoted to you, Pierce."

"I know. I love her more than I love my life."

"Then why haven't you married her?"

"Because I can't give her what she deserves."

Marc raised his eyebrows a fraction. "And what's that?"

"A family. Children. A chance to grow old with the person she loves."

"But you two love each other."

Pierce shook his head. "We're not talking 'bout me and Sherrie. We're talking 'bout you. You and McKenzie. You love her, admit it."

Marc opened his mouth to deny it, but realized it was futile. "Damnit, I tried not to fall in love with her," he said in a pained voice. "Lord knows I fought it tooth and nail. And after it happened, I believed she loved me, too. I was such a fool."

"McKenzie does love you, Marc. I can see it as plain as day. Don't let a misunderstanding keep the two of you apart. McKenzie needs you."

His expression turned bleak as he watched McKenzie smile and laugh with David. She looked absolutely ravishing in a black body-hugging dress. *No doubt she had dressed for David,* he thought jealously. "McKenzie Ashford is a survivor. Believe me, she'll do just fine without me." He spoke with explosive calm. A tiny muscle in his cheek pumped rhythmically, indicating a barely controlled rage.

He summoned her with his eyes, wanting her to see the anger there. Marc was secretly delighted when she glanced his way, smiling timidly, and met his black scowl. The smile quickly vanished. Her expression seemed to say, *How dare you sit there and glare at me as if I'm guilty of something?* He could tell she was fuming. That knowledge gave him little satisfaction, however.

Pierce watched the silent angry exchange between the two of them. His concern turned to Marc. "You dumped her, Marc. But what about you? How are you gonna make it without her?"

Marc smiled ruefully. "I'll survive."

"Sure you will," Jim said sarcastically. "Just like you have all these years? Hell, if you think you were miserable before, it ain't nothing compared to how you're gonna feel when McKenzie isn't around anymore."

"I appreciate your concern, fellas, but don't worry about me." A strong sense of defeat pulled at him.

Marc's eyes continued to drift across the room to where McKenzie and David were seated. The look of pain and longing on his face tore at Jim's heart.

Marc resisted the urge to go over to their table and yank McKenzie out of there. Instead, he got up hastily. Looking at his watch, he said, "I'd better head back to the office. I have an appointment in forty-five minutes." They paid their bill and left the restaurant. Just as they were about to get into Marc's car, they all turned when they heard someone call Marc's name.

Marc's face hid the disappointment when he spied Glenda headed toward them. He had hoped it was McKenzie.

"Marc, how are you?" She turned to acknowledge Jim. When she laid eyes on Pierce, her gasp of surprise brought laughter from all around. Glenda looked from Marc to Pierce and back again. "Oh, my!" She turned to face Marc. "I didn't know you were a twin, Marc. Why didn't you ever tell me?"

Marc shrugged, but said nothing.

Turning around to Pierce, she held out her hand. "I see Marc took a rude pill this morning, so I'll just introduce myself. I'm Glenda." She glared at Marc. "A sometime friend of your brother."

Pierce chuckled. "I'm Pierce. It's very nice to meet you, Glenda." He shook her hand and quickly released it.

"Marc, you must have a lot on your mind, today," Glenda said from behind him. "You walked right past me a few minutes ago without even seeing me." She found him staring as McKenzie and David headed toward David's car. She added with a smirk, "I wonder what's on your mind? What—or should I say who—it is, it serves you right!" Glenda flounced away.

"Witch!" Marc hissed under his breath.

Pierce and Jim both doubled over with laughter.

"Hello, McKenzie."

McKenzie looked up to find Pierce standing in the lab. She had been so engrossed in her work that she'd failed to hear anyone come in. Her nostrils flared with fury. *"What do you want?"*

"I thought we could talk . . . about your mother's . . . death."

"It's too late, don't you think? My mother's dead because of you and the drugs you gave her! You weren't even man enough to hang around or call for an ambulance."

"I was young, McKenzie. Young and very scared. I didn't know the drugs were bad."

"You could have called for help, but you were nothing but a coward. *A coward.*" Rancor sharpened her voice.

"You have every right to be angry, but you shouldn't let yourself be eaten up by hatred and sorrow. Don't give in to it. It can only hurt you in the long run. I should have called for help, but I didn't. I ran. There is nothing I can do now that will change what happened. You'll never know how I agonized over leaving Barbara like that. I've always wished I could've turned back the hands of time. But I can't. Even knowing how you must feel about me, I felt I had to come here. To face you and apologize. I came to ask for your forgiveness—"

"*Forgiveness*. You have to be out of your mind. I'll never forgive you. My mother died and left me. You have your life."

"Just barely."

"What are you talking about? Oh, that's right—Marc mentioned you're supposed to be sick." She laughed harshly. "I don't think you're sick at all. I think you're out to take him for every penny you can get your—"

"You're wrong." Pierce stood silent, his eyes closed. Finally he spoke, his voice a whisper. "I'm . . . I have . . . I'm dying, McKenzie. I'm HIV positive."

In that instant, she knew he was telling the truth. She could see it as clear as day in his eyes. Among the emotions she felt was a deep sense of shame. "Oh Lord, Pierce. I'm so sorry. How . . . long?"

"I've had it for a while."

"Do you know what your T-cell levels are?"

"They're below two hundred right now." He coughed.

"I'm . . . sorry about what I said to you, Pierce. I would never wish that on anybody. I'm working so hard to find a way to fight HIV."

"I know. Sherrie praises your efforts all the time."

"You came out here to meet your brother, but you also knew about the company's AIDS research. I thought you were after money."

"I never wanted money. My brother is why I'm out here. If I can get into the one of the test programs I want that, too."

McKenzie knew she had misjudged Pierce, also. He reminded her a lot of Marc in his mannerisms. She hastily wrote down a number. "You can call this number, and they'll direct you from there. The experimental vaccine is getting very positive results. I'm really sorry about what I said earlier."

He stared through piercing eyes, so much like Marc's. " believe you really mean that."

"I do."

Pierce suddenly reached for the counter and leaned against it. He placed a trembling hand to his head.

McKenzie was beside him instantly. "Pierce, are you okay?"

"I-I feel a little dizzy, that's all."

McKenzie led him over to a nearby chair. "Can I get you something to drink?" She placed the palm of her hand against his cheek. "Oh Lord, Pierce! You're burning up. We have to get you to the hospital."

She quickly called for an ambulance. Then, while they waited, she tried to locate Sherrie and Marc. Neither could be found. McKenzie was still trying to find them when the paramedics arrived. She left a message with Clara, then rode with Pierce to the hospital.

Her heart saddened over the fear she saw in his eyes. Placing his fevered hand in hers, McKenzie whispered, "It's going to be all right, Pierce. It's going to be all right. Sherrie and Marc will meet us at the hospital. I left a message for them."

"T-they had l-lunch to . . . together. They wanted . . . wanted us t-to t-talk."

"Ssssh, try to rest." McKenzie closed her eyes and said a quick prayer for Pierce.

McKenzie flipped through the pages of a magazine in the emergency waiting room at the hospital. She glanced at her watch several times. When would Marc and Sherrie get there? Pulling her calling card out of her purse, she headed toward the pay phones. Just as she was about to dial, she heard herself being paged.

She rushed back to the nursing station. "I'm Dr. McKenzie Ashford."

"Would you follow me, please? Mr. Phillips has been moved to room 5221A. You can take this elevator to the fifth floor."

"Thank you." She took a deep breath and headed up to see

Pierce. McKenzie felt guilty about the way she'd treated him. She had no right to act as his judge and jury.

Seeing him in such a fragile state tore at her heart.

His thin body lay still—so still that it frightened her. McKenzie moved closer, relieved to see the rise and fall of his chest. As she neared, she found him staring off into space. A lone tear stained his cheek.

"I'm so sorry, Pierce, about the way I've treated you. I was wrong to blame you for what happened to my mother. I know you didn't kill her. I guess I just needed to believe that. Please believe that I don't want to see anything happen to you." Tears filled her eyes. "C-can you ever f-forgive m-me?"

He wouldn't look at her. "N-nothing to f-forgive. I understand how you must feel. And I don't want pity."

"I don't pity you, Pierce. I'm ashamed. Very ashamed of how I've acted."

Tears filled his voice. "I got scared. I got scared and ran."

McKenzie placed a hand over his. "Let's forget about it, okay? The past is the past. Nothing can change it. Right now I want to concentrate on your getting better. Sherrie and Marc should be on their way by now. They should be here soon."

Pierce looked at her, then. "You know, Kyla . . . McKenzie . . . even though I asked for your forgiveness, I will never be able to forget what I did."

"Pierce, you've got to forgive yourself. I can't do that for you."

"You . . . you should take your own advice. Forgive yourself over what happened between you and Marc. Learn from it. From where I'm lying, you and Marc have your whole lives in front of you. Don't waste a minute of it fighting."

She smiled through her tears. "Maybe you should take that up with Marc."

"I will." He reached up to wipe her tears. "Y-you look just like y-your mother with your hair cut so short."

"Really? I never thought so."

He nodded. "Yeah, you do." His eyes drifted shut.

She could tell he was getting tired. "Don't try to talk any-more, Pierce. Just rest."

"Sure, Doc," he mumbled. The medication was working, and Pierce drifted off to sleep.

She checked her watch, wondering what was taking Marc and Sherrie so long. McKenzie heard a noise behind her and saw Sherrie tiptoe in. "How is he?"

She could see the fear in Sherrie's eyes. "What happened?"

"He came to the lab to see me. To ask for my forgiveness. I wasn't very nice to him, and then he collapsed. I feel so bad, Sherrie. I don't want anything to happen to him. I don't." She put her hands to her mouth to keep from crying out loud.

"I believe you." Sherrie walked over to the bed and gently placed a kiss on his forehead.

"S-Sherrie."

"I'm here, honey. I'm here."

McKenzie turned to leave, to give them some privacy, and found Marc standing in the doorway. When she saw him standing there, her initial impulse was to run to him and throw herself into his arms, but pride held her back. She smiled as he entered the room.

Ignoring her friendly greeting, Marc strode through the door and right past her.

McKenzie's smile vanished instantly at the rebuke. Her chin quivered. Not one tender word, not one loving gesture. Nothing about how he was feeling. His brother was sick and in the hospital. It had to bother him. Wanting to give comfort, she reached out to him. Walking up to him, she placed a gentle hand on his arm. "I know you must be worried about Pierce."

"How is he?"

"I don't know, Marc. He—"

He grabbed her by the arm and pulled her outside the hospital room. He whispered loudly. "What happened?"

"He became dizzy. When I checked him, he was burning up, so I called the paramedics."

"Is this for real, or are you pretending to care about Pierce?"

"How dare you ask me something like that?" McKenzie clenched her fists tightly at her sides, furious that he would not believe her.

Marc was first astounded by her angry words, then became sheepish. "Under the circumstances, I felt I had to ask. I'm sorry if I've offended you. Now if you will excuse me, I need to go check on my brother." With one final look, Marc walked away.

How that brusque dismissal hurt! "Well, don't let me get in your way," she muttered.

Sherrie followed Marc out into the corridor. Pierce was sleeping peacefully. She glanced around. "What happened to McKenzie? Did she leave?"

"I don't know, nor do I give a damn!"

"Why are you being so distant to her?"

Marc stared at Sherrie as if she were from another planet. "I can't believe your memory is so short. How can you and Pierce be so damned forgiving?"

"Put yourself in her shoes, Marc. Try to understand what she's been through."

"It was all lies, Sherrie. She never cared for me."

"You know that's not true, Marc. McKenzie loves you."

A spasm jumped along his lean jaw. "She couldn't. She thought I was Pierce. How could she love me, thinking I was him?"

Sherrie was quiet.

Marc put a hand to his mouth. "I don't think I could ever trust her again. I try not to make the same mistake twice."

"She said she was sorry."

"Doesn't mean a thing."

"I know you love her, Marc."

"I don't love her, and I never will!"

At the sound of a gasp, they turned and saw McKenzie. She stared up at him in an unsettling silence. Her expression betrayed the pain of a broken heart. She gulped hard, hot tears slipping down her cheeks. "I'm sorry. I didn't mean t-to eavesdrop. I-I c-came back . . . t-to . . ." Her voice broke. Humiliated, she turned and fled.

"I hope you're happy, Marc. Look what you've gone and done. How could you do that to her?"

"I wasn't talking—" Sherrie stomped away before he could finish. Marc felt like a big heel. He had not meant to blurt it out like that. It was a lie to begin with, but he would not admit that to anyone.

He flinched, recalling the pain etched on McKenzie's face. Marc doubted he would ever forget her expression. It was the look of a heartbroken woman.

In the safety of her car, McKenzie stilled her trembling body. Once more in control, she sped out of the hospital parking lot and headed to the security of her home.

Arriving home, McKenzie threw down her purse and jacket, leaving them on the sofa, and headed upstairs to her bedroom. The room was dark, and she stumbled and fell, bruising her knee cruelly as she missed her step. The pain was the final assault on her spirit, and McKenzie burst into heartrending tears.

Twenty-six

McKenzie stayed away from the hospital the first week for fear of running into Marc. She had avoided him at work, with little success. During those times, he'd remained somewhat civil.

She wanted to see for herself how Pierce was doing, so she headed to the hospital. She found him sitting up in bed watching TV. "Hello, Pierce. How are you doing?"

He glanced her way and smiled. "I'm feeling as well as can be expected, I guess. I thought you had forgotten me."

"I'm so sorry. I . . . thought it was best if I stayed away. Pierce, I wish there was something I could do."

"There is. Take care of my brother. He needs you."

"Like a hole in the head."

"I mean it, McKenzie. Marc needs you."

"He can't even be nice to me, Pierce. He won't let me get within two feet of him. When I try to talk about anything personal, he just shuts down."

"Give him some time. He's been hurt a lot in the past. It will take a strong woman to pull him out of the past, especially when it involves pain and heartache. We all need to stay out of the past."

"I don't think it would matter one way or the other to Marc."

"Why do you say that, Doc?"

"I don't think I'm what he needs. I've hurt him a lot, and he hates me. I don't know if I have the strength to keep fighting for him."

"Do you love Marc?"

She looked at Pierce. Her eyes held a vulnerable glimmer. "I love him dearly. But I'm afraid he doesn't love me."

"Did he tell you that?"

"He didn't just tell me, he told the whole hospital."

"Huh?"

"I overheard him telling Sherrie that he didn't love me. He didn't know I was standing there."

"I don't believe he meant that."

"I do."

"Why don't you ask him directly? I believe he loves you. Sherrie does, too. No matter what he may have said."

"I can't. I don't think I can bear hearing him say those words again.

"If I were you, I'd ask him straight on. You might be surprised at what you hear. All you need to do is give him love, babies, a reason to live. I think that'll be enough."

McKenzie smiled, but her mood was still pensive. Along with those basic things, there had to be forgiveness. She wasn't sure Marc cared enough to yield up that special healing. No matter. She would, McKenzie decided determinedly, fight for him.

"Since when did the two of you become buddies?" came a deep drawl from behind her. She recognized Marc's voice.

A deafening silence descended over the room. She tried not to stare at him, at his handsome features, the watchful eyes.

McKenzie tried, but she failed.

So she did the only thing she could think of, she turned back to face Pierce. She thought of all the reasons she shouldn't be glad to see Marc, beginning with the way he had been avoiding her and ending with the way he vehemently denied loving her.

Without looking at him, she said evenly, "Hi, Marc."

He paused to stand beside her. "You didn't answer my question."

"Pierce and I have worked out our differences. He may look just like you, but he's not as unforgiving."

"That's probably because he hasn't been lied to like I have."

"McKenzie! Marc! Will the two of you act like adults? I've never seen two people so stubborn. Marc, you know good and well that you want to be with McKenzie."

"I don't want to go into that right now."

"Why not?" McKenzie asked. "You've already announced to the whole hospital that you don't love me. If it weren't for you, I wouldn't even be in town right now. You were the one who was so insistent on my staying here."

"I didn't mean for it to come out like that—"

McKenzie held up her hand. "It doesn't matter."

"For heaven's sake! Are you two still fighting?" Sherrie asked as she walked into the room.

Pierce raised himself up. "I'm glad you're here, baby. They're getting on my nerves with this crap!"

"I didn't come here to upset you. Maybe I should come back later." Marc turned to leave.

"You don't have to leave, Marc. This is your brother. I'll go."

"Neither one of you has to leave. You're never going to resolve anything if you're not going to talk to each other," Sherrie advised.

"McKenzie and I have nothing to resolve!"

McKenzie looked away to hide her sorrow. Marc's comment hurt her far more deeply than anyone could've imagined. Without a word, she moved to the window, staring out into the dusk.

Sherrie went over and put her arms around the trembling McKenzie. "Don't let him get to you. Just be patient. He has to work out his feelings," she whispered.

Stealing a glance at him, she swallowed, fighting a burgeoning feeling of desire. "As far as I'm concerned, Marc Chandler can go straight to hell!" Ignoring Marc, she kissed Pierce lightly on the cheek and said softly, "I'll see you later. And thanks for trying."

* * *

Sherrie confronted Marc. "How can you just let her leave like that? I think y'all are both taking this too far. It was a misunderstanding. That's all. She and Pierce managed to work everything out. Why can't the two of you?"

"What do you expect me to do? Run after her?" Marc asked, sparks of anger shooting from his eyes.

"Yes." Pierce and Sherrie chorused.

"Why would I want to do that?"

"Because you love her. That's why. Don't let your stubborn pride stand in the way of your love," said Pierce. "Life is much too short."

Marc stood there, deep in thought. Suddenly he turned on his heel and left the room. He found McKenzie at the end of the corridor.

"McKenzie, wait."

When he caught up with her, she peered up at him and asked, "What do you want?"

"I want to know why you're really at this hospital. Do you think you can get to me through my brother?"

She answered without slowing her step, her voice oddly strained. "You have a vivid imagination. I came to see how Pierce is doing. That's all. Now that you're here, I'll get out of your way."

"You're not in my way, McKenzie."

"Then why do you make me feel that way? Every time we're in the same room I always feel as if I'm intruding. Each time I've tried to have a conversation with you, I can feel you putting up your guard. I know you don't want me, but can we at least try to reestablish a friendship?"

Marc found the clarity of her expression troubling. It disturbed him greatly that she had such a guileless glance when he knew her to be capable of such treacherous deceit.

"It's going to take time, McKenzie."

She stepped backward, proudly, wanting him to know she

was not in retreat. Arms folded, she looked him straight in the eye. "I'm willing to take the time. Are you?"

"Let's just see what happens."

Disappointment washed over her. She hadn't really thought Marc had been overcome with some miraculous change of heart, had she? No, of course she hadn't. McKenzie hardened her features, determined not to let him know how his attitude had hurt her.

McKenzie walked away from Marc, not daring to look into his piercing dark eyes and see how little he truly cared about her.

"McKenzie—" Seeing the hurt on her face brought a momentary stab of remorse to Marc's heart, but he quickly forced that weakness about her feelings aside in favor of heeding his own.

She stopped and whirled around, facing him. "I'm not going to beg, Marc. Once my project is completed, I'll be out of your life so fast it'll make your head spin."

"I don't want you to leave, McKenzie."

She could see his teeth grinding. *How he must hate this,* she thought, miserable. "I'm sorry, Marc. I'm sorry I hurt you. I never meant to."

Her sudden impassioned claim startled him. He sucked in a quick breath and unconsciously withdrew a step. Wariness and a sudden new hope churned inside him.

McKenzie was watching his face, trying to judge his reaction by the subtle shifts in his expression. She frowned unhappily. "You believe me, don't you?"

"Yes," came his faint whisper.

She waited for him to say more, but he didn't. He simply walked away.

Holding to her heart when her pride failed her, McKenzie impulsively called him back.

"What, McKenzie?"

"Can we please have dinner? That is, if you haven't eaten already."

"I'm not—" Marc glanced up to see an elderly woman slowly advancing toward them, and he smiled. As she neared, he immediately offered to escort her back to her room, seeing her weakened state. Turning to McKenzie, he said, "I'll be right back. Will you wait here?"

McKenzie nodded.

He returned to her promptly. "I'm sorry, but I could tell she was getting tired."

"You are a very sweet and caring man. It's one of the things I lo—" She stopped short. "I-I think what you did was nice."

"What were we talking about?"

"I asked you out to dinner. I thought we could go to The Cheesecake Factory."

"I don't know—"

"Please, Marc. It's just dinner."

"I'll follow you, if that's okay."

"Sure."

They walked out into the huge parking lot. Marc walked McKenzie to her car, and then headed to his.

At the restaurant, McKenzie had no notion of his thoughts. Her eyes kept going to his firm full lips as he ate his food.

Marc stopped eating. "Aren't you going to eat, McKenzie? I thought you were hungry." The husky tremor of his voice seemed to wrap around her and set her pulses rising.

"I . . . I'm not as hungry as I thought," she murmured softly. As his dark gaze held her, she seemed at a loss as to what else she should say.

"What's wrong, McKenzie?"

"I hate all this tension. We can't even talk to each other."

"We're talking."

"Not like we used to. I miss the way it used to be. I miss us." McKenzie placed a slender hand over his.

He eased his hand away. "There is no us."

"There used to be. There can be once again."

"You ruined whatever we might have had."

"Maybe I did, Marc. Even so, I think we should talk about it. Not scream or yell. We need to talk."

Marc laid his fork down. "You know, McKenzie, I really thought you were different. Hell, I wanted you to be different. I feel like an ass for getting involved with you! What's so pathetic about the whole situation is that I can't get you out of my mind. I think about you constantly."

"You've missed me? Is that what you're saying, Marc?"

Marc instantly grew wary, for he realized he'd said far more than he'd meant to say. Her teasing question demanded the truthful response he was still unwilling to give.

"No. I haven't missed you at all. Have you missed me, sweetness?"

McKenzie smiled. "No—yes. Yes, I've missed you terribly.'

He chuckled. "I can see it in your eyes. Right now, you want to wrap me in your arms and kiss me, don't you?"

She was losing the battle in her struggle to ignore Marc's playful banter, and she hated herself for her weakness. Looking away, she said, "Please, Marc. I'm not exactly desperate."

He leaned toward her, whispering, "Tell me, sweetheart, has another man made you feel so breathless when he touched you? Like this." Marc softly traced her fingers, touching them lightly.

McKenzie knew exactly what he meant. His touches were whisper soft. Suddenly she thought she could hear his heart beating rapidly, and his speech was full of emotion. "Does any other woman affect you the way I do?"

Marc's eyes suddenly had a vulnerable look, as if she had exposed his soul. She was right. She held as much power over him as he did over her—maybe even more. Hunger for her surged through him. "You want me to make love to you."

There was no mistaking the invitation in her voice and her eyes. "Yes. Yes I do, Marc."

He raised his hand to signal the waiter for the check. "Let get out of here."

"I'm right behind you."

As soon as they entered her town house, Marc pulled her into his arms and held her tightly against him. He felt her breath, quick and warm against his neck, and felt his desire ignite. He found the warmth of her mouth with his own. Afraid that she would pull away from him, he held her even tighter, caressing her body with his hands. Trembling with passion, he finally released her. Searching her eyes for any uncertainty and finding none, Marc undid the buttons of her blouse and slid it off her shoulders.

He bent to kiss her again, running his hands from her wrists up to her shoulders, then back down again. As he kissed her more deeply, he felt her eagerness, and Marc groaned. Lost in the softness of her skin and the sweetness of her mouth, he traced the curve of her back upward to her shoulders with both hands. McKenzie pulled away. Unzipping her jeans, she slipped them down, letting them fall to the floor, pooling around her ankles. Stepping over them, she grabbed Marc by the hand, clad only in her bra and panties, and led him up the stairs to her bedroom.

As soon as they entered her bedroom, Marc relieved her of her underclothes. Quickly he took off his own clothes and faced McKenzie. He could see the desire in her eyes. He drew her to him, kissing her passionately.

Pulling her down on the bed with him, Marc whispered in her ear, "I want to savor your sweetness."

He turned until McKenzie lay beneath him. Through the ultimate act of union, her world had exploded and reformed.

Marc raised up, placing his firm muscled body on top of McKenzie. As soon as his body touched hers, felt its warmth, his desire grew stronger. Slowly he kissed her again as he moved his hips against hers. He ran his hands up and down her long legs, caressing the softness of her inner thighs until he felt her move against his hand, and finally her moans became too much for him. Marc entered her slowly, making sure she was ready to receive him. His need growing more urgent, he thrust himself harder and deeper inside of her, feeling her take all of him, and he heard himself groan.

Marc sought McKenzie's mouth and kissed her deeply, hearing her tiny moans of pleasure as they moved in unison. As he moved faster and faster, he felt her body shudder, and she cried out. Marc thrust as deeply as he could. Unable to control his desire any longer, he finally let himself go.

McKenzie lay satisfied. Their lovemaking had been wonderful. They had moved together so passionately that everything else in her life before was nothing. Surely it was the same for him. Surely nothing else would matter to him now, after their tumultuous joining.

Turning to look at him, lying so close, McKenzie sought his eyes. They were unchanged, as cold and as hard as they had ever been. What had happened between them meant nothing to him! He had used her!

McKenzie's blood froze. Her chest tightened painfully.

"Damn you, McKenzie!" he said, and in an instant he was out of the bed. With his back to her, he stared out the window into the darkness.

In his anger, Marc had made love to her to ease his fury and appease his body. Their lovemaking——that wonderful experience that had shattered her world before rebuilding it—meant nothing to him. Or perhaps, McKenzie hoped, it meant more than he wanted to admit.

Marc did not turn around. He stood so straight, so rigid, so far away. McKenzie wanted to hold him, to explain the emotions tearing through her. "It wasn't supposed to happen," he said in a voice no longer husky. He sounded angry. "Nothing has changed, McKenzie. We were just satisfying our lust. You were a means to an end, nothing more," he said, as harshly as he had ever spoken to anyone. He put all his scorn into the words. "Do you understand?" His eyes were cold and icy.

An infinite sadness settled over her like a cloud. He had scorned her at every turn. The pain in his voice had been real—

too real. She had no reason to look for anything from him but hurt and rejection. "I didn't force you to make love to me."

"I'm aware of that. I just didn't want this to happen." *Liar!* a little voice inside his head screamed.

McKenzie jumped out of the bed, grabbed her robe, and was across the room in a flash. She was so angry she wanted to take a swing at him. "You were willing enough!"

McKenzie shriveled a little at Marc's expression. "Yes, I guess I was," he said with a brisk nod of his head, but the pain-filled look in his eyes was unmistakable. "A mistake I won't ever repeat."

Marc stepped around her and headed for the door.

His words were a kick to the stomach; his leaving was worse. McKenzie called out to him. "Before you go, Marc, there's something I want to say to you."

"Say what you have to, so that I can leave."

Silent as McKenzie came closer, Marc waited for her to speak. Although the air was cool, he felt only heat for her. His fingers trembled. "I want you so much that you do this to me," he said, holding out his hands. "I'm not going to make love to you again. I can only be a friend to you."

He wanted to leave her place . . . damn it, he wanted her out of his life.

McKenzie, hurt beyond imagining, drew herself up. "I never asked you for . . . anything else."

Marc turned to leave once more, but she placed gentle fingers on his arm.

"Marc, I'm sorry about all this," she said, and then more quickly, "please let me finish. After tonight, I won't bother you again."

He nodded once, curtly.

She fell silent for so long that Marc thought she was finished. He was about to take his leave.

"Wait! The next part is the hardest to say." She took a deep breath. Marc found it hard to breathe.

"I love you, Marc. I've tried everything I could to show you, but you've made it abundantly clear that you don't want me in your life."

She took him by surprise. He hadn't expected her to declare her love for him. He closed his eyes and tried to ignore the heat and hunger that raced through his body.

"After what we shared not too long ago, I find it hard to believe you mean all the things you've said to me, but you don't have to say it anymore. I've gotten the message. Loud and clear I keep hoping—" She looked away and her eyes filled to the brim with tears. "But I keep being wrong."

McKenzie closed her eyes, tears shimmering on her lashes, and when she looked at him again a single crystal teardrop fell on her cheek. She did not brush it away. She stood still, as if wanting to say more. Then, with a sigh, she hurried toward the door, holding it open. "You can leave now."

Marc stopped in front of her, looking at her. McKenzie could not bear his scrutiny any longer, and she walked away. As he took his leave, he heard the door close behind him softly.

Curled up on the cushioned window seat, now wrapped in a blanket, McKenzie dwelled on the whole pitiful picture. She loved him the way a woman loved a man who did not love her in return. Worse, he never would.

Wrapping herself deeper in her blanket, she gazed at the heavens. Tears of frustration burned her eyes, and tears of heartbreak, as well. Everything had gone all wrong. Marc was supposed to be making love to her because he was in love with her, not because he was horny and wanted to punish her.

Why did her heart refuse to believe his words? He had done nothing to indicate that he cared anything for her, but her heart told her otherwise. Maybe there was a chance for them. She would keep her distance, but she would not give up on him.

Twenty-seven

Over the next several weeks, McKenzie threw herself into her work with such abandon that she took herself by surprise. She seldom saw Marc, except for the weekly Monday-morning meetings. She didn't want to see him. Thinking about him was bad enough.

Carla strolled into her office, carrying a storage box filled with papers. "McKenzie, it's almost time for the press conference."

"I'm ready," she lied. Marc would be there, and McKenzie didn't know if she could bear his angry glares.

"You want to ride with me?"

McKenzie picked up her briefcase. "Yes. I think I'll do that, if you don't mind." She watched Carla struggle with her briefcase and the lightweight box. "Give me your briefcase, or the box. If you keep that up you're going to fall on your face."

Marc greeted them at the door. "I was beginning to get worried about the two of you."

Carla breezed by, murmuring, "We got stuck in traffic."

"Hello, Marc."

He smiled. "Hello, McKenzie. I'm glad you're here."

Unspeakable joy filled McKenzie's heart at hearing those words. She wanted to tell him she felt the same way, but he was called away.

Marc walked up to the podium. After a few initial remarks,

he introduced McKenzie. Smiling, she joined him on the platform. She took a deep breath, then said a silent prayer before taking the microphone.

"We've received encouraging results on the first Phase I clinical trials with CP-281, Chandler's orally administered vaccine. One test subject was HIV positive for over four years and exhibiting minor symptoms. After taking the CP-281 for approximately twelve weeks, he tested negative for the first time and his T-cell count had risen dramatically. I would like you to note that a negative blood test does not indicate the absence of the AIDS virus in the body—" She paused to let the resounding applause stop.

As she talked, she could feel Marc's eyes on her. "However based on these data, we believe that CP-281 can be safely administered at the levels needed to halt the further progression of HIV to the point that AIDS will never manifest itself. All indications so far point to that conclusion."

Marc joined her, and she turned the mike back over to him. Together, they answered questions for a few minutes before slipping out of a side door. Carla remained behind to answer any questions.

McKenzie glanced over at Marc and noticed how tired he looked. "Is something wrong, Marc?"

"Why do you ask?"

"You look tense. Come here," She motioned to a vacant room nearby. "Come in here and sit down. I'll give you neck rub."

Marc sat down and let McKenzie ease the tension in his neck and shoulders. He closed his eyes as her gentle fingers massaged his sore hard muscles. Then he grabbed her hands, stood up, and jerked her close to him. Anger flashed in his dark expressive eyes.

"Please let me go," she said, her eyes wide with fear. " only meant to—"

"You meant to what? Make a fool of me again?" he asked coldly. "What were you going to do this time, Dr. Ashford

Try to arouse me enough to take you right here? How convenient of you to find an empty room just to *ease* my tension."

Color flooded McKenzie's cheeks at the insult, and she was suddenly as furious as he. She wanted to cry, but she wouldn't. McKenzie was afraid that if she started she wouldn't be able to stop. "If you'd only get off your high horse for just a second, you'd see I was only trying to help." She made no effort to keep her voice down, her balled fists resting on her hips.

"I don't believe anything you say."

"You've made that abundantly clear. Excuse me for offering to give you a neck rub. I didn't realize you had no control over your libido. Maybe you should try saltpeter. I hear it works great for *dogs*."

Marc jerked her to him. He wanted to hurt her as much as she had hurt him. "I want you to hear this. You once told me I was afraid of falling in love with you. I was never in any danger of falling in love with you. It was lust, nothing else."

Suddenly she lowered her voice. "Why are you doing this? *How can you be so heartless?* I've tried to explain. It was an honest mistake, Marc. I thought you were Pierce."

"Really?" Marc murmured with every evidence of disbelief in his gleaming dark eyes. "One could speculate, Dr. Ashford, that you knew my identity full-well, but relished your game."

"Marc, please. I wish—"

"Go to hell, Dr. Ashford," he sneered as he walked over to the door, slamming his fist into the wall. He tried to vent his anger before doing something he would regret.

She hurt so much she didn't know how to begin to resolve it. It was an overwhelming pain, one without a beginning or an end. McKenzie couldn't seem to cry any more. Her eyes burned from the lack of tears. It was over. Marc didn't love her, nor would he ever forgive her. McKenzie decided it was time to move on with her life.

* * *

Throughout Calvin's wedding ceremony, McKenzie's mind kept drifting to Marc. In the days following the last confrontation, she had seen very little of him.

It was hard to believe they had ever been lovers, she thought bleakly. He had become a total stranger in just a matter of months, it seemed.

Calvin and his bride soon joined her.

"Congratulations to both of you. I wish you nothing but happiness." She hugged each one briefly.

"It's been great to finally meet you. Calvin talks about you all the time." Kissing Calvin lightly on the cheek, Ellen said in a low voice, "Honey, there's my great-aunt, Lucy. I'd better go over and say hello. You stay here and talk with McKenzie."

"She's beautiful, Calvin. I'm so happy for you."

"I care for her a great deal, Mack. She's good to me, and good for me."

"That's as it should be."

Calvin took a seat next to her. "What's going on with you? I can see the sadness. Are you going to tell me about you and Marc? Why did the two of you break up?"

"It's a long story, Calvin. Besides, it's your wedding day. I'm not going to bore you with my problems. Your bride is looking for you. Go on to her."

"Are you going to be okay?"

"Yes. You know I'm a survivor." She kissed him on the cheek and whispered, "Be happy, Calvin," before strolling toward his mother's table.

She sat quietly through dinner, her mind thousands of miles away. She thought about Marc and the brief happiness they shared.

Ellen danced with her father, while Calvin whirled her mother across the floor. He was out of breath as he made his way over to the table she shared with his mother.

"Wanna dance, Mack?"

She smiled sadly. "No, thanks. I'm not in the mood for dancing."

Calvin took a seat next to her. "Come on, girl. Stop worrying about Marc. If he loves you, he'll come to his senses. Now, enjoy the party."

"I'm not worried about Marc. There are plenty of other fish in the sea. I don't need him."

"Mack, it's me you're talking to. You're never gonna love another man the way you love this Marc Chandler. Boy, I sure can't wait to meet him."

"Why do you say that?"

"Because I have never seen you this way. It's written all over your face. You love him with your whole being. You've finally met a man who can make you temporarily forget about medical research."

"I should have told him what I suspected from the beginning. I never should have tried to get revenge. I'm not good at it, anyway."

"You've got too much heart to be vengeful, Mack. He has to understand that you didn't know he had a twin—"

"Marc doesn't care about that. He feels that I used him." A hot tear rolled down her cheek. "I don't want to love him. I don't want to be in love, period. It's too powerful, too consuming . . . too painful."

Calvin cupped her chin, lifted her face, looking deeply into her eyes. "Mack, you don't mean that."

"Yes, Calvin, I do. I can't go through something like this again. When we broke up, Marc got custody of my heart. I love him so much, but he doesn't see it."

"I know the feeling."

McKenzie looked up into his eyes. Reaching, she pulled him toward her. "Oh, Calvin. I'm so sorry." She hugged him tightly before letting him go. "I never meant to hurt you."

"It's okay, Mack. I moved on, and that's when I met Ellen. She's a wonderful lady, and she loves me."

"I'm very happy for you."

"Same here."

"But—"

"Don't lose hope, Mack. If Marc loves you, he'll come around. If he doesn't, then it's his loss. You're a wonderful lady." Looking over his shoulder, he added, "Ellen's waving at me. I'd better go join my wife."

Leaning forward in his chair, Marc inquired, "Where is McKenzie? I haven't seen her all day." He and Carla had just finished their meeting in his office.

Still writing notes on her legal pad, her head down, Carla said, "McKenzie is in Orlando. I thought you knew."

"When did she leave?" he asked after a moment, staring at Carla. "Is she coming back?"

With her pencil nestled between her lips, she managed to shrug. Removing the pencil, she said, "I don't know, Marc, I think so."

He struggled to maintain his composure. "Well, when is she supposed to come back?"

"I'm not sure. Actually, she didn't really say. I guess we'll just have to wait and see."

"Why did she go back to Orlando?"

"Because of a wedding."

Marc felt as if someone had hit him square in the chest. He inhaled deeply. "A wedding?"

Carla snapped her notebook shut. She set back in her chair, meeting his angry glare straight on. "Marc, why are you asking so many questions?"

"Is she the bride?"

"She didn't say. All I know is that someone named Calvin is the groom."

"Calvin."

"Do you know him?"

"No, we haven't had the pleasure of meeting face to face, *yet*." He paused. "Calvin and McKenzie are close friends—at least that's what she told me."

"And?"

"Calvin's in love with her." Marc could barely contain his fury. *Would she marry him just to get back at me?* he wondered.

"Marc? Are you okay?"

"I'm just fine, Carla. And I want you to know something else. If McKenzie's decided to marry a man she's not in love with, then she deserves whatever happens to her." Marc was beside himself.

"I *didn't* say she was getting married. I said she was in the wedding. *You* made that assumption. Anyway, what difference would it make? It's not as if the man she loves is offering marriage, anyway."

Marc scowled at her. "I don't have time for this! I'm getting out of here. I'll be at home for the remainder of the day."

"Marc, wait!" Carla grabbed Marc by the arm and led him back into her office. "Have a seat, will you?" When he was seated, she spoke again. "Marc, why won't you be honest with McKenzie? You love her. Jim and I know it. Pierce and Sherrie know it. The one person who needs to know doesn't."

"As far as I'm concerned, she doesn't deserve to know. McKenzie played me like a fiddle." His tone was bitter. "It was just a ploy to get me to open up to her, so she could find a way to blackmail me."

"Did you read the journal from beginning to end?"

"No. I didn't have to."

"I think maybe you should have. The entries she wrote after meeting you are the ones you should have read. In them, she wrote about her ambiguous feelings for you, and later, that maybe you weren't guilty of what she had assumed all these years."

Marc was quiet. "I wish she had just confronted me about all this. It could have been straightened out a long time ago."

"It's not too late now, is it?"

He shrugged. "I don't really know, Carla."

"Think about it. Think long and hard before you lose her for good."

Marc leaned forward in the chair, his hands covering his face.

Sighing loudly, he stood up and headed to the door. He hesitated before closing the door. "I have never felt this way about anyone, not even Margie. I regret the day I laid eyes on that damn diary." He sighed once more before closing the door.

Twenty-eight

McKenzie rushed into the restaurant. She spotted David immediately. He was seated at a table near the door. Smiling, she rushed to join him.

"I'm glad you called, David. I dreaded coming back to an empty town house. I dreaded coming back to California."

"Did you have a good time in Florida?"

"Yes. It was wonderful. I got to see a bunch of old and dear friends."

"How was the wedding?" David picked up his glass of wine and sipped it.

"It was so beautiful. I think I cried throughout the whole ceremony. Calvin's mother and I kept passing each other tissues."

"I'm glad you're back. Marc has been a beast to work for." He shuddered. Leaning toward McKenzie, David said in a low whisper, "I think it's because he missed you. Carla said he grilled her like crazy until she finally told him you went to Orlando to be in a wedding. He wanted to know if you married Calvin. Imagine that."

"Marc's got a lot of nerve! It wasn't any of his business where I went."

David wagged a finger at her. "Huh. That man loves you, girlfriend."

"David, I wish I could believe that." McKenzie ached with an inner pain. "You know, he thinks you and I are involved."

"What? Get the heck outta here!" he managed to sputter. "You mean to tell me you never told Marc that I'm gay?"

"No. I didn't think it was my place to discuss your sexual preferences. It has nothing to do with your job."

David's attention was somewhere else. "Well, well, well. Talk about the devil—"

McKenzie looked around. Following the hostess were Marc and Glenda. Marc nodded slightly in their direction. He didn't look at all pleased to see her. She fought her feelings of disappointment. McKenzie knew by now that she should expect nothing less than hostility from him. Still, it hurt.

David almost choked. "Oh, God! He's with Glenda. That wench is something else!"

"I hope the two of them will be very happy together," McKenzie said sarcastically. Inside, she was trying to keep tears from falling. It hurt deeply seeing him out with another woman. She caught David watching her, his eyes full of sympathy. McKenzie took a sip of iced tea and shrugged. "He's free to do whatever or whoever he wants. It's not my business."

"Guess she can't mean too much to him. He looked like he wanted to cut my heart out. Like right now, he's just staring over here at us. Girlfriend, if looks could kill—"

McKenzie folded her arms across her chest. "He has no right to be upset. He dumped me!"

"It's obvious he still cares for you. Otherwise, he wouldn't be bugging like this."

"Bugging or not, I'm not going to let him ruin our evening out. Marc had his chance, and he threw it out the window." *Along with my heart,* she silently added.

Anger flared within Marc. Or was it jealousy? Impossible. He meant everything he had told her. Everything between them was over. He had no business feeling like the worst ass on earth.

But Marc could not get her out of his mind. Seeing her here with David angered him.

Glenda touched Marc's arm lightly. *"That man is gay,* Marc. You don't have to worry about him."

Marc was surprised. "How do you know that?"

"I made a pass at him once. He told me. Now don't you go looking at me like that. He wasn't just saying it to keep me at bay. He really meant it."

"I never had any idea. I mean, I did think he was kind of soft."

"Does it matter?"

Marc shook his head. "No. It's his business. What he does outside of company time is no concern of mine."

"Except when it involves a certain Dr. Ashford."

Marc said nothing. His eyes were on McKenzie. Nothing else mattered . . . nothing had mattered for a long while, although Marc had only just now come to that realization. Only McKenzie mattered. And he had lost her.

Glenda gave Marc a gentle prod. "Why don't you just go on over and talk to her? Stop sitting here and eyeballing them." She glanced around the room quickly. "It's embarrassing."

He chuckled. "You're crazy. You know that, don't you?"

Glenda threw back her head and laughed. "What's taken you so long to figure that out?"

Pierce was sitting up in bed when Sherrie arrived. He smiled at her. "Guess what, baby? Doctor Brown said I could go home today."

She clapped her hands together. "Honey, that's wonderful. I've missed sleeping next to you."

"I was thinking . . ." Pierce paused. "I was thinking we could go to Vegas."

Sherrie looked puzzled. "Vegas? What for? You're just getting out of the hospital—"

Pierce grabbed her hand, pulling her to sit beside him on the bed. "I thought we could get married. Tonight."

"Get—did you just say we could get married?"

Pierce laughed. "Yes. Sherrie, if you'll still have me. Wil you?"

Tears of joy poured from her eyes. "Of course I'll marry you Honey, I love you with my body and soul." She wrapped he arms around his neck, and pulled his head down to hers "You've made me so happy, Pierce."

"I love you, too."

Sherrie pulled her ample body up off the bed. She went to stand by the window. "Are you sure you're feeling up to this You're just getting out of the hospital."

"I'm well enough to marry you. I may have to do it from wheelchair, but I'm going to make you my wife. Tonight! realized, lying up here, that I don't want to waste another pre cious moment of my life not being your husband."

She walked back over to the bed. "Pierce, you are one of the sweetest men I know. So courageous. I don't want to wast another minute, either. Let's do it."

"Am I interrupting?" Marc stood in the doorway. "I car come back later."

Pierce waved him into the room. "No. Come on in, Marc You're just in time."

"Just in time for what?" He looked from one to the other Noting the wide grins they both wore, Marc had a feeling h knew what was coming next.

"We're getting married," Sherrie announced.

"It's about damn time! When?"

Pierce added, "Tonight. In Vegas. We would like you to ac company us. What do you say?"

"Pierce, are you up to the trip?"

He nodded. "I want to marry Sherrie."

"You don't have to travel to Nevada. You'll get married thi evening at my house. I'll arrange everything. Now let's get yo home. If you're getting married tonight, you're going to need some rest."

"Thanks, Marc."

He grinned. "No problem, bro."

Sherrie stopped Marc before he left the room. "Marc, I want McKenzie to be there. Is that going to be a problem?"

"No. It's your wedding. You can have whoever you want there."

She kissed him lightly on the cheek. "Thank you, Marc. That really means a lot to me. And I know how awkward it must be for you."

"Don't worry about me. I'll be fine. Now, you get Pierce all checked out and I'll start on the arrangements. We don't have much time."

"Thanks again, Marc."

"As I said before, this is no problem. I'm honored to be able to be a part of my brother's wedding."

Although Marc tried to sound indifferent, Sherrie could still see the pain etched on his face.

Pierce and Sherrie became husband and wife at seven-thirty that evening. A teary-eyed McKenzie and a somber Marc were in attendance, along with Carla and Jim. McKenzie stood by as the newlyweds cut their wedding cake. Not able to take any more of their exuberance over being married, she readied to leave. Carla caught up with her at the door.

"You're not leaving yet, are you?"

McKenzie glanced at Marc. "Yes I am. I don't feel comfortable being here. Especially with the way things are between Marc and me." She felt the heat of Marc's gaze on her. "I think I should leave."

Carla hugged her. "McKenzie, I just know you and Marc are going to work things out. Please don't give up on him. He loves you. He really does."

"So you keep telling me. Pierce and Sherrie say the same

thing. Everyone but Marc." McKenzie shook her head. "I can't take it anymore, Carla. I've done all I can do. It's up to Marc now. I'll tell you this, I won't wait forever." she knew she would, though. She knew she would never love another man the way she loved Marc. He was her soulmate. She glanced at him one last time before leaving. This time he would not look at her. Crushed, she eased out of the room.

Carla marched over to Marc. "You're definitely going to lose her if you don't get your head together."

"What do you expect me to do? Go chasing after her?"

"That's *exactly* what I expect. You love her, Marc. It's a rare thing to find someone who loves you as much as you love them. Why can't you just let go of the past?"

"Carla, I—"

"I know what Margie did to you. I know how you felt when that girl lied about being pregnant with your baby. I know how you felt about seeing Glenda with that guy. I know about all those things. I know you were hurt when you found out your mother kept Pierce's existence a secret."

"But—"

"But nothing, Marc. We all have to deal with hurt and disappointment at one time or another. It's how we react to those emotions that will determine our future relationships. McKenzie loves you, and she's really hurting right now—not unlike you. You need each other."

Marc nodded. He told himself he was being a fool. McKenzie had done more for him than any woman before her. But he wasn't sure he could, or even should, put those sentiments into words. "You're right, Carla. But how do I know I can trust her with my heart?"

"You don't. It's a chance you'll have to take. You know there are no guarantees in life."

Marc glanced around the room.

"If you're looking for McKenzie, she left already. She said

he couldn't stay here with the way things are between the two
of you. She just walked out. Maybe you can catch her outside,
if you hurry."

Marc made it outside just as McKenzie was driving off. He
decided he would pay her a visit tomorrow. The time had come
to bury the pain and heartache.

Twenty-nine

"Open up, McKenzie." Marc's voice was low, almost begging. It fired McKenzie's senses, reminding her of how much she missed him. He had been out there knocking for the past five minutes.

Despondency washed over her. Only an innate sense of pride enabled her to hold back more tears. She stood by the door unable to speak.

"Open up, McKenzie. Please. I know you're in there."

Her heart paused, as if to acknowledge the powerful emotion welling up within her. When it resumed beating, it pumped pure fear. "Go away, Marc."

"No. I'm not leaving. We need to talk."

"No we don't. You've made yourself pretty clear."

"Damn it, McKenzie, open up! I really need to talk to you."

Her heart stopped. She curled her lips together. Breathless seconds passed while his words reverberated through her brain.

McKenzie tried to temper her expectations with a dose of reality. He didn't love her, and he never would.

Weakened by dread, she crossed the room and slowly opened the door. Marc stood there, an arm propped against the door.

He peered at McKenzie closely. The shadows were there under her eyes. Something else bothered him. She was answering him with brief responses that told him little. The fight was missing. Her voice sounded flat.

"Are you sure you're all right?"

McKenzie shrugged. "I'm fine. What are you doing here? I ope you realize it's six-thirty in the morning."

Marc's lips twitched. "I didn't think my presence would be o disturbing to you. Besides, if I remember correctly, you're n early riser. Speaking of which, maybe you should go back o bed."

McKenzie didn't like the hint of a smile. "What is that sup- osed to mean?"

The fight was back.

He shook his head. "Nothing. Forget it."

McKenzie dropped down onto the loveseat in her living oom. Massaging her forehead with the palm of her hands, she sked, "Marc, why did you come here?" Frowning, she looked p at him. "Didn't you have anyone back at Chandler you could orment?"

Marc sat on the arm of her sofa. "I didn't come here to orment you. Just to talk. Would you join me on the sofa, please? don't want to talk across the room."

McKenzie walked over and plopped down on the sofa. "So lk."

Marc took a seat beside her. Placing his large hand over hers, e said softly. "I've missed you, McKenzie."

She reacted by pulling her hand away, as if she had been urned. "You said that to say what?"

"You're not going to make this easy for me, are you?"

"Marc, it's like this. I don't particularly like you at this mo- ent." She moved to the farthest corner of the sofa, away from m.

"I guess I deserve that."

"What is this about, Marc?"

"I don't want you to leave. I know you're planning to move ack to Orlando."

"Carla talks too much," she muttered. Her heart pounded in er chest. If Marc had sprouted wings, she would not have been ore surprised by his admission. "Why? Why don't you want e to leave?"

"Because I want you."

McKenzie's heart plummeted to the floor of her stomach. So that was it. He simply wanted her, he didn't love her. What a fool she had been to think otherwise.

"It won't work." Her bottom lip began to tremble, and she could feel tears begin to burn in her eyes and throat. "I'm tired of trying to prove to you how sorry I am for what I did. I know it was not my place to seek revenge without knowing all the facts. I was wrong, and I've acknowledged that fact. However, I never lied about my feelings for you. I told you how I felt and I'm tired of waiting to see if you'll be kind enough to love me back. You've made it clear that you don't, and that's fine. I'm leaving town in a couple of weeks, and I'll be out of your life for good."

"McKenzie . . ." As much as he wanted to, Marc could not bring himself to say the words she wanted to hear—the words he knew she needed to hear.

"What, Marc?" Her expression was full of hope.

"We have a contract."

"Damn the contract, Marc. *Damn you.* I can't take this any more. I'm not staying. You can sue me. I don't give a damn."

"So you're saying that if we're not a couple you're going to leave town. It sounds like an ultimatum."

"It's not an ultimatum. It's a choice. I can't work with you Marc. It hurts too much. You know, I think you've forgotten all the problems you caused your father not so long ago."

"What are you talking about?"

"You told me yourself that you caused your parents a lot of pain during your teenage years and your early twenties. Did they ever stop loving you, Marc? No! They loved you unconditionally. They never gave up on you. Your mother made a decision many years ago that she felt was the only option she had at the time. You were a baby. You had no idea what she was going through. She didn't know what the future held. Yet, you have the unmitigated gall to sit in judgment of her. You sit in judgment of all women!"

"McKenzie—"

"Let me finish, Marc. You've been hurt. We've all been hurt at one time or another. You refused to forgive your mother on her deathbed. You are not perfect, Marc. Even you've made mistakes."

"I went to the cemetery yesterday. To visit my mother's grave. I hadn't been out there since her funeral. I went to have a long talk with her."

"How did it go?" she asked softly.

"I told her about finding Pierce, about his marriage. I think she was pleased. I asked for her forgiveness." Marc sat up then. "Funny thing is, I think she heard me. I can't explain it, but she forgave me."

"How do you know?"

"Because as I knelt beside her grave I felt a peace that I've not felt in a long time."

"But don't you think it's a little late?"

"No. If I've learned nothing else, it's that the past is the past. I do realize now how difficult it must have been for you. In ways we can't ignore, the past will always be with us. We just have to learn to accept it for what it is. Instead of learning from the past, we often make the mistake of thinking we can get even. Often, we let all our anger and hurt from the past consume us."

"I'm glad you made your peace with your mother. She certainly deserved much better from you. Sherrie told me about the letter she wrote to you and Pierce. She never stopped loving him, and she tried to find him. There's been so much needless suffering in both your lives."

"I know, McKenzie. I realize I have a holier-than-thou attitude, but I'm working on it. I've come to understand that forgiveness is an important part of the healing process."

"That's quite an admission, Marc, and I appreciate it. But I'm still leaving. I don't think we can work together anymore."

"Our personal relationship shouldn't have anything to do with business. I told you that in the beginning."

"I know you've always said that, but I think it will be best for me if I leave."

"I don't want you to go, McKenzie." He could again see the hope that sprang instantly in her eyes. He cursed himself for not being able to tell her how he really felt. "It's too late in the game to bring another scientist on board."

Disappointment spread like wildfire through her body. "I see."

"We can still be together, McKenzie. We can still be a couple, if that's what you want."

This time there was no sign of hope in her eyes. All he saw was defeat.

"Is it what you want, Marc?"

"It's not about what I want. I want you to be happy."

"You want your vaccine."

"You know that I do."

"Another scientist can finish what I started."

The words weren't coming out the way he wanted. "I don't want another scientist. I want you . . . to finish what you started." He was frustrated. "McKenzie, are you interested in our getting back together?"

"I need to know something. Do you love me?"

Marc met McKenzie's eyes for a moment, then he glanced away.

Weary of being hurt again, she said softly, "It's all right. I didn't really expect an answer," she said truthfully. It was better than leaving herself open for another cruel rejection.

"I don't know what to say. I don't want to be apart from you."

"I think you don't know what you want," she managed. The pain inside her was real, devastating, acute. Her head throbbed with it; her heart pounded with it; her lungs constricted with it. She summoned what was surely her last ounce of strength. "Would you please leave, Marc? It's over between us."

Helplessly, he watched her stand, arms gripped around her chest, shoulders tensed.

Hesitantly, Marc reached out and touched her shoulders. He could feel her tense, but she did not move away. "McKenzie—"

She shook her head. "Leave me alone, Marc. We have nothing more to say to each other."

Just when she thought she couldn't stand to remain in the same room with him a second longer, she heard him leave. The door closed gently behind him.

Heartbroken, she watched from the window as he left.

Marc wasn't sure how he made it back to his office. He felt numb. It was over. He had driven McKenzie out of his life. All she wanted to hear was that he wanted her to stay because he loved her. Marc couldn't bring himself to say those words. He just couldn't. He'd thought to use her desire to make a scientific discovery to make her stay.

"Marc?"

"Yes, Carla?"

"Did you get a chance to see McKenzie?"

"She plans to move back to Florida. She doesn't want to stay."

"Did you tell her that you love her?"

"I couldn't."

"Marc, you need to tell her. She really loves you. Don't let her walk out of your life—you'll regret it for the rest of your days."

"Carla's right."

Jim strode in and sat in the chair next to Carla. "Marc, call her. Call her and tell her that you love her."

"She's not going to talk to me. She doesn't want to see me again."

"Did she say that?"

"Yes."

"Why is it so hard, Marc? We've all known heartbreak at one time or another."

"I said those words only once in my life. Margie just laughed in my face. I felt as if my heart had been ripped into. I'd never hurt so much, especially after I was arrested and she had skipped town with all my possessions, leaving me to rot in prison. Fortunately for me, it didn't come to that."

"I remember when that happened. Marc looked as if he'd been dragged through the mud afterward. He really loved that tramp. I tried to warn him about her, but—"

"But I didn't believe Carla. Hell, I thought she was just jealous." Marc placed a hand in Carla's. "She has been a good friend, this lady here. A good friend. And you too, Jim. I don't know what I'd have done without the two of you."

"I'd do anything for you, old man."

"I wish you could get McKenzie back for me."

Carla perked up. "I've got a fabulous idea!" She quickly told them her plan.

Marc was skeptical. "Are you sure this will work? I don't think McKenzie will just go along with something like this without a fight."

"McKenzie loves you, Marc. I know it'll work." Turning to Carla, Jim added, "Count me in. I'll do what I can."

Carla smiled and batted her eyes prettily. "Thanks, Jim. I knew I could depend on you for help."

"Anything for you, cupcake."

Marc screwed up his face. "You two are making me sick! Get out of here with all that sweet talk."

Carla tiptoed to give Jim a kiss on the lips. "He's just jealous, honey bun."

"I know, doll face."

"Will you two get the hell out of my office?"

"Now, Marc. You don't have to be so nasty. Just you wait and see. You and McKenzie will be back together again."

Jim nodded. "If not, no one is going to be able to be around him."

Marc picked up his briefcase. "If you two won't leave, then I will," he snapped. He stormed by a laughing Carla and Jim.

* * *

Three days later, McKenzie answered the door and was surprised to find a messenger standing there. He held a large gift-wrapped package for her.

"I'm afraid there must be some sort of mistake. I haven't ordered—"

"No, ma'am. There's no mistake. I'm supposed to deliver this to you."

"Who is it from?"

"I don't know, ma'am. I just have my orders to deliver it."

"Well, thank you." She reached in her pocket to tip him, but he refused.

"My tip's already been taken care of, ma'am. Have a good day." He was gone before she could respond.

Attached to the box was an envelope. She tore into it as if her life depended on it. It was an invitation of some sort. Ivory vellum with gold ink lettering. An invitation to some elegant event. Probably another AIDS fund-raiser.

Opening the box, McKenzie found an exquisite dress. Reminiscent of the twenties, the gold-colored gown had a silk, ribbed, organza bodice and a plunging scoop back. A pleated silk chartreuse sash defined the drop waistline, while a softly gathered, silk crepe skirt swirled to a sweeping train. Inside was a matching pair of crepe shoes.

Just as McKenzie searched through the box for a gift card, the telephone rang.

"Hello."

"Hi, it's me, Carla. How are you?"

"I'm okay, I guess."

"Did you receive the package?"

"Yes. How did you know about them?"

"I sent them. There's a big fund-raiser on Saturday, and I hope you'll attend with me. Afterward, you, Sherrie, and I could have sort of a girl's night out."

"You didn't have to go out and buy me an outfit. I could have bought one myself."

"I know, but when I saw this one it looked so much like you that I wanted you to have it. It's such a beautiful dress."

McKenzie held up the gown. It was absolutely gorgeous. "I really do like it. I'll tell you what. I'll keep all of this on one condition—you give me the bill so that I can reimburse you."

"Agreed. Now do you want to meet me somewhere for lunch? We can shop for accessories."

"Sure. Carla?"

"Yes."

"Is Marc going to be there?"

"He might, and then again, he might not. He's not been himself lately. Is that going to be a problem? His being there?"

She wanted to say yes, but instead answered, "No. No problem at all. I was just curious."

Thirty

Marc tugged at his bow tie. In the span of five minutes, he had checked his watch three times.

"Marc, why don't you have a seat? McKenzie will be here. She told Carla she was coming," Jim said, clapping Marc on the shoulder.

"I don't think this is going to work. McKenzie is a smart woman. She's not going to go for this."

"She loves you, Marc. I know she'll be here." Carla glanced at her watch. "The limo should be arriving at her place soon."

Marc paced back and forth across the room.

"You're going to wear a hole in the carpet if you don't quit pacing like that, old man."

"I don't want to lose her, Jim. I can't." Putting his hands to his face for a moment, he said, "Lord knows I never thought I'd feel this way in a million years."

Jim chuckled. "I always knew this day would come. I've been waiting a long time for this."

"I'm scared to death. Damn! This woman has me on pins and needles."

"Everything's going to work out. You'll see, Marc."

"I hope so."

McKenzie stood staring out her bedroom window into the starless night. She had decided not to attend the fund-raiser.

She could not bear seeing Marc. Not yet. She was torn with feelings of guilt, though, because she'd practically promised Carla that she would be there. *Surely she'll understand why I can't be there tonight,* McKenzie reasoned.

She eyed the dress that hung on her door. It was so beautiful. Carla had great taste. McKenzie walked over and fingered the soft folds of the gown. Maybe she would go, after all. It would serve Marc right to see how she was determined to go on with her life—without him. He would not know that she was dying inside. She would share that secret with no one. If she did go, she'd need to hurry. The limo would be arriving in forty-five minutes.

McKenzie eyed herself in the mirror. The dress was stunning. She wondered what Marc would say when he saw her in it. Most likely he wouldn't even notice. She chided herself for thinking about the one man she could not have. It still hurt deeply to think about Marc. McKenzie wondered if she would ever get over him. She doubted it. She loved him with her body and soul.

The ringing of the doorbell brought her out of her reverie. *It must be the driver,* she thought as she grabbed her purse and headed downstairs. All the way to the Beverly Hills Hotel, she tried to shut out thoughts of Marc.

"You look stunning," Sherrie exclaimed. "Your dress is fit for a queen. I've never seen anything like it."

Sherrie wore an ivory-colored silk dress with a handbeaded halter-style bodice and a full skirt. McKenzie thought it was very flattering on Sherrie.

"When Marc sees you it will take his breath away," Carla agreed. "You look so beautiful." Her body hugging dress, also ivory, was made of silk crepe with handbeaded straps that criss-crossed in the back.

"Then Marc is here?"

"Yes, he's somewhere around here. I saw him about twenty minutes ago."

"Well, I'm sure he won't care one whit what I look like in this, or any other dress, for that matter."

A husky voice whispered in her ear. "Don't be so hard on the man."

McKenzie spun around. "Calvin! What on earth are you doing here?" She looked accusingly at Sherrie, Carla, and David. Putting her hands on her hips, she demanded, "All right, somebody tell me what's going on. Right now!"

"Mack, it's your wedding day. I'm here to give you away."

McKenzie was sure she'd heard wrong. "M-my wed—what?"

"Calvin's right. You and Marc are about to get married. He's not one for long engagements, you know," Carla added.

"But we've never been engaged." Had they all lost their minds? McKenzie shook her head, thoroughly confused.

"See what I mean? Oh, the music s starting. Everybody get in place."

McKenzie held her hand up. "No! Everybody just stay right where you are. *Now wait one minute.* I'm not about to let the four of you shanghai me into a marriage with Marc. Especially a marriage he doesn't want."

"But—" Carla started.

"But nothing, Carla! Marc has never once told me that he loved me, much less wanted to marry me. Does he even know about this surprise wedding? I'm sure he would be furious if he knew what you were doing—"

"You're wrong, McKenzie."

"Marc!" She gazed at him in shock. "Do you know what's going on here? They're trying to trick us into getting married."

He turned away from McKenzie, to speak to their friends. "Could you all please excuse us for a moment?"

"Are you in on this, too? What is the meaning of all this, Marc?"

"I want you."

Suddenly, the memory of all the pain she suffered over the

past few months surfaced, and with it came anger. She backed away from him, glaring at him.

"Who in hell do you think you are? Do you honestly think you can just walk in and out of my life at the drop of a hat and still find me waiting with open arms? No! You decided a while back that you wanted me out of your life."

Marc caught her shoulders and shook her lightly. "Listen to me, McKenzie," he pleaded. "I want to marry you. I want you to be my wife. I want to wake up next to you every morning. I want to hear you laugh. Hell, I even want to argue with you."

McKenzie's eyes glittered with unshed tears. "Do you think those are the magic words? They're not. I know that you don't love me."

Marc lowered his head. When he finally lifted it, he said in a ragged voice, "I know I hurt you, McKenzie. I hate myself for that. I want to make up for all the pain I caused you. You once asked me for forgiveness. Now I'm asking you. Can you forgive me?"

She answered his question with one of her own. "Do you love me?"

He didn't answer. Hurt, McKenzie pulled away. "You don't have to answer." She brushed away a tear. "I know what you'll say—that you care about me, but you don't love me."

"McKenzie—"

"Just don't say anything!" Tears glittered in her eyes and rolled down her cheeks as she backed away from him, mumbling. "This is the last time I'm going to let you hurt me like this. Is this some sort of payback?" She held her hand up. "It really doesn't matter anymore. I've had enough." Wiping away the tears, she looked up into his brown eyes. "I can't believe you'd go this far to hurt me."

"McKenzie—" Marc pleaded.

"Leave me alone. I'm getting out of here." Lifting up her skirt, she rushed down the stairs, and out of the door.

* * *

Marc realized she had meant what she said. McKenzie wasn't going to marry him. He had lost her for good this time. A pain like none he had ever felt before swept over him and, in its wake it left an aching void. All because he was afraid to say three little words. Three words she needed to hear.

It was then that Marc realized that he feared living a life without her more. He rushed after her. The limo was about to leave just as he raced out of the hotel.

"McKenzie, wait!" Marc was about to call out, but he heard a someone shouting in the background. It was Jim.

"Marc, look out! Get—"

Marc turned around, confusion written all over his face. He saw a car speeding toward him, police sirens blaring, and lights flashing in the distance.

Oh, dear Lord! There was a police chase going on. And Marc was standing in the street. McKenzie stared in horror as she watch the driver of a white BMW bearing down on Marc.

Marc seemed rooted to the spot. Coming to his senses, he started to move, but wasn't quick enough. McKenzie screamed as she caught sight of Marc's body being knocked to the side.

Everything suddenly went crazy. Police cars were stopping everywhere. McKenzie didn't care. All she wanted to do was get back to Marc. He couldn't die.

"Turn around! I've got to get back to him!" she cried hysterically. "Driver, please hurry!"

Thirty-one

Feeling inexplicable pain in his abdomen and in his thigh Marc wanted to cry out, but couldn't because the pain was so great. He felt himself falling, *Oh God, I'm going to die. I'm going to die,* he kept hearing over and over in his head. *I never told McKenzie how much I love her. Now it's too late.*

He felt Jim grab him, gently lying him flat on the ground.

"He took a slam to the thigh," Jim announced. "Lord, there's a lot of blood."

Marc tried to speak, but no words came out. The burning pain wouldn't stop. Tears of regret filled his eyes.

"Marc, old man. Can you hear me? The ambulance will be here soon. Hang on."

He could hear Carla, hear the fear in her voice, yelling for everyone to stay back. McKenzie. Where was McKenzie? Then he heard her voice.

She was suddenly sitting beside him. *"Marc.* Oh God, Marc. Honey, it's me, McKenzie. I'm right here, sweetheart." She quickly determined whether he was breathing adequately, then checked his pulse. Satisfied, she ripped open his pants leg to examine his injury. Bright red arterial blood was pulsing into the wound. Gently brushing his forehead, she said, "I know you're in pain, but I've got to apply pressure to stop the bleeding."

Someone handed her a cloth of some sort.

Marc's vision blurred, and he could no longer see McKenzie, but he could still hear her voice, soft and soothing.

"Marc, honey, you're going to feel some pain, but I've got to do this. I have to stop the blood."

He moaned in intense pain as she applied direct pressure to his wound.

"I'm so sorry, honey," McKenzie murmured. "I've got to stop the bleeding. You just hold on, you hear me? The ambulance will be here soon. Everything is going to be okay." Looking toward heaven, she prayed, "Oh God, please don't let him die."

Marc could feel her tears on his face. He could hear her words, the pain in her voice. He wanted to reassure her, but words wouldn't come out. He swallowed with difficulty, trying to find his voice.

McKenzie squeezed his hand gently. "I'm here, Marc. Don't try to talk, honey." Glancing over at Calvin, she asked, "Where is the damn ambulance?"

"They're on their way. Shouldn't be much longer," he assured her.

With his all of his strength, Marc cried out her name. "Mac . . . ken . . . zie . . ."

"Marc—"

"Lis—lis . . . ten. I . . . love . . . you, Mc . . . Ken . . . zie." Darkness descended, and Marc lost consciousness.

"Wha—" McKenzie checked his pulse. The color drained from her face. "He's going into shock. Marc? Oh God, Marc? *Nooooo!* Where is the ambulance?" she screamed hysterically.

"Oh Lord, Marc can't die! He can't," Carla said, falling into Calvin's arms, weeping.

Pastor Rivers bent down and began to pray.

The paramedics rushed over. Gently, but forcefully, they tore McKenzie away from Marc, and swiftly proceeded to work on him.

Calvin aided a grief-stricken McKenzie to her feet. "He can't die, Calvin!" She sobbed uncontrollably. "I-it can't end like

this. If he dies . . . oooh, God, I don't know how I'm going t
go on." Her voice broke, and she fell in a heap on the sidewalk
crying out her pain. She wept aloud, rocking back and forth.

Someone called her name. McKenzie looked up. It wa
Pierce.

"They're about to leave for the hospital. Marc's in the an
bulance."

McKenzie scrambled up as quickly as she could. Runnin
toward the ambulance, she shouted to the driver, "Wait! I'r
going with him."

Surrounded by Calvin, Ellen, Jim, and Carla, McKenzie trie
to convince Sherrie to take Pierce home.

"I'm not leaving my brother, McKenzie. I just found him—
His voice broke. "I'm not leaving."

"He's going to come through surgery fine. Marc's a fighte
I know he's going to be all right," Sherrie said.

McKenzie nodded. "You're right. He's going to be fine. V
have to believe that."

Several hours later, they still hadn't heard anything.

Unable to concentrate on anything else but Marc, McKenz
paced back and forth down the hall.

Calvin joined her. "Have faith, Mack."

"I do. I just feel so helpless. Like the day my mother die
There was nothing I could do to save her. And now I can't ev
save the man I love." She wiped away angry tears. "I know he
lost a lot of blood, but Marc's got to live. Oh, Calvin, I lo
him so much."

Hugging her, he nodded. "I know you do. And I belie
everything will work out. You and Marc will be married befo
you know it, and starting a life together."

"I want that so much, Calvin. Oh how I wish I had just sh
up and married him—none of this would've happened. V
would be together." McKenzie started to cry harder.

"Come on, Mack. Let's get you something to drink."

The doctor came out.

"Dr. Ashford?"

She turned around. "Is Marc going to be okay?"

Nodding he said, "He's in recovery now. He has a midshaft fracture of the femur. We've cleaned and sutured the torn tissue."

"Is he going to need plastic surgery?"

"Fortunately the tissue loss was not too great. We'll be able to fill in the loss with rotation flaps."

"Is Marc going to be all right?" Pierce asked from behind them.

McKenzie repeated what she'd been told by the doctor.

Joining the others in the waiting room, she once again repeated the news. Calvin and Ellen were the first to leave.

"We're going to go back to the hotel to get some sleep. We'll check in on Marc in the morning."

Embracing Calvin, McKenzie said, "I'm so glad you were here. I don't know if I could've made it without you."

"You've been given a second chance, Mack. Don't blow it," Calvin whispered.

"I won't," she promised.

Jim and Carla stood up. "I think we're gonna leave, too," said Jim. "Marc's not gonna be up for a lot of company tonight. We'll be back in the morning."

Carla smiled. "You mean later on. It's after midnight."

"Thank you both for being here with us. I'm so sorry I acted so hotheaded." McKenzie shook her head. "If I had just kept my mouth shut and married Marc—"

"Don't blame yourself, McKenzie. It wasn't your fault."

"I wish I could believe that, Carla."

"We can see Marc now," Pierce announced.

"You and Sherrie go on in," McKenzie decided. "I'm going to stay with him all night." After Jim and Carla said their goodbyes, she gave each of them a hug. "Oh, Carla, can you do me a favor?"

"Sure. What is it you need?"

"Could you go by my place and pick up a pair of jeans an a shirt for me?" She handed Carla her keys.

"Will do. I'll bring them with me when I come back."

"Thank you." She watched them for a minute before headin in the direction of Marc's room.

"He's been asking for you," Sherrie whispered when she er tered the room.

She stared down into the face of the man she loved with a of her heart. Although pale, his tawny face was still full strength. "Marc, I'm here," McKenzie said in a loud whispe "I'm right here."

He opened his eyes slowly. "Doc—"

"You need to rest—"

"Tell me . . . will I-I be able to w-walk?"

"I think so. You're far too stubborn not to."

Marc grunted. "Damn pain."

"I think you're feeling better already," McKenzie teased.

Pierce and Sherrie smiled.

Placing his arm around McKenzie, Pierce said, "We're goir to take off. Try to get some rest, and make Marc behave. We' see you in a few hours."

She nodded. "Good night," she murmured without takir her eyes off Marc.

"Y-you should get some rest. You look tired, Doc." Ma licked his lips. "Go home."

"I'm not going anywhere. And you should be the one restin You just went through serious trauma. Now close your eyes—

Marc was asleep.

Smiling, McKenzie sank down into a chair beside his bed

She was snoring softly when Carla tapped her on the shou der. Following her out of the room, she asked, "What are yo doing back so soon?"

Handing McKenzie a black overnight bag, she said, thought about you and your dress . . . the blood. I thought you feel more comfortable in something else."

McKenzie smiled and embraced her. "Thanks. Now you

on home and get some rest. Marc's sleeping, and it looks as if he'll be just fine."

"I'm so glad to hear that." Hugging McKenzie once more, Carla said, "I'll see you shortly."

After a quick shower and change of clothes, McKenzie felt better. Seated once more by Marc's bed, she dozed off, her head resting on her hand.

Marc's eyes opened. His vision cleared, and he glanced around the room. He tried to smile when he laid eyes on a sleeping McKenzie. She'd changed into a pair of jeans and a polo shirt. She wore her plaid sneakers.

Shifting in the uncomfortable-looking chair, she woke up suddenly. McKenzie pushed out of her chair upon finding him watching her.

"Marc, honey, how are you feeling?" She reached for his hand, squeezing it gently.

He grimaced. "Like hell, but grateful to see another day."

"I'm so sorry. I shouldn't have—"

"Not your fault," He interrupted. "I should have been more aware of my surroundings."

"We don't have to talk about this now. It's more important that you rest and get well. We have the rest of our lives for talking."

"The rest of our lives," Marc murmured.

McKenzie visited the hospital every day. "You're looking better and better every day, Marc."

"I'm ready to go home," he grumbled.

She kissed his forehead. "Sweetheart, don't rush it. When the doctor feels you're ready, he'll discharge you." McKenzie gently buried her face against his throat. "I wanted to die right there with you, Marc." Covering his hand with hers, she murmured, "I love you, Marc."

"I love you, too." His lips pressed against hers, then gently covered her mouth. She returned his kiss with reckless abandon.

McKenzie quivered at the sweet tenderness of his kiss. When he raised his head, she smiled up at him. "I've missed you so much, and I'm so thankful we have a second chance. I'm so thankful."

"Love," Marc moaned, pulling her to him. "I want to ask you something. It's something I should have done in the first place."

"What are you talking about?"

"Will you marry me?"

McKenzie' s eyes filled with tears. "Y-yes, Marc, I'll marry you." She wiped her eyes with her hand. "Can we do it right away? As soon as possible?"

"Don't you want a wedding?"

"No. I want to get married as soon as you're able. We can always have a big wedding later."

Marc nodded in understanding. "You're afraid of losing me, aren't you?"

"Yes."

Marc propped himself up in bed. "Honey, tomorrow isn't promised to any of us. I don't want to lose you, either, but we both know that death is a reality. I'm alive, you're alive. Let's make the best of the time we have together. We can't dwell on death."

"I know you're right, Marc. It's just that death has been so much a part of my life—"

He kissed her to silence her. "I love you, and as soon as we can arrange it we're getting married. "I love you, Dr. McKenzie Ashford."

"Forever and ever."

Epilogue

One year later

"How are you holding up, sweetheart?" Marc whispered as he placed a supporting arm around McKenzie.

"I'm fine. Just hungry, though."

Marc grinned at her. "You're always hungry. If you keep that up, you're going to gain more weight than you want to."

"I'm eating for two—no, make that three." She watched his face for a reaction.

"I know. Wait a minute—did you just say you're eating for three?" Surprise registered on his face, followed by stark happiness. He grinned from ear to ear. "You did, didn't you? We're having twins!"

McKenzie smiled, her wide eyes shining with love. "Yes. We're going to have twice the diapers, colic, baby food—"

Sherrie walked up. "Did I just hear you say that you're expecting twins?"

McKenzie nodded. "Yes, we're having twins, Sherrie."

"That's wonderful! I'm so happy for you both."

Marc put a comforting arm around Sherrie. "We were thinking of naming a son after Pierce. How do you feel about that?"

Sherrie tried to stop the tears that flowed. "I think it's a wonderful idea. I know Pierce would be honored." She wiped her tears with the back of her hand. "I-I just wish h-he . . . I wish he were here."

McKenzie dabbed at her eyes. "I do, too. I miss him so much."

Marc nodded, unable to speak. He heard his name called, and turned to face Carla. She stood at the podium, and gestured for him to join her. Turning back to Sherrie and McKenzie, he whispered, "I guess it's show time. Carla is motioning for us to join her on the platform."

McKenzie followed her husband to the stage as he moved to stand next to Carla. She watched as Sherrie took a seat near the platform, before turning her eyes to her husband. They had been married for four months now, and they were still acting like newlyweds.

"Septavir, Chandler's oral vaccine has been approved by the Food and Drug Administration in the United States," Marc announced to an audience filled with doctors, scientists, competitors, and the press. When he finished, he turned to McKenzie. "I would like my wife, Dr. McKenzie Chandler, to join me at the podium. I'll let her tell you more about Septavir."

McKenzie walked up and stood next to her husband. He leaned over and whispered, "I love you, sweetheart," before taking a seat next to Carla onstage.

McKenzie cleared her throat and began. "Years ago, President Kennedy looked toward the heavens and proclaimed that the flag of peace and democracy, not war and tyranny, must be the first to be planted on the moon. He gave us a goal of reaching the moon, and we achieved it—ahead of time."

"Today I am pleased to announce that Septavir exhibits the potential to incapacitate the AIDS virus directly in the human bloodstream almost immediately upon contact, before the virus has a chance to invade the cells and cause havoc with DNA . . ."

Later that evening as she lay in bed with her husband, McKenzie turned to Marc and said, "I hope Septavir will save lives. I wish we had been able to save Pierce."

Marc kissed her lightly on the forehead. "I do, too. But I am thankful that I had a chance to get to know him. At least I had a year with him."

"We've both lost family. Now we are about to add to ours. Only this time, we must teach our children that love is an endless act of forgiveness. And that the only ties that bind nearer and dearer are of family. No one should ever let emotions like anger get in the way of being a family."

Marc nodded. "I agree. We almost lost each other because of hurt and anger." He pulled her closer into his arms. "I'm grateful to you for not giving up on me."

McKenzie laughed. "I'm glad you finally came to your senses."

"I still can't believe I made such a fool of myself the night we got married."

"I think it's about the most romantic thing you've ever done."

Marc sat up quickly, moving his arms from under McKenzie, causing her to flop back on the bed. *"What?* Woman, you've got to be kidding!"

"No, I'm not kidding, Marc. You're not a very romantic person. But—"

"But nothing. I'm very romantic," Marc sniped.

McKenzie kissed his cheek. "I didn't mean to hurt your feelings. I love you just the way you are. Honest I do." She wrapped her arms around him, massaging his hairy chest. "I was just saying—"

"Don't say anything. Just kiss me," he ordered. Marc turned, pushing her back against the pillows. "I'll show you just how romantic I can be."

And he did, for the rest of the night.

Coming in August from
Arabesque Books . . .

THE BUSINESS OF LOVE by Angela Winters
    1-58314-150-2 $5.99US/$7.99CAN

The heir to a hotel chain, Maya Woodson is determined to make her plan to go public a success—even if she is at odds with handsome Trajan Matthews, the investment expert who's overseeing the deal. But when a crime endangers the chain's future—and their careers—Maya and Trajan must discover what they cherish most . . . if they are to find a love-filled future.

FIRST LOVE by Cheryl Faye
    1-58314-117-0 $5.99US/$7.99CAN

When shy Lena Caldwell and Quincy Taylor strike up a friendship, it isn't long before a sweetly sensual fire is sparked. But as their attraction grows, Quincy's past mistakes inject doubt into their newfound romance and the two must confront their insecurities to find a love worth fighting for.

SOULFUL SERENADE by Linda Hudson-Smith
    1-58314-140-5 $5.99US/$7.99CAN

Hillary Houston has it all—personality, looks, talent, and now, sexy engineer Brandon Blair. But when Hillary is offered the chance to become a recording superstar, Brandon's threatened with the possibility of losing the woman of his dreams . . . unless he can find a way to keep her forever.

ADMISSION OF LOVE by Niobia Bryant
    1-58314-164-2 $5.99US/$7.99CAN

When supermodel Chloe Bryant settles down in her mother's rural South Carolina town, she is at instant odds with handsome, reserved Devon Jamison. But amid hidden hurt and unexpected romantic rivals, Devon and Chloe begin to discover what they both really desire—to gain the dream they want most and have always waited for . . .

Please Use the Coupon on the Next Page to Order

Have A Sizzling Summer
With Arabesque Books